ALSO BY OLIVIA MILES

This Christmas

Oyster Bay Series
Feels Like Home
Along Came You
Maybe This Time
This Thing Called Love
Those Summer Nights
Still the One (Bayside Brides)
One Fine Day (Bayside Brides)
Had to Be You (Bayside Brides)

Misty Point Series
One Week to the Wedding
The Winter Wedding Plan

Sweeter in the City Series
Sweeter in the Summer
Sweeter Than Sunshine
No Sweeter Love
One Sweet Christmas

Briar Creek Series
Mistletoe on Main Street
A Match Made on Main Street
Hope Springs on Main Street
Love Blooms on Main Street
Christmas Comes to Main Street

Harlequin Special Edition
'Twas the Week Before Christmas
Recipe for Romance

ISBN 978-1-7346208-0-1

MEET ME AT SUNSET

First Edition: February 2020

Meet Me at Sunset

Chapter One

Gemma

Gemma Morgan should have been staring at the blinking cursor on her computer screen, not looking down at her now bare finger, the indentation of her two-carat, brilliant-cut engagement ring still fresh, even though months had passed since she'd taken it off. Five months. Five long, hard months. She rubbed at the skin, trying to banish the mark, but, like the memory it carried, it seemed determined to stay.

She sighed and pushed her chair away from her desk. The rain that had been falling since early morning had stopped, replaced just as quickly with bright sunshine and a clear blue sky, and she walked to the window of her living room, looking out onto Lincoln Park. It was her favorite thing about this apartment—

the view. Ironic, she supposed, that she had come to Chicago thirteen years ago specifically to live in the city and be part of the whole urban experience, and yet the apartment she'd chosen overlooked nature instead of the buildings that had once appealed to her.

The only way she'd even been able to afford this apartment was because of her grandmother, who had left all three Morgan sisters a not completely insignificant trust and equal ownership of Gran's house on a small, carless island in northern Michigan, about seven hours from Chicago. When Gran had passed away last summer, Gemma had used her inheritance to upgrade her apartment, allowing enough left over to quit her rather soulless job as an account executive at the advertising agency so she could write fulltime (in theory). Her older sister, Hope, had put her share into a compounding-interest savings plan for her twin daughters, and Ellie, the youngest, had rented an art studio on the island where she lived year-round in Gran's house, so she could pursue her painting career, or at least try to do so until her funds ran out, as their father liked to grumble.

Ellie's decision was the only decision that their father didn't support, but then, Bart Morgan had never agreed with Ellie's choices, from the way she spent her free time growing up (wandering and daydreaming rather than studying and excelling at music or sports) to where she applied to college (art school). But as their mother was quick to point out, it was Ellie who had stayed at the house and taken care of Gran in her final years, so there was really nothing that Bart could say about anything. He had been free to run his steel company in suburban Ohio, and Gemma's mother, Celia, had been free to enjoy her private tennis lessons at the club.

It had been nearly a year now since Gran had died, peacefully, at the island hospital (something else that Bart didn't agree with, thinking she should have gone to Cleveland for better care). Nearly a year since Gemma had moved into this apartment. And nearly a year since she'd given her notice at the agency and walked home to the smaller walk-up she had then shared with her fiancé Sean, feeling purposeful and excited, knowing that now she would have all the time in the world needed to write the second book on her publishing contract. But the months had passed quickly, almost in a blur, and now that book was due in a month. Twenty-seven days, really.

And she only had seventy-three pages written. Well, seventy-two if you took away the title page.

Gemma turned from the window. The day was slipping away, as the days seemed to do lately. She glanced down at her attire: pink tee and grey sweatpants that still bore the stain of spilled pizza sauce from last night (yes, she had slept in them, too), because she hadn't yet showered. She had cleaned the apartment, though. Scrubbed the floors on her hands and knees and even dusted the blinds. But she hadn't written anything. And now it was already after two.

Was it any wonder that Sean had broken up with her?

Though, really, back when she was with Sean, she didn't walk around the apartment wearing the same clothes for days on end, eating exclusively from takeout menus. Back when she was with Sean, she had written seventy-three (okay, seventy-two!) pages of her second contracted novel.

She could blame it on the time it had taken to undo her wedding plans; the endless calls to the photographer, band, church director, and hotel event coordinator had left her hot with humiliation and unable to do much more than sit in her lovely new apartment in flannel pajamas with a bowl of ice cream on her lap and a box of tissues at her side. She could blame it on the way her mother had cried, "But what are we supposed to tell all our friends? They'll be so disappointed!" when she'd finally broken the news, after three weeks of waiting for Sean to change his mind. But ultimately the blame was hers alone. She was in a funk. And she needed to snap out of it.

If only she knew how.

After all, who was she to write a romance novel when she knew nothing about love?

Quickly, she showered and dressed, cringing a little when she realized how tight the waistband of her jeans had become since she'd worn them last month for Hope's thirty-fourth birthday celebration at a trendy restaurant in the suburbs, where Gemma had felt like a third wheel surrounded by her sister's beautiful family and realizing that, not even three years younger, Gemma was in danger of never having the wonderful things her sister possessed at this rate.

Now the top button of the jeans pressed against her stomach, making it a little hard to bend over and reach for her shoes. Regardless, they would have to do, because she didn't have any time to shave her legs for a skirt or a dress if she wanted to make the three-fifteen train to the bucolic suburb where Hope was throwing a birthday party for her twin girls.

Gemma grabbed the birthday gifts she'd ordered last week, paying extra to have them wrapped in bright pink paper because she knew that if she wrapped them herself, they would have tape marks and creases, whereas Hope's gifts always looked professionally wrapped, even though they were not, and hurried to the elevator at the end of the hall, hoping that she would be able to flag down a passing cab.

They pulled up to Union Station with ten minutes to spare. Enough time for her to stand outside, on the edge of the Chicago River, and take in the view of the skyscrapers across the bridge. There, two blocks to the north and hugging the river to its west, was Sean's office building—once her office building, where they'd first met, years ago, when the city was still new and life still felt full of possibility. His view, she knew, faced this way. And for reasons she couldn't explain, and couldn't even justify, she counted up the floors until she found the twenty-third, and stared until she liked to think he might just sense her presence, and then, she held up her hand, just in case he was working on a Saturday, which he sometimes did when he was working on a big campaign, and just in case he'd swiveled in his chair and turned to look down, catching her in that moment, she flipped him the bird.

She smiled as she hurried through the station and paid for her ticket. And she smiled as she boarded the train and pulled out her latest paperback (that she was reading, not writing), and she smiled when her brother-in-law picked her up thirty minutes later, even though she would have preferred a little one-on-one time with Hope instead.

"Hope would have come but she was busy with last-minute party preparations," Evan said, giving her a wry look. They both knew, after all, how Hope could fuss over details. He turned onto their winding, tree-lined street where large, four- and five-bedroom homes sat beneath the eaves of old elm trees, their lawns professionally manicured, the grass forever green.

Hope's house was not the largest on the block, but it was, in Gemma's opinion, the prettiest: a Tudor-style common in the Chicago area, with original paned windows and a bluestone walkway leading to the arched front door. Inside, Hope had painted out the dark woodwork, leaving only the exposed beams on the ceiling in the living room, giving it a light and airy feeling even if those white sofas did seem a little impractical with twin girls. Still, they were always pristine, every pillow plumped, every surface bare aside from a few cozy touches: a vase of fresh-cut seasonal flowers, a few coffee-table books, a framed photo of the girls at the lakefront, looking absolutely adorable.

Sometimes Gemma didn't know how her sister did it. Her house was perfect. Her kids were perfect. Her husband was perfect. She was perfect.

Whereas Gemma... Well, Gemma realized as Evan closed the door behind them that the top button on her jeans had popped open.

Hope sailed into the room in navy linen pants and a pale pink blouse, looking fresh and relaxed. Her honey-colored hair trailed down her back in a low ponytail. Gemma caught a waft of her peony-scented perfume as she reached in for a hug, and whispered in Gemma's ear, "Thank God you're here."

Gemma pulled back, perplexed, but still smiling. It was only when she held out the gifts that she noticed the slightly wild look to her sister's eyes. It was the stress of the party, she decided. Hope was too hard on herself, always had been. No doubt she wanted everything to look perfect. And it certainly couldn't be easy to host fifteen four-year-olds when you had those white sofas.

They walked into the equally white kitchen, where a three-tiered cake with pink frosting was resting on the center island. It had been doused in colorful sprinkles, looking like something you'd see front and center in a bakery window, but Gemma knew her sister well enough to know that Hope had made it herself.

Through the screen doors, Gemma saw that Rose and Victoria were dancing around with fistfuls of balloons in bright, happy colors that were a contrast to their white party dresses. On their heads they wore gold crowns that matched their gold Mary Jane shoes, to show everyone that they were the birthday girls. The entire patio had been set up with tiny tables for the kids, a food station for the parents (complete with a drinks bar), and centerpieces of colorful spring arrangements. At the edge of the fenced-in yard, Gemma saw that a man was leading a white pony by a glittering gold harness.

Gemma squinted out the window as something caught her eye. "Is that?" It couldn't be! The pony wasn't just a pony. It was...She turned, catching Hope's failed attempt at a casual shrug. "It is! Oh, Hope! A *unicorn*?"

"The girls think it's real, so don't tell them it isn't!"

Gemma laughed and turned back to the window to admire the majestic gold horn that was attached to the pony's head by a strap.

"Did you tell Mom?" she asked, accepting a glass of chilled white wine. It went down easily and helped dull the nagging dread she felt about her deadline. Coming up here was always a good distraction, she thought. She hadn't thought about Sean in—she checked the clock on the wall and calculated how long it had been since she'd gotten off the train—eleven minutes!

Her shoulders slumped. Now she'd have to restart the timer.

Hope took a sip from her own glass. Gemma noted that her fingernails were painted the exact shade of pink as her blouse. Growing up, Gemma always thought Hope adhered to these habits because it was expected of her, but as she'd carried these traits through to her married life, it became clear that Hope preferred it this way.

"I sent her a picture but I think they're in France now, right? Or was it Spain?"

"Neither," Gemma replied. "They're in Iceland. I'm surprised it's not on your calendar," she joked. Everything was on Hope's calendar. Her entire life was planned out by the hour.

The doorbell rang, and Hope sighed, took another swig of wine, and then breezed into the hall. A moment later, voices could be heard greeting each other, and Gemma took this as her cue to go outside, where Evan was now trying to keep the girls from the pony—ahem, unicorn.

"Auntie Gemma!" the girls cried when they saw her. They ran toward her, arms outstretched, baby teeth on full display, and for a moment, all was right in the world.

Gemma squatted down, opening her arms to pull them in, hoping that she wouldn't accidentally spill the glass of wine she was clutching in one hand on the back of Rose's white dress.

"We have a unicorn," Victoria said, whispering reverently and then clasping her hand over her mouth to stifle her giggles.

"I saw!" Gemma rounded her eyes, playing along.

When the twins ran toward the door to the house to greet their friends, she saw Evan raise an eyebrow. "Hope had to have a unicorn."

"Or the girls did?" Gemma tried.

Evan gave her a knowing look before he crossed the patio toward the door to greet some new arrivals.

The backyard filled quickly, and more than once she heard Hope remark that she was happy the rain had cleared. Rain meant no unicorn, Gemma supposed. It also meant a lot of people in a very pristine house, many under the age of five. Really, she was surprised that Hope had been willing to take that risk.

"Next year we're doing high tea, in the city," Hope informed her once the games were underway for the kids and the guests were mingling amongst themselves.

Gemma frowned at her sister, wanting to say that she thought the party was a success, but Hope quickly said, "They'll be five then. Perfect age for that sort of thing."

Gemma smiled. Of course. "I seem to recall we always did that for your birthday, didn't we?"

Hope seemed to frown. "You're right. We did. Meanwhile Ellie always got to have her party at the country club pool."

"Well, she has a summer birthday," Gemma pointed out, but she knew what Hope meant. When Ellie pushed for later bed times, she was met with heaved sighs and resigned nods of the head. Whereas if Hope or Gemma had asked, the answer would have been a firm and immediate "no." Rules were rules in the Morgan household. At least, until Ellie came along.

"Have you spoken to her recently?" Hope asked.

Gemma was quick to shake her head. "I haven't been good at keeping in touch with everything that's gone on lately." She felt uneasy thinking about her sister. They had exchanged words, last summer, at Gran's service. Words that didn't sit right with her and that she couldn't take back. Still, she and Ellie had always gotten along, and surely Ellie had to know that tensions were high then. They were all grieving. And, of course, they were at their childhood home, under their father's roof and his tight control over everything they said and did. They were tense and nervous, just like they'd been as kids.

"Service is always hit or miss on the island." Hope smiled at a passing guest.

Gemma wished it were just that, but she had a feeling there was more to it. "She did call and leave a voicemail after she heard about the wedding..." She trailed off, hating that she'd now broached the topic when all she wanted to do was push it out of her head for an afternoon.

Hope nodded. She was the peacemaker, always had been. The role model. She made monthly calls to Ellie, even had it written on the calendar in the kitchen. Sunday nights were for calls to their parents, and even if she wasn't able to reach them, Gemma knew her sister well enough to know that Hope was dutiful enough to try.

"How's the book coming along?" Hope asked, and the eager smile told Gemma that her sister was trying to steer her off the topic of Sean in a helpful way. She had no way of knowing that she'd just brought up something equally prickly.

It was the dreaded question, and one that Gemma didn't hear very often other than from her editor and literary agent, because she tried not to engage with anyone, especially of late. But this was her sister. She could be honest with Hope.

"Not well. I'm...blocked." There, she'd said it. She didn't know where her story was going. She didn't know the ending.

"Still upset about Sean?" Hope frowned at her. "You know he's not worth it. To just decide one day that he'd changed his mind? After committing? As painful as that is, it's better to know that now than six years from now."

Six years was how long Hope and Evan had been married. That was easy for Hope to say.

"Maybe you need a change of scenery. Something to get your mind off things here," Hope said. Her expression suddenly lifted. "Why don't you go to the lake house?"

Gemma frowned. "Evening Island?" It was far from convenient, and now was the time to buckle down, not take a vacation. Besides, there was the matter of Ellie to think about.

Still, Ellie was her sister, and they had to work through things eventually, and when she thought of the clear, cool water and the breeze flowing through the open window in her favorite room in the house, the one on the third floor that had the desk in the alcove, looking out over the lake, she felt her spirits lift.

"A change might help me to focus," she said. Stop her from thinking of Sean at every turn, picturing their life in the four walls of the apartment they had all too briefly shared. "And it might help to spend some quality time with Ellie. If she'll let me come."

Hope gave her a smile. "Of course she'll let you come. Besides, she sort of has to. It's our family's house, even if we never get back there."

Gemma considered this. Why couldn't she go back to Evening Island? The house was theirs to share. It wasn't like she had any responsibilities keeping her in Chicago—no kids, no husband, no pets. Not even a houseplant.

She pursed her lips and shifted to less self-pitying thoughts.

Evening Island, where the sun seemed to shine every day and even on the days that it didn't, the smell of lilacs and grass just grew stronger. The island where she'd run free as a child, allowed to skin her knees and ride bikes on all the dirt roads, and swim out as far as she dared in the icy water. The place where she could run free, allowing her mind to take flight and her heart to soar.

Gemma nodded. Evening Island. She'd go tomorrow. She wasn't sure why she hadn't thought of it sooner.

Chapter Two

Ellie

Ellie finished washing her paintbrushes in the stainless-steel sink in the back room of her studio, wondering if she should stay and finish that landscape she'd started of the South Bay lighthouse instead of heading home early.

Her stomach rumbled, providing an answer for her. She dried her hands on the skirt of her cotton sundress, flicked off the lights, and locked the door behind her.

Her studio, where she not only painted but also offered a painting class on a weekly basis, was located near the island harbor. It was tucked away at the edge of Main Street, but far enough from the center of town where she wouldn't be disturbed from her work. She'd rented it with her inheritance, selecting it for the beautiful views that always gave her something new and interesting to observe. Occasionally people from the bed and breakfast across the street popped in, usually just to check things out, and the guys docking their sailboats too, even if they were only hoping for a mug of the fresh coffee she kept brewing. Still, she was happy for the company. Life on Evening Island was quiet. Sometimes, even too quiet.

It was the cost of being surrounded by so much natural beauty, she thought, as she hopped onto her bicycle and cycled into town. It was a late Saturday afternoon in the spring, meaning that the street was filled with tourists, and that while this might be good for business, she wasn't exactly looking for a big crowd tonight. Her bike creaked beneath her, not completely uncommon given how much she rode the thing, but she frowned as she pulled to a stop outside Main Street Market and crouched down to inspect the situation.

She muttered to herself as she stood, all too aware that talking to herself had become a regular (and slightly worrisome) occurrence since Gran had passed. She'd be lucky to get this bike home tonight given the air pressure in the front tire.

With a sigh, she walked into the grocery store, which had been around since the turn of the twentieth century. The pine floors were original: wide planks, each scratch telling a story. The aisles were narrow, and carts were not even an option. She grabbed a wicker basket and went straight for the deli counter, where the current owner, Donna Carlisle, prepared fresh soups and sandwiches every day.

For some inexplicable reason, Ellie's heart was heavy as she considered her options, even though she usually loved the spinach wrap and lentil soup, and both were still in stock. Some nights she ate in town, or got together with some of the other locals who had become friends over the years, but tonight there were no plans. The truth was that she was getting a little lonely sitting out on the front porch watching the sun go down. The painting helped; after all, how could she not be inspired by such colors and lighting? But she'd painted enough for today, and tonight...Well, tonight she was bored out of her friggin' mind. There. She'd said it. She was bored to tears!

With surprise, she realized that actually, she *was* crying, that a tear was running down her cheek and that more were sure to quickly follow. She brushed it away, darting her eyes to the right in the hopes that no one would see, but it was just a sea of tourists, murmuring over how quaint everything was.

It was quaint. And beautiful. And her happiest memories were here on this island. When they came up here as children, she and her sisters would play all day, while for once their mother wasn't fussing over them getting their hair messy. She was too busy drinking what she called lemonade (but the girls knew better) and playing cards to notice. Evening Island brought out the best in her too. In all of them, really. Well, except for their father, but his stays were brief: two weekends per summer, one at the start and one at the end.

Back then, Ellie couldn't understand how her father was so restless here, so unable to just relax and take in the surroundings. She still couldn't understand it, but Gran had, and that was why she had left the cottage to her three granddaughters when she'd died.

Because there was no other food in the house and she'd managed to kill the vegetable garden last summer when there was a dry spell and she had sheer forgotten to water that patch of lawn back near the shed (*Please forgive me, Gran*), Ellie grabbed the spinach wrap and a big bag of salt and vinegar flavored potato chips and then, because hey, it was Saturday night, a bottle of white wine. And a pint of double chocolate chip ice cream. Maybe she'd call Mandy or Naomi and see if they were up for something—but she knew that shops held longer hours on the weekends once the ferries started bringing people in from the Blue Harbor dock four times an hour, and most locals worked to serve the tourists.

"Hey, Ellie," Donna said as she rang her up. She pushed a wisp of graying hair from her forehead and gave a friendly smile. Soon the summer staff would start, but lately, Donna always manned the counter. Ellie was starting to get a little uncomfortable by the fact that Donna probably kept a running tab of how many bottles of sauvignon blanc Ellie purchased in a week over the colder months. But there was no other option for shopping unless she wanted to take the ferry to the mainland, and that was just more trouble than it was worth half the time. Sure, Blue Harbor was a change of scenery, and the town was full of shops and people, some faces familiar enough, others new, but the ferry stopped running from January through March, and it only crossed twice a day in the off season, and you had to plan for it. And Ellie, well, she had never been one for planning. Just ask her father.

She pursed her lips at that, remembering that he was far away, that he never came to Michigan to visit, and that their phone calls had been further and fewer between. Lack of quality cell reception had been an easy excuse for that. Still, somehow it didn't make the ache in her chest go away, try as she might. And oh, how she had tried. To tell herself that she didn't care, when she did, deep down. So much. Too much, really.

She grabbed a plastic spoon for her ice cream. The dishwasher had stopped working last week, and she hadn't the time nor resources to call anyone to fix it, and there were quite a few dishes piled up by now...

That was the problem with island life, she decided. It made you lazy. Time slowed down, you went through the day at your own pace, and well, it was wonderful, really. Really, really wonderful. Except when it wasn't.

Outside, she set her brown grocery bag in her bicycle basket. She eyed the front tire and decided that it wasn't worth the risk. She'd walk the bike home and deal with it in the morning. Hopefully it just needed some air in the tires and not a patch. She had time...She may not have much else, but she had time.

At first, the thought of all that time to paint had been a dream come true.

Now...She stopped walking. Blinked. Felt her heart speed up and her stomach do something a little funny.

Now she was staring at the face of Simon Webber. Only it couldn't be Simon. Simon hadn't been back to the island in a decade, and sometime, long ago but probably not as long ago as she should have, she'd accepted the fact that he'd never be back.

And here he was, coming out of the bakery, as casually as if he had never left town, and for a second, she dared to imagine how that would have been. If he'd returned. Like he'd promised. How different life might have been.

That was one fantasy she had harbored for too long. Now, her heart was hammering in her chest. Why now? Why not then? And what would she even say?

He glanced up and down Main Street; his turquoise blue eyes were practically glowing, even from this distance. And that grin, broad and slightly mischievous—oh Lord, that grin!

She brought a hand to her hair, hoping that she didn't have paint gumming up the ends, and wondering if she should turn, hop on her bike and attempt to get up Hill Street on that front tire, compose herself and seek him out another day. Or should she stand here and wait for him to see her? Wait for him to take the lead?

Oh, God. He saw her. He did a double take (be still her heart!) and his grin widened even deeper, making his eyes go all crinkly at the corners and his dimple quirk.

"Ellie? Ellie Morgan?" He was coming over to her in long, purposeful strides, and before she could even react, she was pressed against his chest. His hard, warm, thick chest, and oh, she couldn't help it. She closed her eyes, and, ever so discreetly, gave a little sniff.

He smelled good, just like she remembered, and oh, how she remembered. He smelled like the cedar soap he'd always used, with only a slight undertone of sweat. And he felt warm, and sturdy, and she wanted to hold him even longer, she wanted to take him back to Sunset Cottage and...Well. A lady didn't talk about those things. Not that Ellie had ever been much of a lady. Her oldest sister Hope was the lady. Gemma was the brain. Ellie was the wild child. The artist. The black sheep. The family disappointment.

But none of that mattered. Not when Simon was standing in front of her, looking as good as he had ten years ago, the last time she'd seen him. Even if it wasn't supposed to be the last time.

"I didn't know you were coming back to town!" she finally said, managing to find her words.

"I didn't know you were still spending your summers here," he said with a grin. His eyes were sparkling, and he seemed so happy to see her that she didn't even feel nervous. It was exactly like she had once pictured their reunion to be, well, other than the missing kiss, of course. A kiss by now would have been nice...

"Oh, I live here year-round now, actually," she corrected. She'd gotten used to the surprised reaction people gave to that. Evening Island wasn't exactly a winter destination, especially when the only access became a small air taxi. The months leading up to spring were dark and quiet. Very, very quiet. But they were also ethereal, with frocked trees and the frozen stretch of water leading all the way to Blue Harbor. Some of her best paintings were inspired by the winter landscape. She had to remember that!

"I thought you went to art school in Chicago?"

She tried not to be too flattered that he remembered that. But then, that was all they had talked about that last summer here together. Their future.

The future that hadn't happened.

She pushed back the pang in her chest. They were kids back then, she told herself. It would be irrelevant to bring it up now, to ask where he'd been, why he'd never come back, why he'd gotten busy with his new life and forgotten her. Because she'd never forgotten him.

Instead, she managed a breezy smile and said, "Oh, I did. And then I moved back to take care of Gran." Or, as Gemma had said the last time she'd seen her, Gran had taken her in.

Ellie still felt the sting of those words.

Simon gave a look of sympathy. "I heard about your grandmother. I'm sorry."

Of course he'd heard. The Webbers, like the Morgans, were summer stock, locals of their own right, people who came every summer, year after year, from Memorial Day through Labor Day. Well, most years. Islanders kept tabs on their friends, brought them fresh-cut flowers and homemade cherry pies, and they were up to date on all the gossip, which was how Ellie knew that Simon was a thriving attorney, living a successful life in Philadelphia.

The fact that Simon was coming back to Evening Island had not been mentioned. Surely, she would have heard. She would have prepared herself. She would have made sure she didn't have the faint markings of paint on her dress, and she might have run a brush through her hair, too.

"She lived a long life," Ellie said bravely, but the tears prickled the backs of her eyes again, damn it. She glanced away, forced a bright smile, but Simon's was one of sympathy and understanding, making her feel connected to him all over again, because of course he knew. He'd spent endless summers with Gran just like she had, here on Evening Island. "Makes it feel like the end of an era, sometimes."

And it was. Now, looking at Simon, and the fine lines around his eyes, and the way his chest had filled out from the boyish frame she knew so well, she was all too aware that time had passed. That the summers they once spent together were only a memory.

But a shared one.

"So what keeps you busy here year-round?" he asked, as one would, except that Ellie couldn't help but think he should know this; if he'd asked, surely his mother might have told him?

"I have an art studio here in town," she said proudly. "It's down by the docks. Turquoise paint. Hard to miss."

"We'll plan on stopping in sometime," Simon said with a grin.

Ellie narrowed her eyes for a moment. We? But then she thought, no doubt his parents had decided to get an early start on the summer. Wanted to air out the house. Maybe they hadn't taken advantage of any renters for the upcoming lilac season the way other locals liked to do, choosing instead to return mid-June, when the festivities were over. The Webbers hadn't been back for a couple of years; maybe they wanted to make up for time lost.

"You here for long?" she asked, shifting the weight on her feet. She hoped the eagerness didn't register in her face. After all, he had a career. He had gone to Colgate, then onto law school. (Gran liked to gossip, it kept her busy, and when it came to Simon, Ellie had been all too happy to listen.)

"For the summer," Simon replied, and Ellie felt the smile widen on her face.

The whole summer! And it was only May!

He glanced back over his shoulder into the crowd and then looked at her in apology. "I have to go, but...this was nice, Ellie. Really nice. I'm glad you're here."

She could only nod in response as she watched him turn and walk away, his shoulders broad, his nut-brown hair curling at the nape of his neck like it did when they were just teenagers. And somehow, Evening Island didn't feel so lonely after all. In fact, it felt just as wonderful as it had all those years ago, when it was the one place she could be where anything felt possible.

Chapter Three

Hope

Hope stared at the dish towel that was hanging from her husband's bathroom hook and forced a calming breath. She would bet anyone five bucks that a bath towel (a thick, soft, embroidered bath towel) was currently hanging from the handle to the dishwasher at this very moment.

She reached out a hand and snatched the thin, flimsy, white dish towel from the hook and tossed it into the laundry basket, which was already spilling over with sheets, endless white undershirts that Evan seemed to change three times a day, and of course, the girls' tiny clothes, most of them in various shades of pink.

Once, there had been a time when she could stare at those little clothes for hours. When she marveled in folding each floral-printed blouse, and ironed each and every pink cotton dress. She always dressed the girls in coordinating clothes but never matching. They were fraternal twins, but they looked enough alike to be mistaken for identical, with their honey-colored loose curls and big green eyes. She wanted them to each be unique. She wanted to foster their individuality. She wanted to give them all the opportunities her mother had never instilled in her.

And yet, despite her best efforts, she feared that she was slowly becoming her mother.

It had started with the house. A giant suburban thing that was far too much trouble to clean, and even when they'd hired a housekeeper to come once a week, still required some elbow grease for the sake of her own dignity. Then there were the neighbors who seemed to never run out of one-upping each other at the playground at the end of the block. Hope wouldn't have minded so much if she'd found one true friend in the mix, or if Evan was around more often, or if the girls weren't currently attempting to *eat the piles of dirt* that they had used to "bake" pies in the backyard playhouse that Hope had once found so charming (and yes, she actually tended to the flowers in the pink window box).

She dropped the laundry basket and flung open the window, hollering down at Evan, who was relaxing at the patio table with a coffee in one hand and the newspaper in another, "They're eating dirt! Stop them! They're eating dirt!"

Had this been her, she would have reacted as swiftly as one would in, say, a house fire. But Evan just raised an eyebrow, seemed to adjust to his surroundings for a moment, as if just now remembering that the twins were in the yard and that he was supposed to be minding them while she squeezed in a shower that didn't even leave time to shave her legs, and then slowly folded his paper, set it on the teak wood table surface, and stood. And *stretched.*

Hope narrowed her eyes as she tightened her grip on the windowsill.

Had this been Hope, she would have snatched the trays of dirt from Rose's and Victoria's hands and immediately stripped them down, led them to the house, and carried each girl up to the bathtub. But Evan decided to use his words.

Four-year-olds didn't respond to words.

Summoning every last bit of patience she could manage, Hope abandoned the laundry basket and went downstairs, out the back door, and stood on the patio, barefoot and shivering with her wet hair. Or maybe she was shaking. It was, after all, a warm day for May.

Evan stood on the patio, barely in hearing distance from the playhouse, calmly telling the girls to please stop playing in the mud.

The girls, of course, did not listen. Chances were, they didn't hear either.

Hope waited to see if he would do anything more, but, turning to see her, he sat back down at the table and picked up his newspaper.

Hope's eyes darted to the girls and back to Evan. The unspoken words were clear. She would have to be the one to take action.

Only what course of action?

"I don't think I can do this anymore," she blurted, not even conscience of what she was saying. But there, the words were out. They'd been said. She couldn't take them back. And she wasn't sure she wanted to.

Her heart sped up a little, but Evan didn't react to her announcement. The girls continued to slap mud into plastic bowls and then attempt to feed each other with matching spoons.

Oh, for crying out loud! She stormed over to the twins, took the mud-filled bowls and spoons from their hands, led them by the wrists to the garden hose, and turned on the spigot. Her freshly laundered clothes were now covered in mud as they wriggled in protest and tried to slap her legs.

Evan watched from a safe distance.

"Can you help?" she asked as Rose tried to dash off the moment she peeled the once-white dress over Victoria's head.

"You're just going to hose them off?" he asked, setting down the paper with what appeared to be great reluctance.

"Do you have a better idea?" She stared at him. She was aware, she realized, that she was challenging him.

Evan did not have a better idea. He sighed, heavily, and then urged Rose to "go back to Mommy."

Through gritted teeth, Hope hosed the girls off, thankful that the water was not very cold at all, and then brought them into the house for a proper bath. When she had them dried, clothed in fresh, coordinating outfits, and seated in front of an educational cartoon show with a healthy snack of carrots and apple slices, she added their dirty dresses to the laundry pile.

Evan was still reading the paper when she returned to the patio. Had he not heard? Not cared? Not believed her? The lack of response fueled her, made her realize that she had meant it. Every word. She couldn't do this anymore!

"I could have used a little help," she said, folding her arms over her chest.

"It seems to me that you have it all covered." He gave a little smile at his double entendre and she glanced down at her pants, which bore the marks of dried, splattered mud.

"This isn't funny," she ground out.

He frowned at her. "You know I'm heading to Singapore in the morning. I need a little time to relax after that party yesterday."

"And I don't?" Her eyes widened in surprise.

He shook his head. "Please. You love those things."

"No," she said, realizing that it was true. "I don't. That party was work. A lot of work." And she had done more than ninety-nine percent of it, too, from the carefully chosen cotton-candy-colored paper stock with the gold font for the invitations, to going to three different stores to track down glitter-filled balloons, to having the truly genius (or crazy?) idea of putting a horn on that pony's head. She had stayed up until midnight putting together the favor bags, allowing for extra just in case some unexpected siblings tagged along. She had then woken at three, because she remembered that she had forgotten to buy strawberries for the smoothies, and then she hadn't been able to fall back asleep, so she started on the cake. Of course it was homemade. From scratch. And she had stood with a piping bag, her hair slipping from its bun, sweat on her brow, watching tutorials on the internet for piping the perfect trim on the perfect pink-frosted cake!

And she had chatted. And smiled. And served. And then, when the party was over, she had cleaned up! And what had Evan been doing when the party was over? Sleeping. On the couch.

"Then why'd you plan it?" he asked.

"Because it was a birthday party. I couldn't *not* have a party for them!"

"You could have made it more simple," he said.

She considered this for a moment. A sheet cake. Maybe cupcakes. Store bought. Some pizza. Juice boxes. Beer and wine. Chips and dip. Could she have done that? Would she have been happier? That had never been her life, not before Evan, and not with him. Before the girls, she had worked in public relations, and she'd taken her job as a mother as seriously as she had her former career, even if the effort went unnoticed more than half the time. But still, she'd tried, done her best, because she didn't know any other way. She didn't know how to keep things simple. The only times in her life that were simple were when she and her sisters would head up to Sunset Cottage, the one place where their mother wasn't concerned about keeping up appearances. The only time Hope wasn't worried about not being good enough.

"I wanted to give them a nice party," she finished. "But it's a lot of work. You could have put the girls to bed for me last night while I was cleaning up." She had bottled that one up inside all day, and there, it was finally out.

"You know they settle down better when you do it," he replied.

Hope counted to three. She waited for the anger to pass. It didn't.

"I could use a little help," she finally said. "When we're both home, at night, or on the weekends..."

"I'm working over fifty hours a week! I deserve some time to relax," Evan said.

"And I don't?" she cried. Then, remembering how their next-door neighbor liked to garden on weekends and was within earshot over the hedge, she lowered her voice to an angry whisper. "And I don't? I barely sleep. I'm exhausted. I'm lonely." And she was. She was with the girls all day, she was never alone, but she was somehow very lonely.

Evan looked at her in astonishment. "You're always at that playground talking to the other moms."

"But all we talk about are kids!" She remembered the days when her interactions with other adults were about something current, or even intellectually stimulating. "All we talk about are recipes and nap schedules."

Evan raised an eyebrow. "You have nap time to do as you please. I don't get that time in my day, Hope."

"And then who would do the laundry? Who would get dinner going?" She sounded shrill, even to her out ears. Did he really not see all she did? Did he think it happened like magic? "Besides, they won't nap much longer," she pointed out.

"Well, they go to school," he said.

"Three mornings a week!" She pulled in a breath. It would be easy to get derailed, to get into a tit for tat argument, but that was not the point of this. The point was that she was not happy. And she needed a change. "I want to be challenged. I want to be...inspired."

"What are you saying?" he asked, looking confused.

"I'm saying that...I think I'd like to go back to work. Or start a business. I do have skills. Heck, I can plan parties." Not that she wanted to plan parties, but she wanted to do something. Something outside the confines of her home. Something that brought her around other adults. Something that made her think. Something that made her feel rewarded for her efforts. Something that was more than just being a good, dutiful wife, mother. Daughter.

Evan's eyebrows rose so far up his forehead that she wasn't entirely sure how he felt by that. But then he gave a little smile. "You want to stay home with the kids. That's what you want to do."

"That's what I *wanted*," she said. "Now I think I need something for myself."

"And who will watch the kids?" He stared at her. "When I got the promotion, we discussed this. My travel schedule is crazy, and working in the city was too far of a commute for you to get back to the girls. And you wanted to stay home, Hope."

It was true, she did. She wanted to be the perfect mother. She just hadn't realized how much it would take out of her. That it would be so...unbalanced.

"Look, I put fresh towels out. In the kitchen. Did you notice?"

Now Hope had to count to ten, like she did when Victoria decided five minutes after a movie had started that she needed to use the bathroom instead of five minutes earlier, when Hope suggested she try.

"Can we talk about this when I get back?" Evan looked weary. "I have an early flight and I still haven't packed for my trip."

Trip. When was the last time that Hope had taken a trip? And Gran's funeral didn't count. They didn't take vacations. Evan couldn't get away from the office, and she had convinced herself it would be too challenging with the girls anyway. But now she thought of a change of scenery, of sand between her toes. And Gemma on her way—today—to Evening Island, to be with Ellie. It was going to be a reunion at their summer place, just the women, like it always was, after all these years.

"I'm taking the girls to the lake house," she announced. Ever since she'd suggested that Gemma go to Evening Island, she couldn't stop thinking of it. It was the one place she could escape, the pressure, the expectation, the feelings of restlessness and guilt and confusion that filled her days more and more. She needed to clear her head and think about what she really wanted. And she wanted to be around her sisters. She wanted to feel the way she did the last time they'd all been there together, when she was still in college, and her entire future was still wide and open.

"Your grandmother's house?" His brows pinched. He'd never been. She'd never pushed for it. She'd let it go, somehow, years back, when their lives merged. "When?"

She shrugged. "I'll drive up tomorrow."

"And when will you be back?" he asked.

She paused. "I don't know," she replied honestly.

He stared at her, and for the first time, she saw something close to fear in his eyes. "Well, you'll be back by the time I return from my business trip. We have our company outing with the firm coming up," he reminded her.

"I know," she replied. It was in her calendar, along with every other social event, school event, neighborhood event, and appointment. If it wasn't another birthday then it was a Saturday barbeque, another opportunity for the women on the block to show off their newest furniture. Her mother would have relished in it. Hope, she had come to realize, did not.

"So you have to be back in time for that," he said, seeming to relax a little.

"Actually," she said slowly, letting a thought take hold. She pictured her calendar, filled with obligations, and imagined skipping each and every one, and not even caring about the social consequences. She wouldn't (gasp!) even make a polite excuse. She wasn't going. That was all. She was not going to attend any more events that she did not want to attend. "The spouses don't all attend. I don't *have* to be back for that. And I'm not sure I will."

She lifted her chin, feeling the thrill of rebellion. Hope had always been a good girl. She opened the door to guests at her parents' annual New Year's Eve party, she smiled and remembered names. She knew every one of Evan's colleagues. She stood at his side. She did everything she was supposed to do.

Until now.

"Okay, okay, you've made your point now," he said, pushing back his chair to stand. "I'm sorry. I should have helped more with the party."

She shook her head. "Last year's party was the same. Next year's would be the same, too."

"Would be?" He blinked rapidly. "What are you saying, Hope?"

"I don't know, Evan," she said, swallowing hard. "I just know that I don't want to do this anymore."

And without another word, she slipped into the house, cleaned up the spilled apples and carrot slices that had gone between the white couch cushions, and even though the juice from the apple could leave a small stain, she decided not to tend to it.

She had packing to do.

Chapter Four

Gemma

Having no car, Gemma took the train as far north as it would get her, up through Wisconsin, and then cabbed it to the ferry port in Blue Harbor, Michigan. It was May, but the ferries were operating on a regular schedule now that the tulips were popping up all over the island. Midwesterners who had felt cooped up all winter were all too happy to shed their down parkas and heavy snow boots, even if the weather forecast did say it would only reach a high in the mid-sixties today.

The man who came to sit beside her on the ferry was wearing shorts and a polo shirt. She wouldn't judge, even if the breeze off the lake was particularly cold once the engine on the boat got going.

The old Gemma—the pre-breakup Gemma—might have scanned her eyes higher, to his face, then glance down at his hand, to see if he was wearing a ring. But the new Gemma—the broken-hearted Gemma—kept her eye on the view, watching as the large green land in the distance came closer and the white dots turned clearer, until she could see the details of the Victorian homes that the island was known for.

The ride was quick, less than fifteen minutes, and soon enough she was dragging her luggage across the wooden dock to town, inhaling the smell of fudge that the island was known for. She had called Ellie last night to let her know she was coming, unsure of what Ellie's reaction might be, and to her surprise, Ellie had seemed happy at the news, if not a bit distracted, but then, that was Ellie. She took life in stride. Sometimes Gemma envied her for it. Today, she was just grateful.

By the time she lugged her bags to the line of horse-drawn carriages that were parked at the port, she collapsed into her seat and leaned her head back.

"Where to?" the driver asked, glancing over his shoulder to catch her eye.

"West End Road," she told him. "Sunset Cottage?"

Everyone knew the house, or houses, technically. West End Road was famed for the row of Victorian homes that hugged the shoreline, not too far from the center of town, but far enough to make sure that the tourists didn't disturb the peace too much. It was quiet and peaceful, a total oasis from the bustling city life she'd lived in, and even years back, when she was younger, it had been a respite from their suburban life outside Cleveland. The school year was full of busy days: bus rides, class schedules, and then after-school activities, dinner, homework, and bedtime. But life on the island had no routine. There was no bedtime, and the sun didn't set until nearly ten at the peak of summer. The days were long and unstructured, and wonderfully carefree.

Hope was right; this was exactly what she needed. Here her mind could wander. Here it wouldn't be filled with the daily stressors that plagued her in the city, even if she did spend more and more time alone in her apartment. Here she would get out and take walks without a route in mind. Her mind would be clear of clutter, free to be creative!

She wouldn't worry about the deadline.

She wouldn't even think about the fact that a month from Saturday marked another key date on her calendar: the day she was supposed to be married.

She would soak in her surroundings. The island. Nothing had changed in all these years. Main Street still smelled like a candy store, with rich chocolate wafting through the air from the fudge shops, and the sweet smell of pies from the Island Bakery, who always sold the last slice before they turned the sign for the day.

The sidewalks were crowded, filled with kids licking ice cream cones from Main Street Sweets and women holding pink paper shopping bags from Lakeside Gifts. But as they rounded the bend and began heading north, the sounds and smells faded quickly, replaced with white picket fences lined with tulips and small wooden homes painted mint green, light blue, white, red, and even pink. She turned to stare at the water, letting it soothe her. Calm her. Even though Chicago bordered Lake Michigan, it wasn't the same.

Sunset Cottage wasn't too much farther up ahead now, and she watched in anticipation as it came into view. It had been in the family since Gran was just a girl, a summer cottage for her that had turned into a full-time residence when her husband died shortly after Gemma's father left for college. She took pride in the place, even if the upkeep was difficult with the harsh winters and remote location. But there were always fresh flowers in the planters near the door, her vegetable garden always produced enough for salads and tomato pies for dinner, and the grass was always free of weeds.

At least it had been. Until now.

Gemma leaned forward as they pulled up to the house and the driver hopped down to help her with the luggage. The grass was long, too long, and it was poking up through the fence that divided it from the neighboring homes, each in far better condition, because she knew that the Taylors and Andersons rented out each summer and hired caretakers throughout the year. The flowers in the pots that flanked the front door had probably been there since Gran was still alive, and had probably died around the same time that she had, too.

Gemma fumbled to pay the driver, her mind spinning, and she slowly walked up the path, her heart sinking with each step as the deferred maintenance became more obvious: peeling paint on the porch, rust on the lantern lights that flanked the front door, and she had only given a cursory glance. Whatever she did, she could not blame Ellie for this, even if it was, obviously, tempting. It would start everything off on the wrong foot, and what she needed to do was set up her desk and get to work. What did it matter if some flowers were dead and the yard looked like it hadn't met a mower since last September?

But it did matter, because some strange part of her needed this place to be exactly as it had always been, right down to Gran sitting on the front porch rocking in her chair. She needed one place she could rely on to always make her feel better. One place that promised good things, like Sunset Cottage always had.

She knocked, which seemed like a strange thing to do considering that she owned a third of the house, the same share as Ellie, but still, knowing Ellie, there was no sense in predicting what state Gemma would find her in. Ellie had always been free with her body, not shy about walking around the house in underwear or changing with the door open.

The need to knock was not for Ellie's sake. It was for Gemma.

Ellie answered right away, her cheeks flushed, her brown hair braided into a long rope that slung over her shoulder.

Before Gemma could stop herself, she blurted, "What happened to the yard?"

Ellie frowned. "Looks fine to me," she said with a shrug.

"The planters. The weeds," Gemma said. She mentally kicked herself for saying anything.

Ellie narrowed her eyes, her chin jutting in defense. "I have a career, you know. Besides, you own a third of this house. If you'd like to do something about it, I won't stop you."

She had a point. And Gemma had crossed a line. "Sorry. You're right. Now that I'm here, I can help."

She'd never mowed a lawn before, but how hard could it be? Sure, she'd hoped to get an hour of writing in before dinner, but maybe she'd spend the time helping Ellie instead. She'd cook her dinner, too, as a thanks for taking care of the house.

Except...she wasn't so sure that Ellie was taking care of the house. She willed herself to keep her expression neutral as she left her bags in the front hall and followed Ellie to the back of the house, where the kitchen was bright and sunny, with a view of the backyard, which was starting to resemble a field.

"Don't you just love wild flowers?" Ellie stared at her in the most challenging way.

Gemma swallowed hard and returned her gaze to the window where knee-high weeds that did indeed have some form of white and purple petals on them lined the fence and hugged the hammock she had hoped to use as a reading spot. Oh, dear.

She turned, glanced around the kitchen, which was virtually unchanged from when they were kids: white cabinets and wood floors. A fridge that had seen better days and a butcher block island where many cherry pies had been made.

But her eyes trailed to the overflowing wastebasket, the evidence of frozen meals and take-out containers on full display, along with paper plates and cups.

"Trash day is tomorrow," Ellie said quickly.

Gemma walked to the fridge, hoping to find a pitcher of cold lemonade waiting for her, like Gran always had on hand, but instead she found the light inside had burnt out and there wasn't even a container of milk on the shelf—only a bottle of white wine, which might be nice if she wasn't here on a mission.

She shut her eyes. This was the side of Ellie that drove their father crazy. Their mother was more protective of Ellie, if not a little dismayed. They didn't know what to do with her. While Gemma and certainly Hope had been predictable, willing to follow in the footsteps of the life that had been chosen for them, Ellie was not. It wasn't that she was a rebel; it was that she was simply not interested.

Gemma closed the door to the fridge. She'd go to the store. She'd buy groceries. Then she'd mow the yard. She'd cook dinner for Ellie as a sign of good will, and then she'd clean up the kitchen and get the house in working order. She'd wake up tomorrow and start writing. In fairness, she was probably too tired from travelling to get much written today anyway.

And who was she kidding? She hadn't written a word in five months.

"It's the first time back since Gran..." Gemma faded away, feeling her grandmother's absence more than ever before. She hadn't been back here since her college days—the last summer before she'd started working full time, and even then, her time here was cut down to only two weeks. Hope hadn't come back in years by then, and it was just her and Ellie. They'd gotten along fine, always had, until now. Because now, well, now the house felt like Ellie's house. Her paint supplies were all over the farmhouse kitchen table. The yard was full of weeds that only Ellie could find beauty in. And there was no food, because Ellie didn't cook.

Not that Gemma had room to judge, she thought, thinking of her recent habits. Still, her apartment was always clean, even if it was because she used cleaning as a way to release her stress. And procrastinate.

She could only assume there wouldn't be fresh sheets on her bed, either. Laundry. Another item on her list for the evening.

Ellie nodded. "It's been a long winter."

"The tourists are back now," Gemma pointed out.

"And you! Although, you're not the only one back in town," Ellie announced, her tone was distinctly giddy as she wandered barefoot down the hall and began lugging Gemma's luggage up the stairs.

"I'm not?" Gemma lifted her computer bag, precious cargo, and ran through a list of possibilities, people they knew who came and went from the island, like they once had. "Are the Taylors here?" she asked hopefully. She knew from the gossip that Gran and Ellie had shared over the years that the other family still attempted a family reunion for at least a week or two each summer. The two sets of sisters had always been so close, but after college, they'd lost touch.

Gemma glanced at Ellie now. They'd all lost touch in a way, she thought sadly.

Ellie stopped at the first landing and turned to face Gemma squarely. "No. Simon is here."

Gemma couldn't help but smile. Well, that explained her sister's good mood, not that she was complaining. Simon had been Ellie's first love, and from what Gemma knew about her sister's personal life, her only love. They'd been more than a summer romance in Ellie's mind, and Gemma knew just how deep the pain of their breakup had been for Ellie.

But now, from the joy in her sister's expression, it would seem that a second chance had presented itself. Like something straight out of one of Gemma's stories.

"Is he still cute?" Gemma tried to conjure up a clear image of him, hoping to find some inspiration for the book that was causing her so much struggle.

"Cuter," Ellie said matter-of-factly.

Wow. Simon had always been on the adorable end of the spectrum, if a few years too young for her, and Gemma tried to imagine what he might look like now, as a man. "So you've seen him?"

Ellie was nodding as she climbed to the second floor. "Yesterday. In town. He's here for the entire summer."

"The whole summer? Doesn't he have a job?"

"Of course he has a job." Ellie's smile slipped in defense of her first true love. "He went to Colgate, you know. And after that he went to Georgetown for law school. He's been living in Philly, working as an attorney."

Gemma arched an eyebrow, and Ellie said in a huff, "Gossip kept Gran occupied. Besides, you know how this island is."

Yes, Gemma did. And she wondered if any of the locals were already aware of the change in her relationship status. Gran had been very excited when she got engaged, after all. No doubt she'd told everyone she knew. Now, unless Ellie had set them straight, Gemma would be forced to.

And that was just...great.

She stood outside a row of open doors, suddenly feeling very tired. "Do you care which bedroom I take?" There were five in total, making it far from a cottage in the traditional sense of the word, and each one still held the same floral-printed wallpaper from when they were young girls.

"The one at the end is mine," Ellie said. It was the room their mother had stayed in each summer.

"Of course," Gemma said. "The biggest."

"Gran's was the biggest," Ellie replied. "Besides, I've been living here for six years. It's my home."

Gemma held up a hand at the edge in her tone. Clearly, there was still tension between them that would need to be resolved, but not tonight. Tonight she needed to get this house cleaned up so that tomorrow she could work through the day without any distraction.

"I was just joking," she said, hoping her tone was convincing. "You live here. You should have the biggest room. Besides, I was hoping to take the third-floor room. Is the desk still there?"

"I think so," Ellie replied. "You do know it's hot as heck up there, right?"

"Not at this time of year," Gemma said. "And not in the mornings and evenings when the windows are open." That was when she did her best writing, after all. When she wrote.

Ellie shrugged. "Suit yourself. It's better for Hope to be on the second floor anyway."

Gemma paused. "What?"

"Didn't you hear?" Ellie asked, her blue eyes shining. "Hope is coming too."

Gemma's pulse skipped a beat. "Hope is coming here? But..." But so many things! She settled on one: "But I just saw her. Last night."

"Well, I just spoke to her today," Ellie said rather proudly, betraying a note of sibling rivalry that had once been the only thing that had troubled them growing up. Hope was so gracious, so clearly the favorite, that garnering her approval was nearly as special as earning their father's, but far more achievable. "And she's coming tomorrow with the girls."

"With the girls?" Gemma tried to understand what Hope had been thinking. She knew that Gemma was in trouble with this book, that she needed space to write, and think clearly. Coming here had been Hope's idea in the first place! How was she expected to push out another two hundred fifty pages of publishable material with two four-year-olds running around the house?

"Well, it's not like she can leave them," Ellie said with a laugh. "She knew that you were coming, so I think she thought, why not? All of us together at Sunset Cottage again. Like old times!"

Like old times, Gemma thought. If only.

Chapter Five

Ellie

Ellie dashed to the studio first thing Monday morning, only it wasn't because she was eager to finish the painting of the South Bay lighthouse or because she wanted to get the coffee brewed before the fishermen pulled in from another early morning out on the lake.

The truth of the matter was that Gemma was already posing a problem—something that Ellie had convinced herself wouldn't happen. She'd told herself that Gemma wouldn't come here if she wasn't sorry, that the argument they'd had last summer had been the stress talking. Being at their parents' house was always tense, and this visit had been a sad time too. Emotions were charged. They'd argued. They'd left without saying good-bye.

She'd told herself that she could have been a better sister too. Could have sent a card or something more than a voicemail when Gemma's engagement ended.

She'd been prepared to let everything go. To start fresh. But then Gemma had come in like a tornado, stripping beds and doing laundry, the machine making an awful noise and the dryer shaking so hard that Ellie could feel the floorboards vibrating. Really! Why hadn't Gemma just taken her up on the offer to hang the linens outside to dry, to let the sun do what it was meant to do?

But Gemma was too busy mowing the lawn to think about hanging clothes, and she'd taken a weed whacker to those lovely wildflowers, too, leaving only a handful which she had at least been thoughtful enough to put in a vase and set on the center of the kitchen table—after she'd banished all of Ellie's painting supplies to a corner of the living room.

Ellie had been about to protest, until Gemma returned from town with a bicycle basket full of groceries and got to work making a simple dinner of chicken salad and fresh bread that she set up on the front porch, with a citronella candle to ward off the bugs. That had been lovely, and because it was possibly leading up to a peace offering, Ellie had said nothing. They chatted about the island and reminisced about their happy times here, and Ellie had gone to bed feeling nervous but hopeful that the worst was behind them.

But this morning, when she woke to the horrible smell of cleaning detergents and ammonia and the sound of buckets clanking and Gemma cursing under her breath, even though she insisted that she hadn't, well, Ellie knew she had to get out of there.

And so here she was. At seven in the morning. In her studio.

She decided that she may as well be productive.

She brewed a pot of coffee and finished her painting and then went through her recent inventory to see which ones she might drop off later this afternoon at the gift shops in town. On a good week, she could sell a dozen, on a bad week, none. On average, she was happy to sell five or six. They didn't go for much, a couple hundred each, some of the smaller ones less, but each sale made her heart swell, validated her effort, her time, her passion.

And it made her curl her lip, just a little, and think, *Told you so.*

After all, her father—and Gemma—couldn't exactly accuse her of being a starving artist if someone was paying for her work, could they?

It would be better when Hope arrived, she told herself. Then the dynamic would be balanced. Dinners on the porch, sisterly bonding. A carefree summer. It would be like old times, just like Hope had promised on the phone.

Thinking of old times, Ellie's mind wandered to Simon. He was on this island, at this very moment. She barely suppressed a squeal, and made a promise to herself that no amount of tension between her and Gemma could ruin this good feeling. Besides, Hope was such a calm, maternal force, always so in control and diplomatic—she'd smooth everything over in no time. She always had that effect on things, always had an eye out for Ellie when she was younger; even if it was just silent solidarity, she had been a comforting presence.

Ellie decided to bring three of her newest watercolors with her into town, before the shops opened for the day. They were cheerful, showing the island in the spring, with new buds on the trees and colorful flowers sprouting up from the fresh green grass. A few she couldn't part with, and those she hung in her studio, for a premium price, or kept with her at home, back at Sunset Cottage. Most were landscapes, all of the island, or the boats in the water surrounding the island, or some, just of the water (blue was one of her favorite colors to work with), but she sometimes felt inspired by the old homes along the coastline, the quaint architecture that was so unique to this location, and the feeling of simpler times that could only be experienced by biking through its winding paths.

The paintings she'd chosen for today were easy to carry, all done on the same size canvas, a popular seller, she'd been told, because the large ones were simply too difficult for tourists to transport home via the ferry, and she walked down the cobblestone street that led directly into the center of town. Mandy, a year-round resident who had grown up on the island, was already stirring fudge in the window of the candy shop that had been owned by her family for three generations, and Ellie could smell the waffle cones baking, as Mandy no doubt prepared for another unseasonably warm day that would hopefully stir up some desire for ice cream.

It was Monday, so there was bound to be less street traffic, but Ellie didn't mind. Who needed tourists when she had Simon looming about? She held her free hand to her stomach at the thought.

The sign to Lakeside Gifts read closed, but she knew from experience that the door was technically open. She turned the knob just as Naomi was stepping out from the back room, her brows up in surprise that relaxed into a smile when Ellie greeted her.

Ellie greeted her friend as she always did, with a "hi" instead of a "hello." Still, she glanced over at the large birdcage near the entrance, where Naomi's pet parrot, Jewel, was perched. The large, handwritten sign warning patrons not to say hello was fair warning, even if often missed. Or ignored.

Luckily, Jewel showed no reaction to Ellie's greeting. He blinked his beady eyes and stayed perfectly quiet.

"Dropping off a few more paintings, if you're interested," she said.

Naomi smiled. "We sold two yesterday. A set. So yes, let me see what we have here."

Two in one day. To the same buyer. Ellie imagined them side by side in a sunroom, or maybe in a guest room. She tried not to think of them hanging in a bathroom, though she knew that some of them ended up there nonetheless. Just last week a woman had popped into the studio after noticing her work at the gallery on Hill Street and had decided the stunning painting in shades of yellow and peach that Ellie had taken particular pride in and had risen before sunrise to capture would be "perfect" over the woman's master bathroom toilet.

Ellie set down the paintings, telling herself she couldn't take offense if Naomi chose only one.

Naomi studied each canvas and then said, "I'll take all three."

"Really?" Ellie felt her heart begin to pound. She'd assumed that Naomi would take two, to replace the pair that had sold. "Great!"

Naomi gave her a rueful look as she moved the paintings to the side of the counter. "Don't look so surprised. You're really talented."

"If you say so," Ellie sighed. She couldn't shake the feeling of needing to be something more than what she was. All she could be was herself, she knew, and she'd remained true, even when it hurt, but sometimes it felt like it would never be enough.

"I do say so," Naomi said. "And if you don't take my word for it, ask the client who bought your set. She had plenty to choose from."

It was true. There were many other paintings and prints for sale in the store—most by local artists that Ellie respected.

She felt a swell of pride. She couldn't wait to tell Gemma about this, even though she knew that Gemma, being creative as well, had always supported her work more than any other member of her family. But Gemma had street credit: a major publisher had invested in her work. In her parents' eyes, Gemma's work was legitimate.

Well, who said that Ellie's wasn't? Naomi was her friend, but she was also a tough islander who didn't sugarcoat the truth.

Ellie wondered what she would have to say about Simon being back in town, and what this meant for Ellie's future. Naomi had never met him, only heard the stories. Originally from Blue Harbor, she'd taken over the store about five years ago, and had quickly become one of Ellie's biggest supporters and closest friends.

Ellie pulled in a breath, wondering where to start, and then decided not to say anything—yet. She'd rather wait and see for herself. For the first time in a while, this island was full of possibility again, and that was a feeling she wasn't ready to part with just yet.

She waited for Naomi to hand her a check for her sales, tucked it into her pocket, and then pushed back out into the street, her hands bare, but her heart full.

Only one thing—or rather, one person—could make it fuller.

Fighting off a smile, she hurried her step down to the Trillium Café, which had always been Simon's favorite spot in town mostly because it was right on the water and no one served better pancakes than Marge, who had owned the place forever.

She walked into the restaurant, which she frequented a little too often since she'd become a permanent resident of the island, even if that meant having to sometimes chitchat with the more eccentric residents. Sure enough, Ches was perched at the counter, and he grinned a little too widely when he saw her, revealing what was now three missing teeth (she grimaced to remember that one had been wiggly around mid-January) and patting the seat next to him.

"Oh, I—" Her eyes darted around, but it was just a sea of locals, and none of them young, because young people didn't live on a remote island in the middle of the Great Lakes, did they? Young people went out into the world, made something of their lives, and then vacationed here.

She tried to think of an excuse fast enough, something that wouldn't take too much light out of poor Ches's eyes, when she felt a hand graze her lower back, ever so briefly.

"She's actually grabbing a table for us both, Chester," Simon said, ever so smoothly.

Ellie inhaled a breath. Her knees felt more than a little weak. And her heart, well, it positively soared like the seagulls that swept and dove all along the shoreline. If only she could capture this feeling as permanently as she captured the birds on canvas. She wanted to hold onto it. Never let it go.

And maybe, if Simon stuck around a little longer, she wouldn't have to.

"Thank you," she whispered, once they were out of earshot.

Simon grinned as he slid into a booth near the window. "You weren't waiting for anyone, were you?"

Just you, she thought. She'd spent an entire summer waiting for him once.

Best not to think about that heartache, she told herself. She opened her menu, even though she of course had it memorized. The blueberry pancakes were the best in the Midwest, and she had travelled enough to be able to say that, despite the fact that she now hadn't left Evening Island since...she frowned. Well, there had been that shopping trip to Blue Harbor last November, before the big snow hit. And stayed.

"No, my sister Gemma arrived last night and she's taken over the place so I thought I'd get out for a bit." She'd dared to think that having Gemma around would be fun, like all the other summers growing up were. That Evening Island brought out the best of them, and that Sunset Cottage was a place of good memories, not the usual arguments that bogged them down once they got back to the "real" world.

Except that this was her "real" world now. And she liked it just the way it was. Wildflowers in the yard and all.

She glanced at Simon across the table. Well, she liked it a little better now that there was some excitement to be had.

"Gemma's back in town?" Simon smiled fondly.

Ellie pursed her lips. "Yes, well." No sense in dragging down this special breakfast by talking about the recent shifts in her family dynamic. "And Hope is coming with her twin girls today."

"Everyone is back then!"

Simon's grin was broad, and oh, so appealing, that for a moment she just stared at him. It wasn't until the space between his brow knitted that she realized she had gotten a little too caught up in the moment.

Quickly, she cleared her throat and closed her menu. "Yep. Everyone is back." She smiled at him, hoping he couldn't hear the pounding of her heart across the table.

She glanced down at his hands, still clutching the menu, thinking how wonderful it would be if he just moved them a few inches closer to hers.

The waitress approached (new seasonal hire, college kid) and they placed their orders. She filled their coffees and hurried off to the next table, looking so nervous and flustered that Ellie had half a heart to warn her how things would be by Memorial Day.

But she had better things to think about right now. Like how blue Simon's eyes were. And how intensely he was looking at her, just like when they were younger. No one had ever looked at her that way since. Surely that still meant something?

"So, tell me everything you've been up to." He leaned forward, giving her his full attention, and her heart began to race. "What's it like living here year-round?"

"Quiet. Lots of inspiration for my work, of course." She wasn't so sure that she sounded convincing.

"Winters must be tough," he remarked, looking at her as if genuinely wanting to hear what she had to say about that.

Oh, she had to a lot to say. Being a resort island, most of the businesses closed down in winter. Many restaurants were seasonal—their owners had primary residences in Michigan or Wisconsin, and the gift shops took long breaks too. Sales were low, she'd expected that, telling herself it gave her time to boost her inventory, and that she had done. She had an entire closet full of winter landscapes. But there were only so many snow-frocked trees that you could paint, she realized...

"Christmas is really magical here," she said, holding onto the one shining moment of that long, cold stretch. She didn't say that after the holidays, it was all downhill until April, when the snow finally began to thaw. "They put a tree right there—" She motioned out the window to the edge of Main Street, but Simon didn't follow her gaze. Instead, she realized with a flutter, he was looking at her.

She felt her cheeks heat. She took a sip of her coffee. She'd forgotten to add sugar to it, but she found that she didn't even care.

"And you?"

She glanced up to see the waitress already delivering their food, looking rather smug about that, if Ellie did say so herself. Couldn't she have postponed things a little longer? Really, did the kitchen have to be quite so efficient?

Simon swallowed a mouthful of hash browns. "I started my own law practice, actually. It's not easy, but it's given me the opportunity to spend some time out here this summer."

She didn't let on that she of course knew he was a lawyer, just as he'd planned to be. It was forgivable, she supposed, given how small the island was and that all the locals knew all the locals and all the seasonal people too. And Simon and his family were seasonal people. They were property owners. That made them islanders. And that made their business, well, everyone's business.

"My mom hasn't been well," he explained, "She wanted to get back here for the season and it seemed like an opportunity for me to help."

"It isn't anything serious?" She felt guilty for not knowing, even though she hadn't seen Mrs. Webber on this island in at least two years.

"She had pneumonia over the winter," he explained. "And she's been struggling to get back on her feet. I'm hoping the warm weather will help her improve." He grinned, and Ellie set a hand on his arm. Warm and soft, she let it stay like that for a moment.

"I'm sure that having you here will help her improve." She grinned. Like old times.

"I'm fixing up the house for her, not doing much, of course, but more than my father can do. He's getting on in age."

"And you work remotely?" she asked, sipping her drink. She couldn't peel her eyes from him. She feared that if she did, she would wake from a wonderful, delicious dream, one that she had had many times over the years, flashbacks, really, to the last summers she had spent on this island before it became her permanent residence. When Evening Island and Simon Webber were interconnected, one and the same, where it seemed that one couldn't exist without the other.

He nodded. "I'm a contract lawyer, not a trial attorney. I spend a lot of time reading." He went on to describe a current case.

Ellie nodded, opening her eyes, pretending to find this not only interesting but also new information, despite Gran filling her in on all she'd heard in her weekly quilting club. But what she was really thinking was that his smile was just as adorable as it was ten years ago.

"And you're doing all that while helping around the house too?"

"Well, my fiancée is better with the domestic side of things..."

She felt the blood drain from her face. For a moment, she wasn't even sure she was breathing. She stared at him, and his brow flinched, forcing her to recover, and quickly.

"Fiancée? Well, this is news!" She smiled brightly, even though her heart felt like it was breaking into a million pieces, just like it had all those years ago, when he'd left the island, gone to college, and the year after that, when he'd stayed at college to take summer classes instead of come back to the island like he used to.

Like he'd promised.

He shrugged, looking nonplussed. "Thanks, I guess. It's what people do, right? Grow up? Get married?"

She nodded, smiled tightly. Yes, it was what people did. But not what she had done. It wasn't by choice. It was more that her life had never been one to follow a conventional path, even if she'd tried.

And just like that, it seemed all too clear. Simon might have been the guy who splashed with her in the water and kissed her on the sandy shore and trotted alongside her through the woods that divided their two houses, always going faster than her, even though her horse was definitely faster, who picked berries with her off wild bushes and then biked home, only to stop and eat them all before they made it to the kitchen. His skin was always bronzed, bringing out the blueness of his eyes, but even then, way back then, he had plans.

And she...she didn't.

She glanced at her watch, pretending to find surprise in what she saw, even though she barely registered the second hand. "Oh! I completely forgot that I'm meeting a client to hand over a commission."

"A commission?" He looked impressed.

Ellie slid out of the booth. On a few occasions, someone saw her work in one of the shops in town and then made a point of finding her studio, where they asked for something specific to be made, a portrait of their child playing down near the water, or one of their sailboats, docked at the harbor. But today, there was no commission to hand off. The season had just started.

And now, she realized, it was going to be a very long season indeed. Just as bad as the winter.

Maybe, between her sisters and now Simon's fiancée lingering about, worse.

Chapter Six

Hope

Hope was prepared for the drive. That was the thing about her, she thought, as she pulled into the ferry lot at the northern tip of Michigan. She was always prepared. She had snacks for car trips, Band-Aids in the small pocket of her handbag for scraped knees, and an extra five hundred in cash in her bedside drawer, for emergencies. She had spreadsheets made up for all their family vacations: detailed daily schedules right down to the exact outfits and hair bows the girls would wear. She packed accordingly.

She had not been prepared to leave her husband, if that was what she had done. She wasn't sure, actually.

They'd gone about the rest of yesterday as if the conversation hadn't happened, and Evan had only brought it up again when he saw her pull their suitcases out of the spare room closet.

"I'll see you when I get back," was all he said that morning as he slipped out the door for the cab that was waiting to take him to O'Hare. He wouldn't be back for three weeks or until the merger closed. She'd said nothing.

She hadn't prepared to go to Evening Island, either. She hadn't bought the necessary staples required for such a trip! She knew that if she took the time to go to the store, load up on sunscreen and new swimsuits, got the girls haircuts, and fretted over snacks for the car ride that she would lose her nerve, stay put, and she didn't want to stay put. She was frankly starting to fear that if she did stay put she would go crazy.

But now, sitting in the car at the ferry dock in Blue Harbor, staring at the lake and the island off in the distance, she feared she had gone crazy. She'd done it. Loaded up all the clothes that made sense into the suitcases, stuffed in toiletries and hairbrushes and a hair dryer and her cosmetic case, all without a list. She had the unsettling feeling that she had forgotten something (contact lens solution, or her toothbrush) but then she told herself to calm down, that she could just buy it there. She just needed to get there, first. She needed to get out of the car and go.

She turned to the girls, who were quietly eating their crackers. The backseat was covered in crumbs. Empty (at least, she hoped they were empty) sugar-free, organic juice boxes were splayed on the seat between them.

"Ready for some girl time?" That's what she'd called it, because that's what it was, really. A little time with her sisters, her daughters, not much different than the summers she'd spent here with Gran and her mother.

The twins cheered, even though she suspected they had no idea what girl time meant and were only picking up on her enthusiasm, even if it was coming from her strangled throat. On the drive here, she'd received no less than four phone calls from various neighbors, and one from the dentist, whose appointment she had skipped, literally clear forgotten and skipped, scheduled for ten o'clock this morning! She religiously went with the girls every six months, all three of them keeping their oral hygiene in order, checking that box and moving on, and now, she had played hooky.

Would she like to reschedule for another day this week, they had asked. And she had experienced the strange thrill of saying no, she couldn't, and she actually couldn't reschedule at this time at all!

For the first time in her entire existence, her calendar did not contain a dentist appointment on it for the foreseeable future. She felt scared. She felt rebellious.

She felt freaking wonderful.

She took the bags from the trunk and, with a daughter on either side of her, managed to get everything to the ticket booth. "Three to the island," she said.

"Round-trip?" When she didn't respond immediately, the man inside the booth added, "Good for a week."

"One way then," she said, fighting back a wave of nausea as he handed her a long-term parking sticker for the car.

But it wasn't until they were seated on the boat, her hands now gripping the bodies of her wiggling children so they wouldn't slip and fall as the motor started and the boat began to slide over the smooth water of Lake Huron, that what she had done finally sank in.

She had done it. Done what she had said she would do. She hadn't just muttered under her breath or gone to bed angry or passive aggressively left Evan's dirty mug on the counter instead of placing it in the dishwasher with the others. She had packed up her girls, driven four hundred miles, and now she was on a boat, the wind in her hair, the air so fresh and clean that she could almost smell the island, and Chicago, and her life, was so far behind her that for one glorious moment, she nearly forgot it ever existed.

That moment ended quickly, when Rose tapped her on the leg, looked at her with round, scared eyes, and then vomited all her crackers, organic juice, and carrot sticks into Hope's lap. Onto her white capris, technically.

Rose started to cry, and Victoria, seeing what had happened, started to scream.

And for a moment, just one moment, Hope began to wonder if this had been such a good idea, after all.

"Oh, let me." A man was beside her, handing her a wad of napkins that bore the logo of a fast food chain she would never allow her girls to eat at, not on her watch. (Evan, she knew, had snuck them there the very few times he had "babysat" so she could attend a meeting at the preschool or, once, the neighborhood book club, that only lasted one session when it was clear no one wanted to actually read the book—well, Hope had read the book, and taken notes in the margin.)

"Thank you." Flustered, Hope took the napkins, using them first to wipe Rose's face and then attempt damage control on herself.

Rose's face was chalk white now, and Hope was intensely afraid that she would throw up again, but by her calculation, there was probably nothing left in her.

She pulled her daughter down into her lap. "We're almost there," she said, as much to herself as to the girls. They were almost there. They'd actually done it. And once there, everything would be better. It always was.

"I have some..." The man, whom Hope finally looked at properly, pulled the sticks of what appeared to be a couple lollipops from his pocket. "I always grab a few when I stop by the bank."

He was attractive, a few years older than she was, with kind hazel eyes and a rather amused smile, all things considered. Dressed in a white polo and khakis, it was hard to determine his reasons for travelling to the island. Hardly vacation attire, and he didn't look familiar.

His grin quirked and she felt her shoulders relax. Normally, she never gave her girls high-fructose corn syrup, let alone red dye, but normally she didn't feel a little flutter at the kindness of what she now realized was quite a handsome man, either.

"Thank you," she said again.

"My pleasure," he said, holding out the two lollipops for the girls, who glanced at her for approval before greedily yanking the candy from the man's hands. He laughed and, seeming satisfied with that interaction, said, "Have a nice time."

"You too," she said wistfully. She watched him go, until he was at the far helm of the boat, thinking that this was the most help and support she had received in a very long time and that she sort of loved him for it, more than she probably should.

She watched to see if he was alone, or going to meet someone who was waiting, but then Victoria was thrusting a sticky wrapper at her, and Rose was asking her to help peel the wrapper, and she thought it was just as well.

He probably had children of his own, she thought, reining in her disappointment. After all, she was a married woman. For now.

*

They took a carriage to the house, something that thrilled the girls to no end, and something that made her smile, too, and not because of the smell of manure. Her car was part of her life back home, and she wanted to forget about that life for a while, the way she used to every summer as a girl, before the pressure of school and grades started all over again.

The house came into view and she inhaled sharply, all at once sure that she had made the right decision in coming here. With its white gable and wraparound porch, it was just as wonderful as she'd remembered it, maybe more so.

The sky was blue and the grass was green and the water was right there, sparkling and still. Later, she'd take the girls over to wade in it and collect rocks.

Now she hurried to unload everything and bring it all up onto the porch. The paint was peeling, she noticed, showing signs of age that hadn't been there last time she'd visited, marking the passing of time that she tried to ignore.

It would all be the same. It had to be the same.

"Hello?" she called as she turned the knob of the front door and let it swing open. The girls ran inside, ahead of her, and she braced herself that they wouldn't knock over one of Gran's porcelain figurines, until she remembered that Gran was not here.

Her heart gave a little tug. She should have visited more, she knew. But there was college and then Evan and then the girls. And life was so busy. Too busy.

From upstairs she heard the floorboards creak, and a moment later, Gemma appeared at the top of the stairs.

"Surprise!" she said brightly. She was feeling downright giddy really, now that she was here, on land, on the island. An entire body of water was separating her from the real world. No need to focus on the fact that it was only a fifteen-minute-long ferry ride.

Gemma didn't look as pleased to see her as Hope had expected. She looked wary, and tired, really, as she came down the steps slowly, stopping at the base. "Ellie told me you were coming. Why didn't you tell me?"

"No time!" Hope was a little breathless. True, she'd had time to tell Ellie, but that had been a requirement, seeing as Ellie was living here now, even if the house did belong to all three of them.

"What made you decide to come?" Gemma pressed.

Hope glanced around the room. The afghan that usually hung from the back of the loveseat was missing and some of the heavy paintings had been replaced with Ellie's light and airy watercolors. "Oh, you know Evan had that business trip in Singapore, and the girls are finished with preschool for the year, so I thought, why not?"

Gemma pursed her lips together, but said nothing.

"The house looks good," Hope commented.

Gemma's look was rueful. "You can thank me later."

Hope gave a wry smile. She should have known this was Gemma's doing. Left to her own devices, Ellie would pick her clothes from a pile in her closet and crawl into an unmade bed each night, and that wasn't just when they were children. They'd shared enough recent events at their parents' house for her to know Ellie hadn't changed her ways yet. If ever.

In a way, she hoped Ellie never would.

"You didn't have to," she started.

Gemma's eyes widened. "Believe me, I did. Or you would have!"

Hope wasn't sure what to make of that remark, so she said nothing. Really, was it assumed that her standards were so high? That she liked everything just so?

Her sisters may be surprised to find out that her life was absolutely nothing like it appeared on the surface. Had Gemma not noticed the stain on Hope's pants?

She looked over to see Rose wander out of the kitchen, without her clothes on. Gemma had to laugh at that, and she did.

Hope, however, was far from amused. While Rose had no problems with modesty, Victoria was the opposite, and had refused to wear the tankini with the lemon-wedge print that Hope had ordered for the summer.

"Where are your clothes?" she asked, giving her sternest, no-nonsense look. It came naturally. Once, she had imagined motherhood to be baking cookies and cuddling under the blanket with a picture book. Now it meant wiping throw up off yourself in public and wrangling nude children.

This was what Evan didn't understand. He had never idealized parenthood. He never had...expectations. Evan's life hadn't changed much from before the twins came along to now. But her life had. Her life, as her own person, had officially ended. Maybe, she thought, it had never even begun.

"It's hot in this house!" Rose pouted, pushing out her lips and narrowing her eyes in Hope's direction.

"Right," Hope said crisply. "It's nap time." It wasn't, not really, but it was also eastern standard time zone here, so technically they were an hour ahead of their routine, meaning that it was nap time, on island time.

"No!" Rose wailed, fueling Hope's decision.

Hope took her by the hand and led her into the kitchen, where sure enough, the sweet little pink romper was lying in a heap next to her bunny-printed underwear. She glanced around. Her heart sped up. "Where's your sister?"

She stared at Rose. Rose stared back with round eyes.

Gemma was the one to walk through the back door, and Hope hoisted Rose onto her hip, her heart pounding as a million thoughts raced through her mind. Her child had escaped. Gone off around the house, crossed the road, and was now floating in Lake Huron. Evan would never forgive her. She would never forgive herself! It wouldn't have ever happened if she hadn't come here. She shouldn't have come here! She should have woken up, eaten her standard half a cup of Greek yogurt with a cup of fresh fruit and a black coffee and then gone to the dentist for her semiannual cleaning. If she'd wanted to see a lake, she could have driven fifteen minutes down the road to Lake Michigan.

"Victoria!" Her voice was shrill. She never would have screamed like this back home—the neighbors would be sure to talk. But Sunset Cottage was remote, and the two houses on either side, by the looks of it, were still unoccupied for the season.

"The playhouse!" she suddenly said. Frantically, she swiveled her head to the left, her eyes falling on the old shed that the Taylor girls had been allowed to turn into a playhouse. Their father had painted it white and their mother had made curtains for the window out of floral-printed pillowcases and Hope could remember being just as envious as her sisters were, not over the tiny playhouse but over just how involved the Taylor girls' parents were with them. Hope had vowed to be like that when she became a mother. And she had. She'd given up her career—one that she was good at and enjoyed. She did all the crafts, and did all the groups. And now...she had lost her child.

Gemma was the first one to make it to the playhouse, with Hope trailing behind, Rose bouncing on her hip, still in the buff, not that Hope cared just now. She hoped there were no garden tools in there, no sharp objects like axes or saws that Victoria might find tempting to touch.

She held her breath as Gemma pulled open the door, which was already half-open, Hope now saw, and out popped a little smiling face. "Surprise!"

Gemma whooped in relief, but Hope clenched her jaw so tight that she was afraid she really might have to go the dentist soon, and she doubted very much that the dentist on the island would take her insurance.

"That's it!" she snapped, turning into Mean Mommy, the mother she had sworn she would never be, the mother she was rapidly becoming, because it was just so much, all day, all the time! It was so...thankless! There was no promotion to strive for. No paycheck deposited into her account every other Friday. Evan hadn't even commented on the unicorn, well, other than with an eye roll. "It's time for a nap!"

Only as soon as she saw Victoria emerge from the shed, her bottom lip now quivering, she knew that there would be no nap, at least not without a bath. This was her life, she realized. Feeding, bathing, cleaning. Repeat.

"But I don't want a nap!" Rose screeched into her ear.

"Well, I do!" Hope ground out.

She was aware that Gemma was watching her with wide eyes. That she had slipped, shown a side of herself that she wasn't proud of, a side that she didn't want to reveal, or even own. But there it was.

"You've had a long drive," Gemma said, taking Victoria by the hand. "I can bathe the girls if you want to get started unpacking?"

Hope could have wept with gratitude. For the second time that day, someone was showing her kindness, someone was offering to help her, and that was more than Evan had done since...well, before conception.

They went into the house, and she decided to take the two small rooms at the end of the hall on the second floor where she and her sisters had stayed as girls, dividing them as they saw fit, Gemma usually alternating between the two, or sometimes all three squeezing into the one room's double bed. She immediately realized that, if she had planned this better, she would have thought to include a gate to put on the girls' room so that they couldn't easily escape in the middle of the night, get lost in a strange house and then, say, fall down the stairs.

Then she remembered that this particular set of bedrooms had a Jack and Jill connecting bathroom. "Thank God," she breathed, deciding she could close the girls' room and only give them entry and exit access to the rest of the house through her own room.

Gemma was already loading the girls into the bath. "You sure everything is okay?"

Hope felt shaky and out of sorts. She nodded, wandering into the room the girls would share to set their clothes in the dresser.

"It was a long drive," she said again.

She started folding each individual piece of clothing and setting them in the drawer, and then stopped herself, because really, what did it matter? Tidy drawers and ironed tiny T-shirts didn't matter, not on Evening Island, and that was why she was here. So she didn't have to worry about all those little things that were making her so miserable. Here the children could roam free (well, under supervision) and her sisters could help her out, and she could think clearly without having to play "the quiet game" in order to hear her own thoughts!

The girls came into the room, wrapped in towels, their hair wet, and she turned down the covers, questioning only for a moment if Ellie would have bothered to put fresh linens on the beds, and then decided it was fine. Fine. It was the cottage. Here they could relax.

The girls fell asleep quickly, and she pulled the blinds, letting only a bit of sunlight glow through the cracks near the window frame. Gemma had already left, and Hope crawled into her own bed and shut her eyes, just for a moment. And she thought about the man on the boat.

Her hero.

Chapter Seven

Gemma

The noise would not stop. Even from the third-floor room she had claimed for herself, she could hear the voices, the singing, the crying, the arguing when it was time for a nap or a snack that didn't quite meet the girls' approval. She'd been listening to it for over forty-eight hours. But Hope had to deal with it every day.

For not the first time, she didn't know how her sister did it.

"I don't know how you do it," she said when she came downstairs, her laptop in hand, after admitting defeat and knowing that she would never get any work done in the house so long as the twins were there. It had been a rainy morning, but the skies were clearing. Her plan was to carve out a spot at the Cottage Coffeehouse. At this rate, it would become her regular table.

Hope was wiping down the kitchen table while the girls scampered away, leaving their half-eaten snack behind.

"It all becomes very routine once you're in it. You'll see when you have some of your own someday." Catching herself, Hope looked alarmed. "Gemma. I'm sorry."

"It's fine. There are even days when I forget about my broken engagement," Gemma said with a wave of her hand, but that wasn't true of course, and her sister understood her well enough to know that.

"You'll find someone else. Someone better," Hope said.

"Will I?" Gemma saw the sympathy in Hope's eyes, and she wondered if her sister really believed her encouraging words or if she was just trying to lift Gemma's spirits. "Maybe I don't want to find anyone else."

"Oh, you say that now..." Hope gave a knowing look.

"It's not easy to find someone." Gemma had dated a bit in college, but Sean had been her first serious relationship. She'd thought it was true love. Now she didn't know if such a thing even existed.

For her, at least, she thought, looking at Hope. Hope had found her happy ending, after all.

"I think someone will come along eventually," Hope said. "If you're open to it."

Gemma grabbed a piece of fruit from the overflowing bowl on the counter and studied it. "Do you really think it's that easy to find more than one person that you could feel something for?" She wanted to believe it, but she was struggling. And the only thing lonelier than feeling like everyone else had found love except her was writing about it in her books.

Hope gave an evasive look and pushed a strand of her hair from her face as she straightened. "I do actually."

Just then, there was a shattering sound, and she and Hope froze. Gemma knew that she should stick around, offer to help, but then she thought of her deadline. She was down to twenty-two days now. She couldn't afford to give up even an hour at this point.

"I should get to the coffee shop," she said, wincing. "Don't wait on me for dinner. I don't know how long I'll be tonight. I need to finish this chapter." And start the next one, she thought, feeling the panic build again; but for now, just finishing this chapter would be good enough.

"I was hoping we could all have dinner together tonight." Hope gave her a look of obvious disappointment, and Gemma pushed back the guilt.

"Tomorrow night. I have to work, Hope," she said, expecting her sister to understand.

But Hope just said, "It's a convenient excuse, isn't it? Work?" Catching Gemma's frown, she waved her away. "Don't mind me. I know you have your deadline. I'm not upset with you."

Perhaps not, but it would seem that Hope was upset with someone. Evan?

Nonsense. Hope had the fairy-tale life. Maybe if Gemma focused on her sisters' love lives instead of her own, she wouldn't feel like such a fraud every time she sat down to write.

Gemma didn't have time to think about that just now. She turned, closed the door to the house behind her, and instead of feeling the guilt that she knew she should have for abandoning her sister in the midst of domestic chaos, she instead felt a sense of freedom that she hadn't even known existed or that she even needed until she had spent four days sharing a house with her sisters.

She was used to being alone. The only unwelcome disruption to her routine was the occasional siren or the barking of her neighbor's teacup yorkie down the hall who couldn't have scared off a burglar if she tried.

She walked down the gravel driveway to the road, pinching her mouth when she saw how quickly the grass was growing back. The rain hadn't helped matters, and now she would either have to take more time away from writing to handle it or see if Hope might help out, and she already knew how that would go. Hope had a yard crew for that type of thing. She would suggest that they do the same.

More money, Gemma thought as she wandered down the road, taking in her surroundings, trying to push away the nagging worry that she had only written fifteen pages since she had been here, and while that was better than what she'd accomplished in five months, most of it was just scenic description. She couldn't bring herself to get to the heart of the story, to bring two people together, when she was no longer convinced that any promises were real. Not long ago, she'd dared to think of getting another contract after this book was handed in; now she didn't know what would be worse, no contract, or another deadline looming over her?

But her savings wouldn't last forever. And unless she found another stream of income, writing was her best bet. It was the only thing she had left, she thought, pushing back the heaviness in her chest. Without Sean, what else was there?

He had been a part of her life for the better part of her twenties. They'd started dating when she was only twenty-two, and he was just a year older. That was the problem, he'd told her when he ended things. They were too young to know better then. Too young to know what they wanted.

In other words, he now knew what he wanted. And it wasn't her.

Sighing, she walked south toward town, past the robin's egg blue Victorian where the Taylors summered with their three girls, each redheaded and pale skinned, requiring their mother to lather their arms and legs and cheeks with so much sunscreen that their skin would be slick for the entire morning. The Taylors hailed from the Detroit area, a wealthy suburb not much different than the one that the Morgans had grown up in.

But that was where the similarities stopped. While both families had daughters, lived comfortably, and summered on Evening Island, Mrs. Taylor was warm and funny, with a laugh that was infectious, and the girls all had a giggle that was contagious. The whole family was happy and smiling, whereas the Morgans felt uptight by comparison—a little uncomfortable when it came to expressing emotion or being casual. Unless they were here, away from the stern gaze of their father. Did their mother pull them into their arms and braid their hair and have pet names for them the way the Taylors did? No. But at least up here, she wasn't nagging them to stand with their shoulders back or straighten their hair bows or parade them around like a trio of dolls either. Here they could be themselves, their own individuals. Back in Cleveland, that wasn't allowed.

Even now, she thought, thinking of Ellie, it was thinly tolerated.

Ellie. She really had been too hard on her. And no one ever said that it was her job to take care of the house. Now that they were all here, they should all share in the work. It was just that Gemma hadn't factored in just how much work that would be. She'd talk to Ellie, once Ellie was around long enough to talk to. The past few days Gemma had rarely left her room other than to eat the meals that Hope was forever cooking and offering, and usually Ellie was out, at her studio, or somewhere else she hadn't made known.

Maybe she was with Simon, Gemma thought, thinking about what Hope had said about finding love again. Contrary to what Gemma led her readers to believe, it just wasn't that easy. At least, not for her.

She stopped to admire the annuals that were popping into full bloom beside the tulips in various shades of pink, purple, and white that lined the path to the Taylors' porch. She knew the property as well as Sunset Cottage—soon there would be peonies, big, puffy balls of gorgeous pale pink and fuchsia flowers, and cream ones, her personal favorite.

The very kind that were supposed to be tied together with a blue ribbon for her wedding bouquet.

She must have been standing outside the gate to the Taylors' home for quite some time, because she hadn't even seen the man come around the side of the house. Now, feeling his stare, her eyes shifted, and her cheeks heated at what she saw. A tousle-haired man not much older than herself, in jeans and work boots and, God help her, nothing else.

She tried to pull her eyes away from his chest, but that would have made her not human. He was broad in the shoulders, and his muscles were lean, and on full display. Even though it was only May, his skin was bronzed from the sun.

"Can I help you?" the man asked in a tone laced with enough amusement that Gemma had to wonder if she'd actually been gaping.

Being holed up with her sisters and alone in her apartment before that clearly hadn't been good for her. It was just a man, and many men in this world were good looking.

Her mouth felt dry as she tried to look natural. "We own the house next door," she explained. She got a better look at his face as he approached. *Yes, focus on the face, Gemma.* Piercing green eyes, nut-brown hair, and a strong jaw. But it was the grin that made her stomach do something funny. She tried to compose herself and had a bad feeling that she was failing. "Do you work for the Taylors?"

As if that wasn't obvious. She hadn't seen him before, and she thought she knew all the locals on the island, but then she hadn't been back in a long time either. Caretakers usually required year-round residency, because by the summer season, the houses were occupied by owners or renters.

"I do." He grinned, but his look was suspicious. "I'm the new caretaker."

"What happened to Edward?" she asked, thinking of the sweet old widower who used to bring her Gran a bouquet of flowers once a week, even if she insisted that nothing was going on between them.

The man raised an eyebrow. "He retired. Spends his time fishing now. It's a physical job."

She blinked. Of course. Quite physical, she thought, forcing her gaze to remain on his face. She felt flustered, like he was waiting for her to say something. She blurted out the first thing that came to mind: "Do you mind if I ask what you do for them?"

She realized by the squint in his eye that this had come across as suspicious, maybe even interrogating. "I'm not checking up on you. I just...Well, my sisters and I are staying in our house for a bit and we might need some help." That was an understatement.

He didn't look surprised by this omission. She wondered if he'd already noticed the place, formed an opinion about the state of it.

"I do whatever they ask," he said with a shrug. "Keep the furnace going in the winter, and make sure the pipes don't freeze. Clean the windows in the summer. Rake in the fall. Keep an eye on tenants that they aren't so sure about." He grinned. "I'm pretty new here, though. This is my first season."

"Do you mind me asking how much you charge to mow the lawn?"

He glanced at the cottage and back at her. "For you? Twenty bucks."

Twenty bucks or two hours of writing time. "It's a deal," she said, feeling relieved.

His eyes held hers until she felt the need to look away. "I'll stop by today if I have time."

"Tomorrow is fine. We're not out to impress." At least she wasn't until now. Now she wished she'd changed her clothes from the comfy but not exactly flattering T-shirt and leggings that she lived in most days, and sometimes slept in, too.

"I'll be by tomorrow then," the man said. "I'm Leo, by the way. Leo Helms."

"Gemma Morgan," she replied, smiling shyly. He held out a hand and she extended hers, her stomach tightening at the contact, before she abruptly pulled her hand back. The racing of her heart was pure non-sense. Honestly!

He grinned, picked up a flannel shirt that he'd dis-carded on the brick-paved path, and wandered back up the lawn around to the side of the house.

Cute, Gemma decided. Inarguably, cute. But no need to go there. She had a book to write. And besides, she had given up on love.

Or rather, it had given up on her.

*

Sean and she had met when she was still working at the ad agency, back when she was dabbling at her first book, still getting used to life in the city. He was tall, cute, and he'd taken her for pizza after work one night.

Sean, unlike her, loved his job at the ad agency. It was exactly what he wanted to do, but he'd always en-couraged her to do what she wanted. When she first got "the call" that her book was being published, he'd been just as excited as she was, insisted on champagne and a proper celebration.

When she'd called her parents to tell the news, her father had gotten right down to business. "How much are they offering?"

Even now, Gemma could still remember the hurt she'd felt in her chest at his reaction. It wasn't about the money, she'd tried to explain. It was about the accomplishment.

Still, when the book came out and another was on the way, her father came around to the idea, even seemed proud of it, something that had triggered her argument with Ellie last summer. Ellie knew how much their father disapproved of her aspirations, and when she tried to make Gemma feel bad about not helping out with Gran more, Gemma had taken the bait, said something that her father had said many times and shouldn't have, even if it was true.

She didn't bring up her writing much around Ellie. Or Hope, come to think of it. When her first book released last year, it was Sean who came with her to all the local bookstores to see the book in the wild. They'd celebrated with champagne and take-out.

Those were the happy times. Sometimes, thinking back on them hurt more than thinking of the bad times.

Lena appeared at her side with a chocolate brownie on a plate. "You looked like you could use it," she said with a little smile.

Lena was a local, the daughter of innkeepers and the same age as Ellie. Gemma remembered her from all the summers she spent here, but she was surprised all the same when she'd walked in to the coffeehouse to see that Lena was still on the island.

"Thanks," she said, eagerly reaching down to break off a piece.

Lena tilted her head. "I heard about your fiancé."

Gemma stopped chewing. Of course. The brownie wasn't a reward for the hard work she'd been doing for the past two hours at this corner table. It was a sympathy brownie. And she must have been frowning.

"Ellie told you?"

Lena shook her head. "I heard it from Darcy Ritter. She runs the quilting club here in town? She was good friends with your grandmother. She takes a painting class at your sister's studio, and she heard all about it."

Along with everyone else in the class, Gemma assumed. She felt her eyes hood. She knew Darcy, and she knew that Darcy liked to keep her pulse on the community.

Lena tsked. "Terrible thing that man did. Jilting you like that!"

"Oh, I don't know if I'd use the word *jilted*." Gemma skirted her eyes, catching he curious glances from the patrons at the nearest table. "It wasn't like he left me standing at the altar."

"Still, you had to call back all those vendors!"

Gemma nodded, and then remembered that she still hadn't heard back on the full refund from the caterers yet. They could only give a full refund if they booked another gig for the same night. She made a mental note to email them as soon as Lena went back to the counter.

Right now she could use every penny she could find. Especially if she kept getting too distracted to finish this book.

"Well," she said, forcing a smile she no longer felt. "Thank you for the brownie."

"Chocolate does wonders," Lena said, giving her a wink.

If only. Gamma pushed the plate to the side and put her attention back on the computer screen.

She stared at the page count on the bottom of her screen, stricken when she realized she had only accomplished ten pages today. And another day had come and gone. She could work all night, she decided, or at least once the girls went to bed, though who knew about what. She was still blocked. Still unable to tackle the central romance in her story that her readers craved. If she didn't believe in her own work, how could she expect anyone else to?

And now all she could think about was her catering deposit, and how large the sum was, and then she was thinking of how Sean didn't have to worry about any of this, because Gemma had been foolish enough to offer to use her inheritance to pay for it. It was that, or ask her parents, and she could never forget how her mother had controlled every detail of Hope's wedding, until Hope had laughed good-naturedly and said, "Maybe you should wear the wedding dress, Mom!"

Gemma fired off an email to the caterers, her anxiety mounting when she saw a new email from her editor at the top of her inbox. Her stomach tightened into a hard knot and she closed the laptop before she could linger too long, or be tempted to click on it, and feel the pressure escalate. Where was the manuscript? Would it be ready on time? She knew what the email would say without having to read it.

With a shaking hand, she ate the rest of the brownie. And Lena was right, because she did feel a little better afterward. She gathered up her belongings and decided to take a walk through town. Sometimes that was all it took for her mind to open up and ideas to strike. A walk. A shower. Something that didn't feel so forced.

It was quiet in town, and warm. Shop owners had embraced the season and most had pots of tulips flanking their doors, their large bay windows displaying brightly colored items, inviting passersby to stop in, browse, hopefully to buy something.

Gemma would have loved to poke around, maybe treat herself to some stationary supplies from the paper store on the corner, but then she thought about her budget, and her book, and her future.

Ten pages. She'd been so optimistic when she'd set out into town!

She stopped outside the next shop she came to, the local real estate office, whose windows were covered in sheets for summer rentals and properties for sale.

She stared at the real estate listings, her eyes popping when she saw how much some of the homes were listed for—homes not even on the west side of the island, homes that were smaller, tucked into the forest, not even walkable from town.

The answer to her problems, it was starting to seem, would be to sell Sunset Cottage.

Chapter Eight

Ellie

Hope was sitting on the front porch when Ellie hopped off her bike, tired from another long day at the studio.

"Come join me!" Hope said with a smile. "The girls are already down for the night."

Ellie glanced in the house through the open screen door. She'd been dodging Gemma since her arrival but now the thought of joining her sister for a glass of wine on the porch sounded exactly like what she needed to push aside the pain in her chest over Simon. For a little while at least.

"Gemma's inside," Hope said, as if reading her mind. "She feels bad, Ellie."

Ellie froze. This was the first time that last summer's argument had been broached directly, and she wasn't sure she wanted to have this conversation right now.

"Come on. Don't make me enjoy this sunset alone," Hope encouraged. "This is our chance to relive all those wonderful summers. Like old times."

Like old times. There was that line again.

Her sister had a point, and Ellie nodded. "I'll be right back." She had barely entered the front hallway when Gemma approached, the anxiety in her eyes at odds with the smile on her face.

"What's going on?" Ellie asked, feeling uneasy. Was it the yard? It had grown again, but she'd told herself she would get to it this weekend, when she had more free time. She'd dared to think that tonight might be different, the kind of night she'd been hoping to have since her sisters announced that they were coming to visit.

But now, it seemed all that would have to wait.

"I was in town today," Gemma said, and for one horrible moment, Ellie wondered if this had something to do with Simon. Had Gemma seen him? Had she said something about how happy Ellie was to have him back, without knowing of course that he was engaged to be married to another woman?

The humiliation! Ellie braced herself.

"And I saw the real estate listings for properties for sale," Gemma continued.

Ellie nodded, waiting for Gemma to say more. Her stomach grumbled and she realized that she hadn't eaten much today. Hadn't eaten much since Simon's big announcement, really.

She inched toward the kitchen, eager to get on with things. "So?"

"So...this house is worth even more than I thought," Gemma said, raising an eyebrow.

"Wait. You want to *sell* Sunset Cottage?" Ellie felt her eyes bulge as she stared at Gemma. Gemma, who had not been to the island since she had graduated from college, had decided to waltz back in, after Gran was gone, and tell Ellie what she wanted to do with the place? "No. No way. Just *no*."

"Hear me out—" Gemma said, stepping forward, but Ellie brushed by her, shaking her head until her ponytail whipped back and forth.

Her heart was hammering in her chest as she pushed deeper into the house and made her way to the kitchen. Tears blinded her eyes as she opened the fridge, only to be reminded that the light was still burned out. She cursed under her breath as she grabbed a bottle of wine by the neck (there were now several, along with cheese and bread and lunchmeat and vegetables, thanks to Hope's trip to the market this week) and poured herself a glass. To the rim.

"Ellie! Come on out to the porch! Let's talk!" That was Hope's voice now. The traitor.

"Talk?" she asked angrily. "Or hear you out?" No one asked Ellie for anything because Ellie was...well, Ellie. Black sheep of the family. Starving artist. Irresponsible Ellie. She may as well have had it tattooed to her forehead. Ellie who had killed the vegetable garden. Ellie who wasn't much of a handyman.

But they had no clue. None of them. This was an old house, and they each had a share in it. And up until now, she had been the only one contributing to its upkeep, and she couldn't sink all of her money into it, not when she had the studio rent.

And without her say, they couldn't do anything. Not even sell this cottage.

"We wanted to have a discussion," Hope called out.

"Oh, so I'm being ganged up on now?" she cried, hating the hurt that crept into her tone. They'd discussed it, planned it, all before she'd come home. Because like it or not, this was her home. Not theirs. "What is this? Some kind of ambush?" She took a long sip of the wine.

"Please, Ellie! I didn't mean to upset you!" Gemma called, and Ellie, despite her anger, wavered. She loved her sisters, and the truth was that she *had* been lonely here. But selling this house?

For starters, where would she go?

She took another gulp of the wine, letting it cool her throat. It was a hot day for May, and it was sticky in the house, even with the breeze floating off the lake. They needed to open more windows. Let the fresh air circulate. Evening was quickly approaching, and here on the island, the evenings were perfect.

Except tonight wasn't shaping up to be.

"Look," she said as she walked onto the wraparound porch through the side kitchen door. Hope had lit candles and set them on the wicker side and coffee tables, and the big round table where their mother and Gran and Mrs. Taylor and Mrs. Anderson would sit and play cards for hours every evening, their laughter rising in the air, carrying itself all the way up to her cracked bedroom window. She loved the sound of it, even if she did feel mildly left out of the fun. Still, she'd made her own fun. She had Gemma and Hope and the Taylors and the Andersons. They were a staple, a presence that was ingrained in their stays at the cottage. There was an unspoken promise that the fun would start all over the next day. Even when it rained, they could explore the old homes. And they had. She knew every inch of the three homes that hugged the southern bay of the West End.

This house was ingrained in her too.

"Gran gave this house to us," she said, pleading with Gemma's emotional side. Gemma had a tender heart, whereas Hope was always the more practical one. Ellie supposed this was why the strain with Gemma hurt so much, because Gemma was supposed to care. And right now, the only thing she seemed to care about was her financial stake in this house. "Gran could have given it to Dad, but she didn't."

"Because she knew that he didn't want it," Gemma pointed out.

"Exactly. She knew that if she gave it to Dad he would turn around and sell it!" Ellie shot back, and Gemma raised her eyebrows at that, because really, wasn't that the truth?

Ellie was no fool. She knew how much homes went for on the island, especially on the lakefront, with views as far as the eye could see. Someone with a fat bank account and a crew of men would come in and turn it into a summer paradise or yet another small inn.

But Gran didn't want that. And Ellie didn't either. She wanted to hold onto the memories. To this island. She wasn't ready to let go of this house.

"But do you really want to live here long term, Ellie?" Gemma asked now, her tone gentle, her eyes a little wary. They were entering tricky territory, and she had the impression that Gemma was hoping to avoid another argument like last summer.

Did she regret her words? Ellie could ask, but she wasn't sure she wanted to hear the truth.

"I...I..." Ellie licked her lip. The truth was that she hadn't considered living anywhere else. Evening Island was her home. She'd returned every summer during college before moving in with Gran after graduation. Yes, she had island fever during the cold months, but that didn't mean she wanted to leave it, did it?

"Because your share of the sale would allow you to find something else," Gemma said.

Ellie narrowed her eyes. "Are you again implying that I am living here by some sort of charity? I'll have you know that my painting class is filled every Friday and I may be offering up another soon. And I sold two paintings over the weekend in one shop alone. And I sell others, regularly."

"That's wonderful!" Hope said, and Gemma beamed a smile so genuine that, for a moment, Ellie almost dared to believe that she was happy for her. That she didn't see her as a failure, the way she had implied last summer, tapping in to Ellie's deepest insecurities.

"I love this house," Ellie said. "And I thought you both did too."

Gemma looked down at her hands, quieted by that, and Ellie glanced at Hope, who was resting on a lounge chair, her legs propped up in front of her, a baby monitor on the end table next to her.

"We don't need to decide anything right now," Hope said mildly, looking as if she couldn't care either way, and why should she? She had a rich husband. She lived a comfortable life. A big, beautiful home all of her own. Like Gemma, she hadn't come back to the island for years. The money didn't matter to her anymore than this house did. She'd never even brought the girls here, and they were already four! She always said it was too far to travel with twins. Gran had only met them once, at Christmas at their parents' house a few years back.

Ellie's jaw tightened at that memory. It was the last time they were all together, before the funeral, and it was just like old times, with their parents fussing over Hope and Evan and the girls and her father inquiring about Gemma's then job at the advertising agency. By then, Ellie had been living with Gran for years, and she knew how her father felt about that.

She just didn't realize until last summer that her father wasn't the only one.

"I know that you think I've been staying here rent-free because I have no other alternatives," she said to Gemma, tears burning her eyes.

"I never said that," Gemma insisted, but Ellie shook her head.

"Last summer you made it very clear that Gran had been kind enough to take me in all those years."

"And she was, Ellie," Gemma said gently. "But I didn't mean it the way you took it."

"Like a charity case?" Ellie folded her arms across her chest. "You did. Partly. You didn't see then that I have a home here. A life. It might not be perfect, and I may not be perfect, but I'm doing my best, for Gran, for this house. For me."

"I'm thinking of you right now," Gemma said. "This house is worth a lot of money. And this island is a small community for someone as young as you. I know Simon is back for the summer, but when he goes back, wouldn't it be nice to have the option to go too?"

"Simon's back?" Hope jumped in, smiling fondly. "Simon Webber? Oh, I'll have to look for him." She smiled suggestively at Ellie.

Ellie took a deep breath, trying to steady the emotions raging within her. "I'm not going to follow Simon back to Philadelphia," she said firmly. Neither of her sisters looked completely convinced.

"You were so in love with him," Gemma said, her eyes shining as if picturing a memory. "And now here he is, after all these years."

"It's not as magical as you make it seem, Gemma," Ellie replied. "It's not like some story out of one of your books. His parents have a house here. He was bound to come back eventually, just like the two of you."

He hadn't come back for her, she reminded himself. Not then. Not now.

"True," Gemma said with a little shrug. "But this isn't our parents' house, Ellie. It's ours. And we have to think about this. If we sold it and split it—"

"*We* don't need to *decide* anything. You two don't get a vote!" Ellie said, tossing back such a large slurp of wine that she had to smother a cough. The last thing she needed was one of her sisters jumping in to pound her back or play nursemaid. She didn't need them now. She needed them back then, when she was fresh out of college, nervous about her options and worried that her father had been right, that she had set herself up for failure, while Gemma and Hope were already settled into their new, successful lives in Chicago. And she'd needed them when she was all alone here, caring for their grandmother. And now they thought they could waltz in and have a say in how she was caring for this house? Nope.

She set the wine glass down on the nearest end table, not caring that some of it spilled onto the whitewashed floorboards. Let one of her sisters wipe it up. After all, they were so keen to have a part in this house, maybe they could pitch in for a change.

"Where are you going?" Gemma called out.

"Out!" Ellie said, because the truth was that she didn't know where she was going. She just knew that she wasn't going to stick around here being told yet again how she was going to live her life.

She ran down the stairs to pull her bike from the side of the house. The sun hadn't completely set yet and there was enough light for her to make her way into town. She had, once, attempted to ride down in the dark, only to end up misjudging where the road turned and ended up squashing a hydrangea bush.

She muttered the whole way into town, trying to rid herself of the hurt that had landed heavily in her chest, stirring up years of resentment that she thought she had finally escaped here on the island. It wasn't just the birth order; it was who she was. Hope was perfect. Gemma was good enough. And Ellie, well, wasn't. She wasn't good enough back then, and according to Gemma, she wasn't good enough now.

She *really* should have watered that vegetable garden more, she thought, as she pulled her bike to a stop on the corner of Main and tied it to a lamppost. Here in town, the bars were open, and some of the local bands were setting up, getting ready for a slim crowd, gearing up for the weekend tomorrow. She decided on Hackney's Pub. It was the most low-key of the bars, mostly frequented by locals, and open year-round. Mack, the current owner, knew her well. He kept her popcorn bowl refilled all night long. Sometimes, that was dinner.

She waved to him and went to sit at her usual seat, the one with the view of the television screens, since the one at the house didn't work very well, when she heard someone whisper her name.

She kept her pace steady, only glancing back on second thought, and there he was. Simon.

Engaged Simon, she reminded herself firmly.

"Oh. Hi." Her greeting, she knew, was decidedly chilly, and maybe that was unfair of her. After all, could he be blamed for falling in love with someone else after all these years? He'd gone to college and law school, started a life and a career. As he had said himself: it was what people did.

She pushed back the heaviness in her heart.

"You here alone?" Simon asked, and she almost had to laugh at that. Of course she was alone. If he thought she had found love on this island, he would be sorely mistaken. Sure, Mack was cute, but she was pretty sure that a few of the other girls in town had their eye on him.

He motioned to the seat beside him.

Ellie frowned. "You're not with your fiancée tonight?"

He shook his head, but his grin slipped in a telling way. "Erin went back to Philly for the weekend."

Erin. She had a name. Ellie conjured up an image in her head: blonde, blue eyes, perky, petite. She hated her already.

Knowing that what she was about to do would probably only lead to more heartache, she took the seat beside him. Oh, she hated that it felt so good, and that all that heaviness in her chest was now replaced with a fluttering sensation when he caught her eye and grinned.

Really, could he still grin at her like that and be engaged to this Erin woman? Sadly, it would seem that he could.

"What'll it be?" he asked, and she noticed that he was drinking a beer, on tap.

Their eyes met as they smiled and she glanced away, at the menu, even though she knew that she preferred the white. "I'll have a white wine," she said, keeping it simple. She'd nurse it, have one only, and then leave. Maybe she'd find Mandy or Naomi, see if they were free tonight. They could sit out on Naomi's back deck and play cards.

Only she didn't want to play cards. She was a twenty-eight-year-old woman and her first love was sitting right beside here. She didn't want to be anywhere else but here.

But did Simon feel the same?

"So how does it feel? Being back on the island?" she asked. She kept darting her eyes in his direction and away again. It hurt too much to look at him. To know that what they had was over, a part of her past, like all those other long, lazy days of summer that she could never seem to get back. It was all slipping away.

"Honestly? Great. Can't say that Erin feels the same, though."

Was that so? Now Ellie swiveled her chair only slightly so that she had a better view of him.

"Who doesn't love Evening Island?" she asked. It was beautiful every day of the year, from the clear water to the lush foliage. Sure, there were moments of cabin fever, but that could happen anywhere. It was a destination spot; tourists flocked here for as many months as the weather permitted.

"Seriously." He shook his head. Shrugged. "She's a city girl. All this nature and slow pace isn't her thing." He seemed to want to say something else but took a long sip of his beer instead. Finally he said, "To be honest, I'm not sure she plans on returning at all."

Ellie fought off a smile, even though she knew that there was really no room in her heart for hope at this moment. But she'd never been much of a realist, at least that's what her father had told her. She thought with her heart, not her head. She didn't focus on practicalities and life's inconveniences, like...Simon's fiancée, for example.

The fiancée who had left the island. While he remained.

Even though she was tempted, she did as she had promised herself and only stayed for one drink. He'd left her wanting more once. It was probably time to turn the tables.

"I should call it a night," she said, standing.

Her stomach flipped over at the look of disappointment that flashed in his eyes. "So soon?"

"I've got an early start tomorrow," she explained. It was true. She was desperate to get out of the house before either of her sisters woke. She'd almost forgotten how they'd left things, and now she felt uneasy about returning home.

She checked the clock on the wall. She'd stayed later than she thought, meaning that she had a dark walk home with the bike.

She looked at Simon. He was worth it. He always had been. And that was just the problem.

"Well, hopefully I'll be seeing you again soon," he said, giving her a slow grin.

She was counting on it.

By the time she got inside the house, it was dark and quiet. Hope and the girls were clearly asleep, and if Gemma wasn't, she hopefully knew better than to leave the third floor tonight. Still, Ellie tiptoed up the stairs to her bedroom and closed the door before turning the lock, thinking how much different a few hours could mean.

Tomorrow, she knew, would be full of more tension, more unresolved issues with her sisters she would have to deal with.

But tonight... tonight she was certain of two things. She was still in love with Simon. And maybe, just maybe, there was a chance that he could fall in love with her again too.

Chapter Nine

Hope

The weather was finally warm enough for the girls to venture at least knee-deep into the water, even if Hope did find it alarmingly icy for herself. She sat on one of the weathered Adirondack chairs that had been on their stretch of beach for as long as she'd been coming here, a notebook in her lap, her eyes on the girls.

When they were like this, playing in the sand, transferring buckets of water to their castle and back again, she couldn't imagine missing out on such a thing, the way Evan did, now by being in Singapore, and daily, when he went to the office. How often had the girls done something so cute that she couldn't find her camera fast enough, and she thought, *How fortunate am I*?

Now, guilt twisted inside her because she knew that she was fortunate. She had a big, beautiful house and was blessed with two gorgeous girls. She had a husband who held down a good job, was moving up in his company, and came home every night that he wasn't travelling, unlike Cindy's husband at the end of the block, who was most definitely sleeping with his secretary—something Cindy pretended not to know about because she didn't want to lose her membership at the country club, or have to get a job.

But Hope did want a job. Or better yet, a career. She remembered how it felt once, to dress for work, not an active day with toddlers. To feel like she was needed and wanted for more than cleaning up spilled milk or preparing yet another snack. To be asked questions, and to have her opinion matter.

Could she make a mean chocolate chip cookie? You bet. Could she whip together a snack for twenty-two kids with various diet restrictions and allergies without a blink of an eye? Absolutely. Was she good at being a mother?

She hoped so.

But she could be good at other things too.

She'd fallen into public relations after college because she was good at writing, and she'd taken the job seriously, applied herself, and moved up at the firm. Before the twins were born, Evan had received a big promotion, too good to turn down, that required a lot of travel. It would make no sense for them to both work, and she couldn't scale down her hours and still commute to the city. And Evan was right: she wanted to be home with the girls. She wanted to give them a different kind of childhood than she'd had. She didn't want to just supervise, she wanted to engage. Take the classes that required participation, not drop-off. Bake the cookies for the bake sale, not pick up something at the store.

And while she had been good at her career, she couldn't say that she longed to go back to it, specifically. What she longed for was the feeling it gave her.

The feeling she had finally admitted she was now lacking by giving it up.

Unlike her sisters, she'd never had any hobbies or passions. Even as children, Gemma had her writing and Ellie had her painting. Hope had instead been the neighborhood babysitter, the responsible teen on the block who could wrestle three kids without complaint, and entertain them, too, not just flick on the television and raid the pantry. She collected her earnings at the end of the evening and deposited it into the high-interest savings account her father had set up for her. Ellie, on the other hand, spent all her birthday money on toys and candy within days of receiving it, seeming to feel that she almost wouldn't be satisfied until every last penny was gone.

Hope had interests: she liked to read, and she liked her tennis lessons. She could play the piano and she maintained a strong grade-point average. But it was Gemma and Ellie who were exceptional.

She'd never given that much thought. Until now. And now, she was, well, she was jealous, she realized. Jealous that her sisters knew who they were and that she didn't.

"Okay, girls," she said wearily, when Rose started tossing sand into the air, causing it to fall like rain onto Victoria's head. "Time for a nap."

"No!" came the inevitable protests, and she was reminded again that the glorious days of naps were coming to an end. Then what? Usually she used those two precious hours to meal prep for dinner, straighten the house, and pick up all the toys that had been dumped all over the living room that morning even though she knew that they would be upturned again before evening. Those two hours were the only time in her entire day, other than after eight, when she was too tired to do much more than sip a glass of wine and zone out in front of reality television, when the house was quiet. And in the evenings, she had to shift her attention from the girls to Evan, of course, to go from serving her children to serving her husband. To hear the latest updates about work, to give her insight, to be supportive.

Was it so wrong to want something, anything, for herself? To have her own day to talk about, one that didn't revolve around playground happenings?

The downside of naptime on Evening Island was that she was bound to the house, and the house was not hers, much as she'd tried, with some little touches like colorful throw pillows to replace the faded floral ones that Gran had kept on the patio furniture all those years, and the lanterns and flowers, and fresh linens that she'd bought for all of their beds, even if Ellie did look more disturbed than grateful.

Gemma's announcement hadn't helped matters, she thought, as she gathered all the toys into her canvas beach tote. She'd had the sense to pack it, and the toys were faded remnants of her own childhood, found in the hall closet on the top shelf, a relic from another era, much like the old wicker furniture on the porch, or the juice glasses that still bore the faded print of lilacs on the edges. She hadn't even thought of those in so many years, but once she saw them again, she was overwhelmed with nostalgia and longing, for another time, another place. Another feeling.

She looked back up at the house. When Gemma had broached the idea to sell Sunset Cottage, it seemed to make sense. It was a big house that they rarely visited, worth enough that her share alone would fund the girls' college bills and Ellie would be able to find a comfortable alternative. The house was so large, and in need of routine maintenance. Hope hadn't thought about it in so many years; she'd been too wrapped up with her day-to-day life to look back on the past. But now, being here, it seemed that it was all she could think about.

And it was safer than thinking about the future.

At that, her stomach twisted and she set a hand to her waist to settle it. Evan had called already, as she assumed he would, and she'd answered, only to hand the phone to the girls, but the reception had been lost partway through the call. When he'd called again, he'd asked when she was coming home, and she couldn't answer that because she didn't know. She couldn't stay here forever, especially not if they sold the house.

She focused again on the house, on the front porch where her own mother used to sit and play cards and chat with the other mothers. It seemed impossible to believe that she was once the girl who would run barefoot on this beachfront, and splash in the water, and not care if her shoulders got too much sun or if she got sand in her hair.

Now she was the mother who was brushing sand out of her children's hair. The cycle of life had continued, just as she somehow always knew it would, that life would carry on for her as it always had, as it had been so carefully laid out for her.

Suddenly, the thought of going into the house, confined to the memories and the reminders of the past, and the horrible, sinking thought of what might have been, what path might have been chosen, became almost less appealing than the thought of two cranky girls who had missed their nap. She longed to walk through town, without the double-wide stroller that was another part of her routine the girls were quickly growing out of, sooner than she wished. Sure, it was hard to wrestle that thing through standard doors, but without it...She tried to picture walking hand in hand with the girls for any length of time and felt herself almost tear up. They'd resist. They'd get tired. She'd be even more housebound than she was now, with even less to talk about with her husband when he came home, with even less interaction with other people, and that was...unbearable.

It took ten minutes to pack up the beach toys and cross the street to the house, and another fifteen to rinse off in the tub because Victoria had so much sand in her hair that it had to be washed, and that always caused a howling fit.

From upstairs she heard Gemma say something she couldn't make out and then close her door with more force than Hope felt was really necessary. Yes, she was writing a book, and yes, she had a deadline, but did she really need to show how much more important that was than what Hope was doing?

Hope stared at her two girls in the tub in dismay. She was rinsing sand out of a child's hair, and Gemma was writing a book that would soon be shelved alongside her other, in bookstores across the nation. Who was she kidding?

With record speed, she drained the water, dried the girls with fluffy striped towels that she had also purchased (again, with a questioning frown from Ellie) and tucked them into their side-by-side beds and drew the curtains.

They fell asleep quickly, thanks to the fresh air and endless activity, and Hope walked up to the third floor and knocked quietly on the door. From behind it, she heard Gemma curse. A moment later, she opened the door. Her hair was pulled into a wild-looking bun and her mouth was pinched.

"Sorry, but I was going to head into for a bit. The girls are asleep. Would you mind just listening out for them? I should be back before they wake up."

Gemma's eyes bulged. "I'm trying to work."

"And they're asleep."

"I don't think you realize what kind of pressure I'm under here," Gemma replied in a steely voice.

Now this was completely unfair! "I was the one who suggested you come up here, remember?" Hope pointed out.

"Yes, and then you came too, and what I thought was going to be a quiet place to write has turned into a raucous family vacation!"

Hope knew deep down that Gemma loved the twins, but she couldn't deny the sting of her sister's words. "I thought it would be nice for us to all spend some quality time together, as sisters."

"It would be. But not until this book is finished," Gemma said. "I don't think you understand—"

"Oh, I understand," Hope said, giving her sister a long look. "I did have a career too, once. And I understand when I'm not wanted."

"I just wish you had mentioned that you wanted to come too—"

"Because then you wouldn't have come? I do own a third of this house." Hope tried to keep the hurt from creeping into her tone. "And I have been preparing the family meals, too."

Now, she wondered why she bothered. It was a thankless job, no matter where she went. "Besides, when was the last time we were all together?" She shook her head. "Forget I asked. You're right. I shouldn't have come."

She could leave. Take the ferry back on Monday. She could be back in time for Cindy's daughter's fifth birthday party next weekend. She realized with sudden panic that she hadn't RSVP'd before she'd left and now she wouldn't have to worry about canceling.

Still, she waited for Gemma to call after her, to say something, anything that would lessen the ache in her chest as she made her way back down to the second floor, the floorboards creaking underneath her. But instead, all Gemma did was close the door, reminding Hope that she was all alone when it came to this parenting thing, and that her dreams of a fun time with her sisters had been as much a pipe dream as her desire to have a career of her own.

And while she hadn't thought much of the argument between Gemma and Ellie last night, today she had to agree. It was time to sell Sunset Cottage. It was nothing like it used to be.

Chapter Ten

Gemma

Gemma only stopped writing when she glanced up through the window and saw a figure crossing the front lawn. A shirtless figure. A handsome figure. A distracting figure, not that she entirely minded.

She looked down at her word count in the bottom corner of screen, closing her eyes in relief with what she saw. Yes, she'd spent another day avoiding the main point of the story and focusing instead on the filler scenes, but it was something, and she could call it a productive day, mostly because Hope had decided to vacate the house with the twins for an extended period of time, both before and after their naps, and Ellie had yet again left the house before even the twins were awake—and when they woke up, the entire house knew it.

She felt bad about her argument with Ellie last night. And the words she had exchanged with Hope earlier. But she also couldn't take back what she'd said, either. And she certainly wasn't complaining about how much she'd accomplished when the house was so empty.

Deciding that she was at a stopping point, she saved her document and closed her laptop. Then, for inexplicable reasons, silly really, she walked into her en suite bathroom, brushed her hair into a neater ponytail, and changed from her pajama pants and tank top to cut-off jean shorts and a cotton pleasant blouse.

Confidence, she told herself. It was something she hadn't felt in a while, not since Sean decided that she wasn't the person he wanted to spend the rest of his life with after all.

Five months later, it still hurt, and with each day closer to her wedding day, the more it brought up all those bad feelings she'd experienced when the breakup was raw and the pain was fresh. The date was now four weeks from tomorrow. Did he still have it on his calendar? Had he forgotten?

Would he even think of her at all? Would he stop and think, even for one second, that he had made a mistake? He'd already picked out his tie. And together they'd selected matching wedding bands—platinum, to match the engagement ring she'd returned to him two weeks after he ended their relationship.

And the honeymoon, the trip to Paris, the one that she had dared to think might be the setting for her third novel, would he cancel it? Or would he go? One thing was for certain: she wouldn't be going. Not even for research. The ticket could be exchanged for a voucher, but even the thought of a getaway to clear her head felt tainted, knowing what the trip could have been.

Should have been.

She sighed heavily and forced herself to open her bedroom door. She'd been tucked away since breakfast, and she hadn't even stopped for lunch. Now her stomach rumbled and she walked down the stairs to the kitchen, happy to find the fridge still stocked, and the pantry, too. The bowl of fresh fruit was now front and center on the farmhouse table—again, Hope's touch.

Guilt reared strong, but she pushed it back. If Hope hadn't interrupted her at such a crucial point in the chapter she'd been writing, she wouldn't have been so short-tempered. She'd offer to watch the girls one day when she had her book more under control. If she could finally break through this panicked feeling she experienced every time she reached the part of her book where the main characters met and eventually fell in love, then she could afford to be generous. And she wanted to be generous. It didn't feel good to take advantage of Hope's hospitality or Ellie's willingness to share the cottage, even if it was just as much hers.

She ate a banana and one of the muffins left over from breakfast, purchased at Island Bakery yesterday by Hope, one of the best spots in town for homemade scones and sandwiches. Growing up, the girls used to pack thick turkey sandwiches from there and spend the day at the beach, before cycling over to Main Street Sweets for penny candy before they came home, full, tired, and smiling.

Home. That's what they had always called this house when they visited, and Gran hadn't minded. Now, it technically was her home, a third of it at least, and Gemma considered that for a moment. Then, feeling that it was time to contribute something to the household, she walked out onto the front porch and admired Leo as he pushed the mower back and forth, in straight lines.

Really, that's all she was doing. Watching from afar. Because getting any closer...well, that was definitely not an option. And really, she was only seeking him out for professional reasons. He was handy, and this house needed work. It had absolutely nothing to do with the fact that he was easy on the eye. Very easy, she thought, as she watched his muscles strain as he turned the mower around.

He stopped when saw her, flashed a grin and wiped the sweat from his brow with a handkerchief that he pulled from his back pocket. He certainly wasn't making this easy, she thought ruefully. Or maybe, it was the other way around. Maybe he was making this too easy. Too easy to think about someone other than Sean. Too easy to believe that she could actually be attracted to another man again.

But attraction was one thing. A relationship was another. And love...she couldn't even think about that.

"I noticed that vegetable garden in the back," he said, sparking a snort from her.

"It *used* to be a vegetable garden," she corrected. Gran had taken such pride in her plants, and when the girls visited in the summer, they'd found endless satisfaction in selecting the tomatoes, beans, and peppers for dinner. One of her favorite memories was of sitting on the porch with her sisters and Gran, shelling peas and looking out over the water, her feet bare, her shorts sticky over her wet bathing suit, her smile tired but sincere.

Those days, she thought heavily, were over. The vegetable garden was proof of that.

"My sister killed it."

He barked out a laugh. It was a nice laugh, rich and heavy, but warm, like his eyes. "I've met Ellie a few times over the last couple of months. She's an artist, right?"

Gemma nodded. "This house is a lot of work for one person."

He lifted an eyebrow. The intensity of his gaze not wavering. "Good thing you're here then."

She looked away, down at her feet. She was vulnerable, out of sorts, and she'd probably latch onto anyone who showed her a little kindness about now. But just as much as she wanted to stay out here, in the warmth of the late afternoon sun, talking with a nice, friendly, good-looking guy, another part of her wanted to go inside, close the door, and stop her heart from beating like this. Inside she was safe. Inside she was protected. Comfortable.

"I could try to revive it," he offered.

Here, she had to raise an eyebrow. "That's very optimistic of you." Last she'd checked, the leaves on the tomato plants had turned crisp and brown, and the peppers looked like they hadn't had a drop of water except for what Mother Nature decided to offer to them.

"I consider myself a bit of a green thumb. I'll have a go." He shrugged, and she knew that she should leave it at that, boundaries and all, but she couldn't help herself. A good-looking man, here on Evening Island, who didn't seem to own a shirt and who knew how to bring the dead back to life?

She followed him around the back, past the old hammock where she used to lie for hours, scribbling in her journal, or late at night, staring up at the stars which seemed so much brighter here on the island than they did back at home. Gran knew all the constellations, and they were happy to stand out on the porch and study them all, well past their usual bedtimes.

"You okay?" he asked, tossing her a quizzical look as he bent down to brush away some of the debris at the base of the plants.

"I was just thinking about this house," she said, a little wistfully. "It's been in my family for a long time, and we had a lot of happy memories here."

"You don't get back very often?" He continued to work while he talked, the muscles in his arms taut as his hands moved expertly over the plants.

"No," she said, distractedly. "It's not easy to get to. I wish I had come back more. But...well, life."

"Has a weird way of doing that, doesn't it?" He grinned up at her and she felt something in her gut twist.

She cleared her throat, eager to break the moment, and focused on the vegetable plants, which were already looking better now that Leo had cleared out the brush.

"Where'd you learn to do all this?" she asked. She raked her gaze over him. His skin was tawny, his brown hair tipped with gold, but there was something about him, maybe it was the smoothness of his hands, or something about the way he spoke and carried himself, that told her there was more to him than what he revealed. He may be handy, but he hadn't always been a handyman, that much was clear.

"My mother was into gardening. I used to follow her around, see what she was doing. She taught me everything she knew. I liked it. It was...peaceful."

She narrowed her eyes. Peaceful. People came to Evening Island seeking peace, that much was for sure. But from her personal experience, they also came to Evening Island for another reason.

To escape.

*

Gemma couldn't help but notice that for the fifth night in a row, Hope fed the girls separately and then tucked them into bed before the rest of them ate their dinner. She checked her watch, it was seven, later than she usually ate at home, not that she watched the clock. Her life, after all, no longer had any structure.

Ellie had not yet returned, but she wasn't surprised by that, and she imagined that Hope wasn't either. Besides, the island was Ellie's home. She had an entire life here that they weren't part of, and for all Gemma knew, on Friday nights, she had somewhere to be.

Still, she felt sad at the thought that Ellie might be avoiding her.

"I feel bad about last night," she admitted to Hope. "I think Ellie's avoiding me."

"Ellie teaches a painting class on Friday evenings," Hope reminded her. "But I feel bad too. And the thought of selling Sunset..."

Gemma grew quiet. She knew. She felt it too. But she had been relying on Hope's practical side to keep her strong.

"I can always eat earlier," she suggested, hoping to make amends for their earlier conversation that day. "Before the girls go down."

Hope piled pasta into two bowls and handed one to Gemma. "I can't eat earlier," Hope said, pulling two forks from the drawer.

"If I'm going to spend an hour, or sometimes more, preparing a delicious meal that I've shopped for and prepped and then have to clean up afterwards, then I deserve to enjoy it!" Tears seemed to fill Hope's eyes but she blinked them away rapidly.

Gemma waited until they were seated on the porch to press. She'd never seen her sister like this, and she was still thinking about her comment yesterday. Could there be trouble in the marriage? Is that what had prompted Hope to come to the island?

She'd always considered herself close to Hope, in the sense that they were easy company, could laugh and talk and stayed up to date on each other's news. But Hope rarely revealed her deepest feelings. Gemma realized with shame that she'd always assumed that Hope didn't have any troubles.

"Is everything okay, Hope? I'm sorry that I couldn't help with the girls today. I'm just in such a bad position with this book and my deadlines." She thought of that email from her editor still sitting in her inbox, unopened. She shoved some pasta into her mouth and chewed in an effort to push away the knot in the pit of her stomach.

"I know." Hope shook her head. "Of course. I shouldn't have asked. I just..." She stared out onto the water, where the sun was dipping into the horizon.

It was a beautiful sunset, and even though they were almost always blessed with beautiful sunsets at this cottage, it never lost its magic. They stopped, sitting in silence, and Gemma soaked in the colors of the sky. Like cotton candy, she used to say as a girl, and this would make Ellie giggle, say that she was suddenly hungry, that she wished she could eat the sky.

Gemma smiled sadly now, wishing that Ellie was sitting here beside them. That just for one evening, they could go back to feeling the way they used to when they came to this cottage.

"Maybe I was out of line last night," she said, when the last sliver of the glowing sun faded into the distance. "But this house is a lot of upkeep, and I'm not sure that Ellie is up to the challenge. It's a lot of space for one person. And a lot of work." She glanced at Hope, not wanting what she said next to come out the wrong way. "A lot of money, too."

They could ask their parents to help them get it in order, she knew, especially if a sale was involved. After all, this was their father's house just as much as it was theirs, though not in any legal sense. Still, somewhere deep inside of him, he must care, must have some memories of this place that made him smile?

This house, with the weather-worn paint and windows that swelled shut on the hottest days of summer, and the ancient fridge and oven that took an hour to preheat, held no value to Bart Morgan.

Hope seemed to consider something for a moment. "Who mowed the lawn?"

"Leo," Gemma said, causing Hope to raise her eyebrow. She quickly added, "He takes care of the Taylors' house."

"The shirtless guy?" When Gemma gave a tight nod, Hope slipped her a smile. "He's cute."

"Is he?" Wrong thing to say. She'd never been a good liar, even a casual one. And Leo being cute wasn't a matter of opinion. It was a fact. "I thought that he could help us out while we're here. Ellie doesn't seem to have the ability, and I certainly don't have the time, and you're busy with the girls."

Hope fell silent. She took a bite of her soup. "Believe it or not, I don't mind doing something else once in a while."

"Still, the yard is big, and it's in bad shape." And if they were going to sell... She'd compiled a mental list of all the other things they might ask Leo to help with, once she had her sisters on board to sell the property. It would take some money, but she considered it a worthwhile investment.

"I've been thinking of doing something else," Hope said, and Gemma took a moment to realize that her sister wasn't talking about the yard or even Sunset Cottage anymore. "I've been thinking of going back to work."

"A few years from now? When the girls are in school?"

"They still have another year of preschool and kindergarten is only half day, so...sooner." Hope's voice had risen to a tinny pitch and Gemma stared at her, knowing that there was definitely something going on that she wasn't fully aware of. She'd always assumed that Hope loved being a stay-at-home mother. She was so devoted to it.

"What were you thinking of doing?" she asked carefully.

"I don't know," Hope said, staring at her plate. "That's just the problem. I don't know."

"That makes two of us," Gemma said. She leaned back into her chair and stared at the water, hoping that it might provide the answer, or at least the inspiration, that she needed to get through to tomorrow when she again faced a blank page...and an equally open future.

Chapter Eleven

Ellie

Ellie offered her class on a weekly basis, open to the public, but it was rare for a newcomer to attend. Today she had her usual crowd: Sally Hayworth who ran the island newspaper and always posted a little advertisement about Ellie's classes at a discounted rate in exchange for extra help on her brushstrokes; Donna from the grocery; Joan Kessler who ran the inn up near the old lighthouse, though rumor was they might be selling soon, and who liked to hang her paintings in the lobby, even if they weren't very good, not that Ellie would ever let on. There was Darcy, who led the quilting club and was one of Gran's oldest friends, and then there were Ellie's friends: Mandy, Naomi, and Lena, who came for support and the company.

Usually she liked her Friday night class. It gave her an opportunity to socialize, to catch up on all the island news, to have a few laughs and to remember the purpose of this all. She usually left the studio after each session thinking how much she loved the island, loved the people, loved what she did.

But tonight, all she wanted was for this class to end. It was Friday. Chances were strong that Simon was out and about. And from the looks of it, he wasn't going to be joining her class, even though she had signs posted all over town. And yes, she had been watching the door, long after her last regular had come in and taken her usual seat.

Darcy, who missed nothing and forgot even less, caught her eye. Ellie felt her cheeks burn as she turned back to the canvas where she was meant to be demonstrating trees tonight. They were surprisingly difficult to capture well, and some of her students were more adept than others.

"I hear that we have had some surprise visitors in town this past week," Darcy remarked as she swirled her paintbrush in her cup of water.

Ellie nodded and said, "Both my sisters are back, and Hope's daughters are here too."

"I saw Gemma at the coffeehouse the other day," Lena chimed in, even though her eyes never strayed from her canvas. "Such a sad face. Terrible that the man would jilt her like that."

"I don't know if he really jilted her," Ellie said, a little uneasily. She didn't want to think about Gemma today, but now, when she did, it wasn't with the same anger she'd felt last night. Gemma had experienced a life-altering setback in recent months. Could that be the sudden interest in selling the cottage? She'd talk to Hope, find out more. Hope was always reasonable; maybe together they could work things out. After all, if Gemma was willing to pull Hope onto her side, why couldn't Ellie try to do the same?

"I'd rather be jilted than alone forever," Mandy said with a sigh, and Darcy let out a loud snort.

"You'd rather have loved and lost than never to have loved at all?" she demanded, with a raised eyebrow arched, oddly, in Ellie's direction. She dabbed at her canvas, even though Ellie was forever explaining the best technique with the brushstroke.

"I'm just saying that it might be nice to be loved...even for a little while."

Ellie gave Mandy a sympathetic smile. It was no secret that Mandy had harbored feelings for Mack for the better part of three years. In other words, since the day Mack stepped foot on the island as the new owner of the pub which was located just next door to Main Street Sweets. Since then, Mandy found every excuse she could to visit the place. There were rumors, of course, that Mack had a few brief summer affairs over the years. There was never a shortage of seasonal hires, after all. Now, with summer upon them, she could see the anxiety in Mandy's eyes.

"What about you, Ellie?" Darcy asked. "Do you feel the same?"

Ellie sighed and went back to her demonstration. "Oh, I don't know...right now I don't have time for romance, anyway. I have my business, and I'm trying to build up my inventory."

"I meant to tell you, Ellie," Naomi cut in, giving her a proud grin. "You know those three paintings you brought me on Monday? I already sold two."

Ellie was astonished. That made four paintings in one week, and just at Lakeside Gifts. She hadn't even checked on her inventory at the other shops in town. She made a mental note to do that this weekend.

Everyone cheered their congratulations, and Ellie felt her chest swell with pride. This was what Gemma had forgotten about, living in Chicago, where she could walk down the street every day for a month straight without seeing a single person she knew. But here, Ellie knew everyone, and they knew her. And even if there were some quirky personalities, and some downright difficult ones, she thought, glancing at Darcy, everyone cared. This was a community. It was special. And she wouldn't leave it. She couldn't.

Still, something in her chest was heavy when she thought of Darcy's comment. A part of her did want love. Romance. Connection. Happiness. And right now, the only man on the island who could offer that was...

"I hear that Simon Webber and his parents are also back for the summer," Darcy announced.

Naomi darted a glance in Ellie's direction. Ellie did her best to feign nonchalance.

"Is that so?" Naomi remarked, and something in her tone told Ellie that she shouldn't bother pretending this was brand-new information.

"I saw him around town," Ellie said simply. "He's engaged to be married."

Naomi's expression folded in disappointment that Ellie tried hard not to let bother her. But Darcy quickly jumped in, saying, "And the girl has already run off to Philly."

My, word did travel fast around here.

"I'm sure she'll be back," Ellie said mildly.

"Perhaps," Darcy said as she blended some shades of green paint and brought her brush to her canvas. "At the end of the day, most people end up exactly where they were meant to be."

She glanced over at Ellie and gave a little wink, and because Ellie wanted to believe this, and because she knew support when she saw it and wasn't one to turn away, she smiled, straight to the heart.

*

She wasn't stalking him. Evening Island was small, and the locals knew all the best places, the ones that were tucked on cobblestone side streets, off the main strip, the ones that didn't have quite as cute doors or signage or flowerpots flanking the windows. The ones that were understated. The ones that had been around forever, since Ellie first could remember.

The next afternoon, she happened to bicycle past his family property on her way back from the north side of the island, where she'd captured the most beautiful painting of the rocky shoreline and the light glistening over the surface off the water. She loved the way the water was so clear, as far as the eye could see, that you didn't know where the shore ended and where it began. And, truth be told, she loved that her sisters wouldn't think to look for her there.

Satisfied, she may have taken a slight detour on her way back to the studio, for the exercise, she told herself. Besides, it was a beautiful day for a bike ride. She didn't often get out this way, and on the off chance that

Simon happened to be, say, sitting on his porch, or working in the yard, she could stop, chat, and...

This was where the plan ended. Her knees had wobbled so hard that she'd nearly lost control of the bike as she'd turned onto his road, telling herself that she was free to go where she pleased, just like all the other tourists on their bikes, who had no idea that they happened to be pedaling past the summer house of possibly the world's most handsome bachelor.

Because he was a bachelor. Until he was a married man. And from the sounds of things the other night, he might not really be getting married after all.

But no one had been outside the Webber house, and it was clear from the way the house looked dark and closed up that no one was home. Here on the island, few people had air-conditioning; really, there was no need for it. Windows were cracked, fresh air was let in, and even the hottest of days were made bearable by the lake effect.

Simon was not home. She felt as let down as she did pleased by this. If he wasn't home, he would be in town. And she intended to find him.

She dropped her new painting and supplies off at the studio, and left her bike parked outside. It was Saturday and it was a sunny afternoon and the tourists were out and about, buying fudge and ice cream and renting bikes for a lap around the perimeter of the island—something she and Simon used to do so often that she had every twist and turn of the path burned into her memory as vivid as the taste of his lips against hers.

Now, she avoided that route. Took her shortcuts around the island. And Simon would probably be dodging the crawl of tourists who used to slow them down, make them share a glance and a smile, and give them an excuse to park their bikes on the closest patch of sand and climb up onto one of the big rocks that was half-submerged in the water, thigh to thigh, hand in hand.

She knew that Simon would be in none of those places. Simon would be at Hackney's, Trillium Café, or maybe even the Dockside Grill. And she might just be frequenting one (or all?) of them today.

Maybe she'd see if Naomi wanted to join her. Or maybe she'd push her luck and go alone, see if her heart could handle another evening alone with Simon and all the emotions that he stirred up inside her.

Even now, if she closed her eyes, she could still feel the sensation of his kiss, the exact pressure of his mouth, the way he was always the last to pull away.

Right, she thought sternly, snapping herself out of it. She clearly needed a chaperone. She'd find Naomi. She needed to collect her check from her anyway.

She turned her bike at the next corner, slowing as she approached Lakeside Gifts. Up ahead, she saw

Naomi standing a few storefronts down from her shop. She had seasonal help—a girl from Notre Dame who lived on the island from May through the end of August. Still, it was unlike her to step away from the store. Unless...

Ellie quickened her step and saw that, sure enough, Naomi was holding the small pocket flask she'd inherited from her grandfather half a decade ago. She rarely pulled it out, and had made a promise to old Pops to only keep his favorite whiskey in it, something that she'd rolled her eyes over at the time but still honored.

Ellie smothered a smile and willed herself not to laugh as she approached her friend. After all, this was a very stressful time for Naomi. Very, very hard on her nerves.

"They said hello," Naomi hissed through wild eyes, and Ellie had to bite down on her lower lip. Hard. Through the open window, she could hear Jewel squawking loudly.

"Hello?" he called. "Hello? Helloooo? Hello. Hello?"

It was truly amazing just how many inflections of a single word that bird could conjure up.

She sighed and rested a hand on Naomi's shoulder. "How long has it been going on for?"

"Forty-five minutes," Naomi said, blinking back tears. "And the shop doesn't close until nine tonight."

The bird squawked louder, desperate to get a response, and beside her, Naomi choked down another sip of her grandfather's favorite libation.

"The thing is," Ellie said gently. "Most people say...hello."

"Shhhh!" Naomi's eyes were huge as she turned to stare at her head-on. "He'll hear you," she whispered urgently. "He was just about to quiet down."

Was he? Ellie wasn't so sure of that. Still, the squawking did get a little louder. Frantic, really.

Naomi screwed the cap back on the flask. "It's going to be a long afternoon," she sighed, staring miserably down Main Street.

"Do you want me to take him to the studio?"

Naomi looked tempted, but then she shook her head. "The cage is too big to carry. Besides, I love the little guy. I just..." She gripped Ellie's elbow as the bird let out another squawk. "That word! It won't stop! I hear it even in my dreams!"

Now Ellie laughed. She had to. "Who was the offender this time?" she asked. It didn't happen often, but when it did, it ruined Naomi's entire day. He didn't stop until the shop closed and a blanket was put over his cage.

"A kid," Naomi sighed. "I shouldn't be mad, but...I'm sort of boiling."

"Let your assistant cover for the rest of the day then. I'm thinking of getting a drink. Or a coffee." Or...or where else could Simon be?

"Thanks, but we're swamped. Nice weather. Can't complain."

"Well, if you change your mind, call me," Ellie said.

Naomi nodded wearily as she stepped back into the shop. The bird calls were at a feverous pitch now. "I will. And thanks."

"That's what friends are for," she said, grinning. And it was, she thought, as she continued down the street. And it was another reason why there was no way in hell she was going to let her sisters talk her into selling Sunset Cottage.

She made quick stops at the other shops, taking down notes of the orders they wanted—taking special pride in Hill Street Gallery's desire to showcase one of her larger paintings in their storefront window next week—and decided to go home, face her sisters, maybe chat with Hope a bit. Maybe Hope would hear her out, guide Gemma down the right path. Make her see that Sunset Cottage was the only thing good from their childhood. The only thing worth keeping.

She was halfway up West End Road when she heard her name being called out.

Her heart gave a lurch, and she steadied the handles of her bike. It couldn't be. It was too good to be true. But as he called out again, she knew that it was him.

She slowed her pace as he caught up beside her, riding, to her complete amusement, a mint green cruiser complete with a white wicker basket.

"Don't laugh," he warned, but it was too late.

"Isn't that your sister's bike?" She hadn't thought of it in years, but it was, she was certain of it. Simon's sister Gina was four years older than him—she used to play with Hope.

"Something seems to have happened to mine in my absence," he said ruefully.

"A lesson in not staying away so long next time," she replied, but even though she was grinning, flirting even, she meant it.

He seemed to see the meaning too, as his grin sobered a bit. "Coming from town?"

It was fairly obvious, and she wondered if he felt as awkward as she did. It made her sad to think that two people who once knew each other so well could be reduced to stilted chitchat. "I was checking on some paintings," she said. She hesitated, and then decided to share the news. "Hill Street Gallery is going to feature one in their window. Tomorrow I'll decide which one in my studio is fit for the job."

"That's amazing, El!" He looked at her with such wonder, such intensity, that she felt herself blush. "I'll have to come by your studio soon and see what you've been up to all these years."

She swallowed hard. Kept her eyes on the road, because it hurt to look at him almost as much as it filled her heart with joy. "I'd like that."

Still, she wouldn't hold him to it. He was making conversation. Keeping things light. It was what adults did, and that's what they were now, even if she didn't really feel like one half the time. Hope was an adult, with her husband and kids. And Gemma...well, Gemma had nearly gotten married. She'd lived with Sean for years, had an entire busy life in the city.

And Ellie had...her art. She had her art, she reminded herself.

"So, what do you have planned for tonight?" Simon asked.

She thought fast, wondering if he could be fishing or just making conversation. *He's engaged*, she reminded herself.

"I'm going to spend some time with my sisters. How about you?"

He gestured to the powder blue bakery bag in his bicycle basket—Island Bakery's signature. "I was just in town to pick up something for my mom. She's still under the weather, so we'll have a low-key night."

"Nothing like a swinging Saturday on the island," Ellie bantered, and Simon caught her eye.

"I seem to remember a lot of exciting nights, actually," he said, wiggling his eyebrows playfully. "Do you remember that time we went night swimming out near the cave?"

Did she remember? Of course she remembered. It was hardly a cave by definition, more of an opening in the cliffs along the east side of the island, but she'd thought about that night a hundred times over the years. She hadn't considered that he'd thought about it too.

She caught his eye as she slowed her bike to a stop. They'd reached the cottage, and as luck would have it, Hope was sitting on the front porch, watching their every move. She waved and called out a big hello to Simon and stood to talk over the railing.

"How's your sister?"

He shrugged. "Good. Married. Happy."

"Tell her I said hello," Hope said.

Ellie toed her kickstand and glanced back at the house. "Well, I should probably get inside." The last thing she needed was for Hope to get the wrong idea, to start implying that she and Simon had a chance together, when they didn't. They couldn't. But oh, how she wished they could.

Simon was looking at her fondly. "We had a lot of fun times, Ellie."

She grinned, her heart warming at all those memories that she'd stowed away, in a locked part of her heart. She wanted to open it, reminisce. But she also didn't want to fall again. "We did."

"Don't go having too much fun tonight without me," he said as he hopped back on his bike and began to pedal away.

She sighed. She never had. And that was just the problem.

But as she walked up the porch to her sister, who was waiting for her with a curious gleam in her eyes, she couldn't fight the smile from her face.

Or the thrill that she hadn't needed to seek him out today after all. That somehow, he had found her.

Chapter Twelve

Hope

Hope had broken down and bribed the girls into good behavior with the promise of an ice cream. She had just been so desperate to walk around town, take in the sights and sounds, to be around other adults!

The trouble had started in the first gift shop, where Victoria had reached her hand out and pilfered a stuffed toy dog without Hope even noticing until they were four stores down the block. She'd been so mortified that she could feel her face flare up right there, in the middle of the street, and she'd pried it from Victoria's clutch, rather than ask to see it, which she really should have done, if she'd been thinking clearly, which she obviously wasn't these days. As she should have expected, Victoria began to scream, one of those screams where she held her breath and turned purple and didn't release the blood-curdling sound until an alarming amount of time had passed. And then... Well, by then Hope was shaking. She was desperate. She pushed the double stroller back to the shop, wrestled the bulky thing through the door, and handed the toy over with a profuse apology. The shop girl hadn't even noticed, but oh, did every one notice the screaming. And from the looks in their eyes, they judged. Oh, yes, they judged.

Disgusted with herself, she reached into her bag and plucked out two of the lollipops that she had purchased at the market last week. That quieted things down. At least until they passed by the toy store, and then it was war.

Pretending she didn't see it, Hope pushed on by and straight into Harbor Home Designs. She knew it was silly, buying things for the cottage when she didn't even live there and they were most likely going to sell it, but she couldn't help herself. She was always drawn to pretty objects, and that house had so much potential! She could just picture it cleared of Gran's worn furnishings, replaced with white slip-covered sofas and rattan chairs and soft, cashmere throws in beachy colors. The walls could be painted over in shady of muted blues and soft grays. The kitchen would be so much brighter in a soft, buttercup yellow, and everything would be so light and airy. The way it was meant to be.

For now, she would make do with what was there. Already she found it was improved with the addition of Ellie's watercolors, and the new linens on the beds had certainly freshened things up. She did feel a tiny bit guilty as she handed over the credit card and bought a pale teal throw and three matching pillows that would liven up the front living room, but then she remembered that Evan never felt guilty for all the lunches he took with coworkers or the tennis lessons he took on the weekends. It wasn't his money; it was their money. At least, that's what he had always told her. But somehow it didn't feel that way. Her job was in the house, yes, but she felt differently when she was earning her own income.

She was just about to turn out of the store when she saw the most darling set of candlesticks in a washed wood near the window display. She reached for one and turned it over to check the price, when she saw the other was suddenly missing. She glanced down to see Rose clutching it close to her chest, her eyes defiant, as Victoria looked on with interest, sucking her lollipop.

"Can Mommy see that?" she asked, smiling in what she hoped was her pleasant face, not her tense face.

Rose giggled. "No!"

Hope swallowed hard. She couldn't handle another scene. "Please? I'll give you a lollipop."

She was aware that a woman beside her was watching her now. Judging, most certainly.

"I *have* a lolly!" Rose pointed out, looking at Hope as if she were crazy. And maybe she was at this point. She had reduced herself to bribing four-year-olds to obey her because she had lost control. And her life was always, if nothing else, in complete control.

Until it wasn't.

"Please, Rose? It would make Mommy so happy."

"No!" Rose lifted the candlestick up and slammed it down, only missing taking out a crystal vase by Hope's swift handiwork. With one hand gripping the candlestick base, she pried Rose's determined fingers from their grip, until the object was free. Sticky, but free. Now she would have to buy it. Even if it was about twenty percent overpriced in her opinion. She may not know children very well, but she knew home décor.

She smiled serenely as Rose wailed, pushed the stroller back to the counter and pulled out the credit card. She managed to continue smiling until she was at the door, and by then, people on the street had stopped to stare at the commotion. It was Sunday afternoon; the tourists were flocking from the ferries that were crossing back and forth to Blue Harbor. Every eye, it seemed, was on her. The woman with the oversized stroller, and a child clutching a lollipop, turning purple in her rage.

She glanced across the street, saw the sign for Main Street Sweets, and whispered in Rose's ear: "Stop screaming right now and I will buy you an ice cream cone."

Oh, she was ashamed. So, so, so ashamed. But it worked. Rose stopped her screaming as quickly as if a light had been switched off, and across the street they went, Hope's pride hanging on by a thread. Through another door they struggled, and then to the counter they went. "Two vanilla scoops," she began, but Victoria shouted, "Chocolate!"

Hope glanced down at her child, and for a moment, she felt herself start to shake. They were wearing precious white, eyelet dresses, coordinating, not matching. Victoria's was edged in a pink ribbon, while Rose's was edged in blue.

"I want chocolate too," Rose said. Then, spotting an older child with a cone dipped in sprinkles, she pointed her lollipop at the girl and said, "I want that!"

The college-aged girl behind the counter was watching, waiting, and a line was forming. "Two of the chocolate sprinkle cones," Hope said, pulling out her wallet.

She handed the treats to her girls, who set their lollies down in their laps, marking an immediate stain, and then wearily moved to the back of the parlor. She'd sit here for a minute, collect herself, and—

An ear-piercing, shrill sound that for a moment, in her fatigue, she almost thought was a siren's wail, cut through the carnival music that played on repeat in this store—no doubt the same soundtrack that had played when she was a child herself. Then, it had delighted her; now, it irritated her. She saw Victoria, red as a beet, holding her empty cone, and there, in her lap, the perfect scoop of chocolate ice cream, already starting to melt.

From beside her a stack of napkins was thrust, and she took them, blindly, silently cursing to herself for attempting this ridiculous trip at all. She should have stayed home, back at the cottage, let the girls play in the sand or wander on the freshly mowed grass, and at the very least, she should not have caved to their demands and purchased chocolate ice cream. They were only four years old and they were walking all over her. She had failed. She was a terrible mother.

There was a chuckling sound, and with surprise, Hope realized that someone was laughing. They thought this was funny? It was so far from funny that she could cry. And she wanted to. She wanted to pitch a fit just like Victoria was doing; she wanted to cry until no more tears flowed.

She turned, about to snap at someone, even if she would probably later come to regret it (more crazy behavior!) when she saw him. The man from the boat.

"Hello," she said. She was surprised to see him here. In an ice cream parlor. Still in town. Few people stayed for a week, and certainly not this early into the season. This time of year, you either had the weekenders or the summer people. That made this interesting.

"We have a strange way of meeting like this," he said, smiling warmly.

"You mean, meeting while my children are making a huge mess and a public scene?" She gave him a weary smile, but there was only kindness in his eyes. They were hazel grey and deep set and something in her stomach fluttered.

"I'm John Bowden, by the way," he said, extending a hand.

She took it. Felt the warmth of his palm, the strength of his grip. She was used to shaking hands with men, even greeting the familiar husbands of her friends (more like acquaintances, really) with hugs at neighborhood and school events. But this was different. This was...personal.

"Hope Morgan," she said, letting her hand drop. Technically, she was Hope Morgan-Lange, but she didn't feel like complicating this conversation, and to most people, she was either Hope Morgan or Hope

Lange. Here on the island, she felt almost like her old self.

She eyed him, wondering if he was married. A man as good looking as he was couldn't be single. And he was good with children. He probably had a few of his own.

She decided to test this theory. "You're good with kids. I take it you have experience?"

"I'm what you might call the fun uncle," he said, grinning wider, as if proud of this role.

Fun uncle? So no kids. She glanced at his hand. No ring either.

She pushed back the flutter in her chest. This man may not be married, but she was. For now, at least.

"So what brings you to Evening Island?" she asked.

He reached across to a nearby table and grabbed a cup of ice cream. His grin was sheepish and, she had to admit, completely charming. "Stress eating, sorry."

She laughed. "Stress eating? Here?" Although, she could probably be accused of it herself. The island used to be a place to relax and unwind. Now it was something different. Their real-world problems were encroaching, maybe even taking over. Last night on the porch with Ellie had been nice, casual, but short-lived. Ellie wasn't in a talking mood, and from the dreamy look in her eyes, she had only one thing on her mind. Or rather, one person.

Hope tried to summon up the feeling of infatuation, the flutter and excitement that new feelings could bring, and failed. Once upon a time, she supposed she had felt that way about Evan, but so much had changed since then.

"I'm here on business," John explained. "I'm an investor."

She frowned. "You mean, like...real estate?"

He nodded. "I'm not at liberty to give specifics, but there's a property of interest."

Hope nodded. As a resort island, there were dozens of inns and larger hotels, too. "Well, the island is great for tourism, as you can see. Where's home then?"

"Chicago," he said, and now her hand began to shake as she scooped the ice cream from Victoria's lap back onto the cone. She'd deal with the dress later.

She glanced at John, to see if he was giving her a weird look like she assumed he would, but he seemed oblivious to the fact that she was salvaging the melting ice cream. She supposed it wasn't as if it had fallen on the floor...

"I'm from Chicago too," she said carefully, and his eyebrows shot up.

"No kidding! Although, I think this island mostly pulls from the Midwest."

She agreed with that. "I'm in the northern suburbs. Originally from the Cleveland area."

"And you're here on a vacation?"

"We have a family house here, actually," she said. "On the west side of the island. It was my grandmother's and she left it to me and my sisters. We used to summer here, and we thought—I thought—well, we're here for the summer. I'm the oldest, and the only one with kids. And my youngest sister lives here year-round—she's an artist here in town. My middle-sister lives near me. She's a writer, and..." She was babbling, because she didn't really know what she was doing here anymore, or how long she planned to stay. As of yesterday, she was still seriously considering leaving, never to return again, but now she had no desire to return home to the big empty house in the suburbs. Now she wanted to stay right where she was.

"One of those big places out on West End Road?" he asked.

She laughed at that. "Don't look too impressed. The homes are big, yes, but they're old, and most are in bad upkeep. Our kitchen is practically from the turn of the century. The windows, too."

"Prime real estate," he pointed out, and she thought of Gemma's idea to list the property.

"So I've heard," was all she said to that.

The man checked his watch and stood. "Well, unfortunately my time is up." He tossed his paper cup in the nearest bin and extended a hand to her.

She took it, wondering if the disappointment she felt in her chest was noticeable on her face. It had been nice talking with him, another adult, and an interested one.

A handsome one.

A strange pull in her chest gave her pause. It was that feeling—that feeling that she had envied seeing in Ellie just last night. No, it couldn't be the same, she told herself. It was the company, she told herself. It was nice, easy company.

His hand was warm, his grip less firm this time, but still strong, and, well, almost tender. He treated her as if he knew her. As if, she dared to think, he cared about her.

"I hope to see you again, Hope," he said, grinning at his word choice.

He'd remembered her name. She liked the way it sounded coming off his lips.

"It's a small island. I'm sure we will," she said as their hands slipped away.

She sat in the ice cream shop, watching her girls, whose faces were now covered in chocolate, their dresses stained possibly beyond repair. And for the first time in a long time, she didn't feel tied down with stress and anxiety and the burden of more baths and more laundry or even the conflict waging inside her about what she was going to decide about her future or what would make her happy. She felt lighter. And free.

And she was looking forward to the promise of tomorrow and what it might bring, not fearing it.

Chapter Thirteen

Gemma

On Monday, Leo came back. Gemma watched him through the window, telling herself that she was allowed a ten-minute break after each five pages that she produced. Sometimes this took an hour. Sometimes it took three. Sometimes it took all day. Still, it was progress, and it was far more than she had been accomplishing in a week back at her apartment in the city.

Hope had been right. But then, Hope was always right. A change of scenery had done her good. And right now, she couldn't complain about her view in the slightest.

Leo was next door, at the Taylors, with a can of paint and a brush he was using to touch up the white trim on the front porch. Yes, Gemma did have to crane her neck to see all of this, but she was a writer, she needed to observe the world, not just sit and stare at a screen, which she'd done too much of lately. Really, she told herself, this was practically research. She had added a gardener into her story just this week, allowing for a plot twist that she hadn't seen coming and which opened up an entire spread of new turns and story development that just might help her finish this thing once and for all.

So really, she should be watching him, even how his muscles pulled at his shirt as he carried his toolbox up the stairs. And right now, he was the only thing to observe, other than the calm, still lake waters or the remnants of the breakfast that Hope had brought up to her that morning, before saying that she would be out with the girls most of the day.

She was certainly taking the girls out more, not that Gemma was complaining.

So that left Leo. He was someone to watch. Someone that might spark another random idea that she could use in her book. Watching him had absolutely nothing to do with the fact that today he was wearing a shirt, one that pulled tightly across his broad chest and shoulders and made his biceps look even bigger than she remembered them.

Her phone pinged, pulling her attention away, and she did so reluctantly. On her screen was an alert, one she must have forgotten to delete five months ago when her world fell apart. Final dress fitting. One hour from now.

She wasn't even aware that she was shaking until she accidentally dropped the phone, letting it hit the wooden floorboards with a thud. Her wedding dress was still in her closet back at the apartment, zipped in its dress bag, hidden from view. She had held onto it for reasons she couldn't explain, even to herself. It had been expensive, but that wasn't a reason to keep it. It was hope, perhaps, that she had clung to. Hope that as the days ticked by, something would change. That her wedding would still go forward, as planned.

Only it wouldn't. She knew that now. And the dress just served as a hurtful reminder of everything that might have been and wouldn't be.

She had no idea if it fit or not anymore. She had let the shop know when she went to pick it up—when she tried to return it and was told that she couldn't, since it was custom made. But she hadn't deleted the appointment from her phone. And now...now she knew that she wouldn't get any more work done today.

She closed out of her document and went to the bathroom to run a brush through her hair. It was after lunch already, late afternoon really, and she hadn't been outside all day. She'd take a walk, and if that walk happened to lead to a chat with Leo, then so be it. She should probably thank him for raking out that vegetable garden, after all. She'd watered it as he'd instructed, letting Rose and Victoria assist, and she thought there might just be a chance to save some of the summer crop after all, if she worked hard at it.

What was she saying? She was selling this house! What did it matter if she saved some squash?

Because it mattered to Gran, she realized. And therefore, it mattered to her.

And even though she knew it was impractical to hold onto this property, she wanted to be sure that it was shiny and polished, taken care of, and loved.

They wouldn't just sell to anyone. They'd sell to another family, a family who would have the time to come here every summer, just as they all once had.

And then... Then she hadn't gotten much further.

Deciding she couldn't think about this anymore right now, especially when Ellie was still avoiding any mention of the subject—and her, at all costs, it would seem from her continued absence—Gemma went downstairs and stepped out onto the front porch, deciding she would take a walk along the beachfront if Leo didn't happen to catch her eye first.

Admittedly, she was darting her gaze in that direction.

Catching her stare, he held up an arm in a wave, and damn it if her stomach didn't flip over a little at that. Honestly, how ridiculous was this? She'd been holed up in her apartment for so long that she now got all weak in the knees over the slightest kindness from a random man?

Only he didn't feel random. He felt...well, like a friend.

"Nice day out!" she said.

He set down his toolbox and took the steps down to the grass. She swallowed hard as he crossed the lawn toward Sunset Cottage. "I don't see you out much."

She grinned, wondering if he had been looking for her and then telling herself that this was ridiculous. It was an observation, and a fairly obvious one.

"Work keeps me busy. I'm under a tight deadline."

"What do you do?" he asked, tipping his head.

"Oh..." She dreaded this part, when she had to state her profession. Once, she had said it with pride. Made the announcement with no hesitation. But lately, she felt like a fraud, like people could see through to her struggle. "I'm a writer."

"Anything I've heard of?"

She raised an eyebrow. "Not unless you read romance novels."

His jaw seemed to harden. "Can't say that I do." He studied her for a moment. "So you believe in all that stuff?"

"Stuff?"

"Happy endings and all that," he said, narrowing his gaze.

Even if she hadn't found it for herself, she knew that it existed for some. Hope was proof of that. She shrugged. "Doesn't everybody?"

"Not everyone," he said briskly, and she had the distinct impression that she had hit a nerve.

She gave a little smile, feeling a kinship that bordered on a connection with this man. "That's why I'm here for the summer," she explained. "I'm finishing up my next book." Finishing up. She nearly snorted on that exaggeration. "There's a room upstairs that I like, with a view of the lake, and well, it's working out better than my place in Chicago." That much was true. She was at least producing words, which she hadn't done since Sean left her.

Leo stood on the grass looking up at her, thrusting his hands into his pockets, little beads of sweat dotting his forehead, and Gemma took this as a reason to invite him in.

"Can I offer you a glass of cold lemonade? I owe you at least that much for helping out with Gran's vegetable garden." She was stalling, she told herself, not flirting. She was avoiding the page.

"A break would be nice. I've pretty much been at it over there since the day I stepped foot off the ferry."He came up the stairs until he was side by side on the porch with her. She could feel the heat off his skin, smell the grass on his body.

She swallowed hard and yanked the door open so hard that it banged against the hinges. Embarrassed, she caught his look of surprise. "Darn thing. Just one of many things that needs some updating around here."

She led him back into the kitchen and poured them each a tall glass of lemonade with extra ice.

"I see your fridge light is out," he observed, fighting off a smile. "I could fix that, but I have a feeling that you're capable of screwing in a light bulb."

She laughed. "Capable, yes. It's finding the time that's the problem."

"I have time," he said mildly. "There's a lot of time on island time."

"What brings you to the island?" She saw the set of his jaw, and immediately realized that she had overstepped. "Sorry," she said quickly. "I can be nosy. Professional habit."

"It's okay, I'm just not one for talking about the past." His brow burrowed before he took another sip from his glass.

"That makes two of us," she said with a grin. She cocked her head toward the parlor. "There are a lot of things that need work around here. Maybe I could show you around?"

She led him through the rooms of the first floor, commenting on the items that would need tended to and fixed up: loose doorknobs, broken window sashes, appliances in desperate need of replacement that would have to make do with a repair.

Finally, they ended up in the parlor, with its shelves of books and the grand piano in the corner of the big bay window. Someone had set a vase of fresh flowers beside it. Hope, no doubt. She was thoughtful like that. She had a way of making any house feel like a home.

Leo noticed a copy of her book on the shelf and picked it up, turning it over in his large hands, his expression blank. Gemma felt her cheeks burn. She'd written that book at a happier time in her life. She didn't like to think about that time anymore, and she didn't like to talk about it either.

Eager to avoid the topic, she scanned the shelves, only then noticing the dozen or so other copies that Gran must have bought, her heart tugging at the silent gesture of support. She noticed Leo following her gaze and said quickly, "I'll donate some to the local library. If they're interested."

He frowned at her as she took the book. "I can't imagine they wouldn't be."

She shrugged. He was probably right, but she struggled to convince herself of this. "Sometimes it's easy to lose sight of your own work when you're too close it."

He gave her a long look. "Not a bad problem to have though, is that? Something you care about?"

"Depends how you look at it, I suppose," she said, her mind trailing back to Sean. She was so close to him she hadn't even seen that he had fallen out of love with her, or maybe, never loved her at all. "Sometimes it's scarier to care."

"Couldn't agree more," he said, holding up his glass to hers, and she again wondered about him. He had a past. Everyone did. But not many people's pasts brought them to a remote island in the Great Lakes.

Yet somehow, hers had.

"This house..." she started, and then stopped. "Well, we're probably going to sell it." *Not probably*, she told herself.

He looked surprised at the news. "Aw, but it's such a piece of history," he said, stirring up the doubts that were already there. "Ellie never mentioned it when I've bumped into her."

"Well, I live in Chicago and so does my sister Hope. And Ellie..." Here she paused and blew out a breath.

He'd seen the vegetable garden, hadn't he? "It doesn't make sense to hold onto it. It's too large, for starters."

He looked around and then nodded. "These old places are hard to maintain, especially up here on the island. But I'd buy it myself if I could afford it."

So he was planning on staying on Evening Island, was he? She tried not to think about that too much.

"Do you have family here?" she asked.

To her surprise, he nodded. "You asked about Edward the other day. He's my grandfather."

"He is?" Gemma was astonished, but now, studying Leo's face more carefully, she saw the resemblance. The same strong features. The same kind eyes. "I don't remember ever seeing you on the island."

"I never visited before. But my mother summered here as a girl before my grandfather moved here full time, and she always spoke fondly of the island. I know she wished she had come back more often."

Gemma knew the feeling all too well. She smiled. "Well, your grandfather was always kind to my grandmother. And to me and my sisters, too." She made a note to seek him out before she left the island.

Left the island. She pulled in a breath, not liking the way that settled.

"Come on out to the porch," she said. "It's stifling in here. I'm afraid of how bad it will be come July."

Not that she would know, she realized, feeling suddenly sad at the thought. She couldn't impose on Ellie forever, and if they were going to list the house, they'd have to do it before the weather turned, anyway. Summer was tourist season. People would come, fall in love with the island, and be tempted into returning on a regular basis.

She'd have to talk to Ellie again soon.

"You don't work out here?" Leo looked around the porch with approval. "If I lived here, I'd be out here all day."

It occurred to her that she didn't know where he lived, but he was private, and determined to remain so, it seemed.

"I never thought about that really, but maybe it would help. I've been struggling with my writing. It's why I came here," she admitted. The table was more than big enough to spread notes out, and her laptop had a strong battery, one that could last for hours without needing to be recharged. And Hope was spending more time out of the house, meaning there was less chance of the twins interrupting her.

"So you came all the way here and stay cooped up inside writing?" Leo gave her a quizzical look.

Well, when he put it like that...

"I guess I'm set in my ways," she thought aloud. "At least, that's what my ex always said."

It was something that Sean had accused her of, once their relationship started taking a turn. That he didn't know her anymore. That she had changed their routine by staying home, writing all day. That he liked her better when she was on the same schedule as him, at the office, breaking for lunch, commuting back and forth from the business district to their north side apartment. They had more to talk about then. It had masked how little they had in common.

She was aware that Leo was giving her a strange look now, and she felt her cheeks warm. "I'm oversharing. I'm sorry. I must not get out enough."

"Let me take you out then," he said. "A writer needs to see the world."

She felt her breath grow heavy, not liking where this going, afraid of where this was going, really. She pulled a face, prepared to let him down, but he held up a hand before she could speak.

"For the record, I've got an ex too. No pressure. Just two friends. Getting out."

Friends. She liked the sound of that, even if it was almost...disappointing? No, she couldn't allow that.

"How does Thursday look for you?"

The same as every other day, she thought. Until now. Now it felt...promising.

"Okay then," she said, grinning.

"Good. It's a date," he said, and immediately Gemma felt a heat flare up in her cheeks.

They stood there, letting the awkward moment pass. Finally, Leo said, "Well, the paint's probably dry on the Taylors' porch by now. I should get that second coat going."

"Of course," Gemma gushed. She didn't want to keep him from his work. And she really shouldn't keep herself from her work either.

And now, for reasons she couldn't quite explain, she felt that she had more work in her.

The gardener was becoming a bigger and bigger character in her story, and maybe, not just in her book.

"And I'll get over here soon to do those repairs. Just jot down a project list. I can work within your budget."

"Thanks. It will really help sell the place."

"*If* you decide to sell," he said over his shoulder as he walked down the porch steps.

Gemma leaned against the doorjamb to the front door, careful not to press against the screen. She didn't need to go damaging anything else in this house. "We'll be selling. This house is too much for my sister to take care of on her own, and my other sister and I don't get up here much."

She watched as Leo's eyes shifted and landed on something over her shoulder. She turned, hoping to see Hope, but dread sinking in when she saw Ellie, standing a few feet away in the hallway, the look on her face telling Gemma that she had heard everything and that she wasn't happy about it at all.

"Ellie," Gemma said. She must not have heard her come home when she was upstairs working, and now she had some explaining to do. But before she could say anything more, Ellie shook her head and pounded up the stairs, leaving Gemma and Leo in an awkward silence at the base.

Leo whistled out a breath. "Hope I didn't get you into trouble," he said.

"Not anymore than I'm already in," she said, only she wasn't so sure that this was true. Because as he held up a hand and crossed the lawn to the house next door, she realized that she couldn't wait to see him again, and that no good could come from thinking that way. About him. Or anyone.

Chapter Fourteen

Ellie

The studio was her special place, even more than Sunset Cottage. Certainly more than her bedroom back at her parents' house, because that one had been decorated by her mother in colors that didn't inspire her: muted mauves when she would have preferred something bright and blue. She hadn't even been allowed to put a nail in the wall; hadn't been allowed to hang one of her own paintings. Granted, some of her early work was amateur, but she had improved over time, gotten a scholarship to the Art Institute when her father refused support of any kind, wanting her to get a degree in education or marketing instead, where she could "apply" her interests in a way that better suited him. He didn't understand that it wasn't the same! "Hobbies are hobbies," he'd said in one of their worst fights. "And hobbies don't pay the bills!"

Now, she wondered if he was right. Between rent on the studio, bills at the house, and the everyday expense of life, her inheritance was dwindling, rapidly, and while the paintings she sold were proving to be a steady stream of income, it wouldn't cover the upkeep needed to keep the cottage running indefinitely. And without her sisters' support as co-owners, she was in a very bad situation.

Would they refuse to pitch in when the roof needed to be replaced? Because it did need to be replaced. She was no dummy. And it should probably be replaced before the heavy snow hit—not only because it would be next to impossible to get a replacement installed once the ferry stopped running, but because she knew that a leaking roof and subsequent water damage would only add to the cost. And what about when the water heater failed? It was imminent, she knew, but she hadn't told them that yet—not when they were grumbling over the washing machine being less than reliable. And now, she didn't feel she could. It would be one more reason for Gemma to want to sell. And why wouldn't Hope agree when it came down to it? Hope was practical. And the house...was not.

She knew it, of course, deep down. It was huge, for starters. Far too big for one person. And it was old.

And any kind of construction or repairs on the island was costly; it was why Gran, like so many year-round islanders, took care of what they had, preserving it, making it last.

And it was also more than Ellie could handle on her own.

Still, she was angry at Gemma. Angry at Hope, for not really sharing much opinion either way. But mostly, she knew in her heart of hearts, she was angry at her father.

And right now, Gemma was sounding more and more like him. Wanting to sell Sunset! He always claimed the house was run-down, in need of modernization. He failed to see that what he saw fit to critique was exactly what made the homes here so cherished and loved. She rather liked the peeling wallpaper; it gave it character! Each squeaky floorboard told a story. But try telling that to her family.

She angrily stroked her brush across the canvas. She was painting a thunderstorm, coming in over the water. Dark clouds and angry waves. Grays and blacks and navy. It wasn't like her usual whimsical, light, and colorful paintings that she was known for on the island. But right now, she didn't feel happy. Right now she felt...scared. As scared as she'd been last summer when Gran was gone and life again felt uncertain, because much as she hated to admit it, even now, the reason she had been so upset with Gemma was because deep down she knew that her sister was right.

Gran had taken her in, unemployed and unwilling to go back to her father for handouts. She could paint all day, Gran had promised, because the island offered endless inspiration. In turn, Ellie had taken care of Gran. At first, she had just served as her companion, but then it moved on from errand running to minding the house, to making sure that Gran was taken to the doctor, that she was comfortable. Weeks and months would go by when she wouldn't even paint. Gemma probably didn't know that.

But despite everything that Ellie had done for Gran, the favor, she knew, was all hers, and that without Gran's invitation, and without the island house, she had nowhere else to go.

The door to the studio jingled and she glanced out the window toward the harbor. Evening was setting in, and she hadn't intended to come back here tonight, but then, yet again, Gemma had to go and upset her. There was no more coffee if one of the guys from the harbor intended on a warmer upper. If she had any now, she'd be awake all night, and she hoped to get some sleep so she could rise early tomorrow and capture the sunrise over on the Eastern Edge.

She dropped her paintbrush into the cup of water and wiped her hands on her apron. She was rounding the bend when she saw him, before he noticed her. The evening sunlight was filtering through the windows, casting rays of gold on his nut-brown hair, and his hands were thrust in the pockets of his khakis. He was studying her paintings, taking time with each one, and he didn't look her way until she stepped farther into the room and said, "Hello."

Simon looked up, the surprise fleeting on his face before his expression turned to one of familiarity. "I promised I'd visit."

"And you always kept your promises," she said, wishing as soon as she'd said it that she hadn't. After all, there had been the one promise that he hadn't kept. He'd promised to come back, and he hadn't until now. As an engaged man.

Because that's what he was, she reminded herself. Whether she liked it or not, he was in a relationship with someone else, and the fact that Erin wasn't here should hold no bearing. But somehow, it did. Because Simon was here, and she was here, and the island...it was their place. And it seemed that it still was.

She eyed him carefully, wondering if he even remembered those words, spoken the final night they were together, ten years ago this August. Ten years, she thought now, thinking that was more than a third of her lifetime, that really, she should be over it by now, except that for some reason, she wasn't. She was eighteen then, same as him. It was a running joke that she was technically an older woman, turning nineteen on the last day of the month. She had three months of age on him, but he seemed so much older and wiser and sure of what he wanted. He was going to be a lawyer, like his father. He would summer at the island. His life would carry on as it always had, whereas she yearned for change.

They'd stayed out late that night, swimming until their skin turned blue with cold, and then huddled together in blankets down at the shore, staying warm next to the fire that he'd built, staying there until the wood burned down and it was just the dying embers and the moon for light.

He'd be back, he promised. And she'd be back, she said. Nothing would change between them, even though it felt like everything was about to change—that their futures held no certainty other than that their lives were about to start. They would be adults, free to finally do as they chose. And he chose not to return.

He'd be back, he'd said. Same time, same place. Next summer. It would be like always, just another year apart, another summer to look forward to. Only she was worried. She knew that this time, they weren't going back to their childhood homes and their usual lives. They were each going out into the world. They'd experience new things. They'd meet new people.

They'd move on from their childhood families. Would they move on from the island too?

She'd kept up her promise. Returned the following summer even though it was just her and her mother and Gemma by then.

But Simon never came. Or explained. Or apologized, either. His parents came—said he'd gotten a great internship that was too good to pass up. Instead, he'd passed her up.

Still, she'd waited. And hoped. For a change of plans.

For a change of heart.

What would she have said, all those years ago, when she'd cried into her pillow late at night, swam in the lake all by herself during the day, and rode her bike all over the island, wishing and hoping that one morning would mark his return, if she knew that he *would* someday return? That he'd be back, long after she'd stopped looking for him. That he'd be standing in her art studio. That she would own an art studio! That she might have another chance.

Except for the small part about him being engaged.

"So you work out of here?" he asked, looking at her in wonder.

She nodded, pride filling her as she stood amongst her work. Her dreams. "I paint out of the studio, but I also paint on location. I run classes once a week, too.

Friday nights. Open to anyone, so long as there's a chair." She eyed him, wondering if she should push her luck, and then decided she had nothing to lose. She'd already lost him once before. "You should drop by sometime."

He grinned at her, and every nerve ending in her body seemed to sing. "Maybe I will."

After a moment, he broke her gaze and motioned to a painting, one of her favorites, that she'd painted last fall when the leaves were at their peak and the entire island seemed to be awash in shades of crimson, orange, and yellow. "This one is remarkable. I never saw the island like this before."

"Most people don't," she said simply. After all, most of the tourists were gone by Labor Day, the summer people too. Then it was just the year-round folks, grateful at first for a chance to breathe, to have their space back, to be able to walk into Main Street Market without having to worry that all the fresh bagels would be sold out, but then, she'd learned with time, eager for everyone to return.

She came to stand next to him, thinking that it would be impossible to give this up, not just the painting but the island, the cottage, the opportunity to see what she saw, every day, to capture with her hand and a paintbrush and some paint.

"I guess I need to come back to the island a little later in the season sometime," he said, slanting her a glance.

Something inside her locked up. She didn't like the way he was looking at her, with that grin, and those eyes...it made her feel things she shouldn't. It made her think that they still had a chance.

Did they?

He was so close to her now that she could feel the heat off his skin, and her heart began to pound at the familiarity of it all. It would be so easy to just fall back into step, to continue the relationship they'd built summer after summer; from the time they were fifteen to eighteen they'd carried on in June where they'd left off the previous August.

Time had never created a distance between them before. Maybe, it didn't have to now.

"I thought you had a job to get back to," she said, trying to keep herself footed in reality.

He shrugged. "I told you. I have my own thing going now. I can technically work from anywhere in the world."

She raised her eyebrows, trying to imagine such freedom. "I'd love to travel the world. To capture it."

"You should," he said, but she just shook her head.

She was exactly what her father told her she was. She was a starving artist. She'd spent all her trust on this studio—because as Gemma was so quick to point out, real estate on the island was prime. The house was paid off, and there was enough set aside for the taxes and the utility bills. But it stopped there. And the money she made selling her paintings in town was far from reliable, and she'd certainly never be rich from it, or even financially secure.

Meaning to her father, it had no value.

She shrugged away the comment and motioned toward the back room. "I have a few from winter, if you're interested."

He nodded and followed her into the storage room. The room was tight and crowded, with dozens of canvases neatly stacked against the walls. Feeling awkward at how alone they were, she began rifling through her stacks, even though she usually knew where every single painting was kept.

"Here we go," she said, pulling out one of her favorites: a scene of Main Street during the first snowfall of the year. Most horses went back to the mainland for the winter months, but here she'd managed to capture a horse-drawn carriage on its way back to one of the family-owned inns, whose residents finally had the house to themselves for a few months. Just looking at it gave her peace, and strengthened her resolve too. Gemma couldn't sell that house. She wouldn't let her. And her vote had to count for something.

Simon shook her head as he studied it. "Wow," he finally said.

He gave her a look of approval she rarely saw from anyone else, but then, she supposed, he had always looked at her like that, hadn't he? Always seen what the others hadn't? Always liked the fact that she was artistic, free-spirited, that she didn't want a conventional life.

But he had wanted that conventional life, hadn't he? And she had never quite fit into that plan.

"You got everything you ever wanted," he remarked.

"Almost," she said, meeting his eye. He squinted, ever so subtly, and she wondered for a moment if she'd overstepped. Her cheeks flamed and she used the time to put the painting back in place, even though she was starting to think that maybe she'd take this one back to the cottage with her. Hope was certainly wasting no time in putting her mark on things around there; perhaps it was time for Ellie to do the same. Maybe if she had tried harder to spruce up the place rather than leave so much of it as it was as a hallmark to her Gran, then Gemma would be more eager to hold on to it.

Except that Gemma seemed to want to cash out. She was becoming more like their father every day. What Ellie really needed to do, she thought, was to appeal to Gemma's sentimental side.

If she could figure out how.

"What's missing?" Simon asked, and Ellie was so caught off guard that she almost dropped the canvas, and that would have been a disaster. Carefully, and with shaking hands, she set it in place, happy for a moment to have her face turned from him.

"Oh, you know." She caught his eye, pushed a loose strand of hair from her cheek. "My parents think I should have a conventional job. Find a husband. Settle down."

"The safe route," Simon said. A shadow passed over his expression. "It's not all it's cracked up to be."

Well, that was interesting. She studied him, waiting to see if he would elaborate, and when he didn't, she said, "But you're happy? Practicing law? Your own firm. Your..." She couldn't bring herself to say it. His engagement.

She wondered if there was a wedding date. She wondered if it was soon.

"I'm happy being here on the island," he said, giving her a crooked grin. "I hadn't realized I missed it so much until I came back. It's...it's easy to get caught up in the daily grind, to forget how much you miss something until you see it again."

He was watching her closely, and Ellie's stomach was positively rolling by now.

For a moment he leaned in, and her heart sped up as their faces grew closer, and she thought he was going to do it, he was going to kiss her. And she knew that she shouldn't. He was engaged. Except, a little part of her said, she had him first. She knew him best. Longest. This Erin woman might know the stuffy guy with the law degree, but she knew the real Simon, the one who chucked strawberries into the air and caught them with his mouth, who shed his shirt and dove into the cool lake water, and swam all the way out, as far as he could make it.

He paused, seeming to catch himself and brushed her cheek with his lips.

"It was good seeing you today," he said, pulling back. He squeezed her shoulder, paused as if there was something more that he wanted to say and thought the better of it, and then let himself out.

Ellie stood in the storage room for several moments after she'd heard the door to the studio open and close. Then she went back into the empty room and stared at the painting that Simon had admired so much, the one with the crimson maple leaves falling at the base of the lanterns that lined Main Street, and she replayed what he'd said over and over, telling herself that she was reading into things, that he was engaged.

But despite knowing this, she couldn't help but feel hopeful that somehow, everything was about to change, and for the better.

Chapter Fifteen

Hope

Hope had established a routine during her ten days on the island. Every morning she woke at six, a solid hour before the girls did, just like always, only here she woke to the light that filtered through the linen curtain panels, spreading sunshine all over her room. She put on her pink cashmere robe, because it was cool in the mornings, when the windows were still cracked from the night before and the day was still young, and padded down the stairs to the kitchen at the back of the house, where she prepared breakfast for everyone, because if she was already cooking for her children, she may as well see it through, and because, it was what was expected of her. Hope hosted holidays. Hope threw parties. Hope was the silent leader growing up, and that dynamic had extended into adulthood.

Hope was not allowed to fall apart.

Sometimes Ellie beat her to it, brewed a pot of coffee and left for the day before Hope had even gotten a start, but more often than not she stuck around, hovering at the kitchen door as if she wasn't so sure she was invited in, or what to make of Hope's hospitality. Hope would hide her smile, pleased to prepare a meal for someone who so clearly appreciated it, just like Ellie had appreciated all those times when Hope was already old enough to drive and responsible for taking Ellie to her much-loathed piano classes, where her posture was forever in question, and where she had been reprimanded more than once for "going rogue" by putting her own spin on a classical piece, and to make up for it, she'd swing Ellie by the ice-cream stand on their way home, their own weekly tradition that only cost her a few of her babysitting dollars and meant so much to Ellie that it was worth it.

Evan certainly didn't appreciate the meals she made for him. He ate dinners quickly, usually with his eyes on the television screen, and then she was left with a sink full of dishes that made the entire effort seem even more thankless. Often he would call to let her know he was working late, and she didn't even bother to mention anymore that she was already roasting a chicken and that she'd just peeled the potatoes.

It hadn't always been like this, she knew. Back when they both held down jobs outside the home, they often met for dinner in the city before heading home. But that was before the girls, and going out to eat with the girls was too much trouble right now.

Around seven, the girls woke, usually together, because they did everything together and because Victoria was scared to walk down the stairs by herself. They'd eat at the table while Hope carried a plate up to Gemma, learning quickly into things that it was best to leave it just outside her closed door. She'd find it when she was ready, even if it had probably gone cold by then.

Then there was the kitchen to clean, and the flower beds to weed, (only thanks to the help of the handyman that Gemma had hired and had been seen chatting with a few times, the yard was looking much better already), and then, when the sun was higher in the sky, she and the girls wandered to their private beach, buckets in hand, a paperback for Hope, not that she could keep her eyes on it much. Oh, she used to love to read! Now, by the time the girls were in bed, her eyes were so heavy that even attempting to read usually put her right to sleep. And she didn't want to sleep! She wanted to enjoy every moment of the evening, not just for the sunsets that turned the sky coral and pink and sherbet orange, but because it was the only time in the day, the only time at all, that was hers. Only hers.

After the beach, there was the bath, and then, usually, a trip into town. Hope had recovered from the weekend's disaster and now made a daily habit of it, to be amongst the land of the living. And, maybe, if she was being completely honest with herself, to have the possibility of running into John again. John who made her take on the same expression that Ellie did any time that Simon's name was mentioned.

Her favorite shop was Harbor House Designs, the home interiors shop just off Main, where Rose had attempted to smash the crystal vase with the candlestick. Now when Hope went inside, she was prepared. Each girl had a lollipop and a promise of another if they behaved. The owner brought in fresh items every three days; she said it was the only way to keep business going with the locals, who were her best customers.

"After all," Sheila said to her today, "there are over five hundred year-round residents on the island."

Were there? That was more than Hope would have thought and the figure felt like one with potential, though she wasn't sure why or how. Still, she picked up a boxwood topiary and set it down, then moved onto some table linens before her eyes drifted to a beautiful armchair in a mint-green buffalo check print.

On a whim, she picked up a charcoal-colored throw pillow with a mint and blue floral pattern and set it on the seat of the chair.

"That's a bold combination," said a voice behind her.

Hope's cheeks flushed as she turned to see the shop owner standing beside her. "Sorry," she said, reaching for the pillow, but Sheila held up a hand.

"Don't be. I like that. I like your style." She tipped her head. "Are you a designer?"

Hope laughed. "No. I'm..." She stopped there. What was she? She didn't even know how to describe herself anymore. A mom? A wife? No one ever asked her what she did anymore. People just assumed. No one really stopped to ask much about her as an individual at all, she realized. Other than John. "I'm Hope Morgan," she said, extending her hand.

Sheila gave it a shake. "I heard that Ellie's sisters were here for the summer. And you have the same eyes." She motioned to a framed print on the wall, and Hope was surprised to realize it one of her sister's paintings.

"Your sister has quite a talent," Sheila said.

"Yes," Hope said, fighting off a rush of contradictory emotions. Ellie had always followed her heart instead of her head, something that their father warned would only lead to trouble. But Hope felt like the one in trouble. The one without a clue as to what the future held anymore. The one who hadn't preserved her own identity.

Whereas Ellie...she always knew what she wanted. And who she was.

"I opened this shop about four years ago," Sheila was saying now as she adjusted a few vases on a shelf. "I'd visited the island before and it was always my dream to end up here someday. You're fortunate to have grown up here."

"We only summered here," Hope corrected, "but...we were fortunate." They still were, she thought. So long as they still had Sunset Cottage, they still had this island. It was always here. It always had been. It just hadn't been...practical for a while.

"It's been a long time since I've been back to the island," Hope said. Too long.

Now, looking back, she felt bad. Maybe they'd expected too much from Ellie. Holding down the fort, taking care of the house. It wasn't like they had offered to pitch in. But they had responsibilities, and Ellie...well, Ellie was Ellie. And as much as she hadn't vocalized it, she understood why Gemma had said what she did last summer. She had a good arrangement here. One that Gran had provided.

"I'm looking for some help, if you're interested," Sheila said, and Hope had to stop herself from gaping.

"Some of my regular clients have been asking for personal consultations. Some of the projects are small—decorating for the holidays or summer parties—others are larger in scale. I've advised clients on everything from wall color to floor tile." She laughed.

Hope didn't know why, but she felt suddenly seized with panic, as if there was a decision to make, and she wasn't prepared to make it. It had all sprung up too soon, and there were logistics. She didn't have childcare. How on earth could she take a job right now? It wasn't practical, but where had being practical gotten her before? And what about Evan? He'd be coming back soon enough, and what was she going to tell him when he did? What about her lovely Tudor house on Willow Lane? And her car. It was still at the ferry station in Blue Harbor, in the long-term parking lot. For some inexplicable reason, she began to worry that she'd forgotten to roll up the windows, even though she never rolled them down. Still, she should check. She could take the ferry over, ease her mind.

Except, if she got on the ferry, stepped foot on mainland, she wasn't sure that she would have the courage to come back. Because she knew how she felt here. Good. Too good, maybe.

"Oh, I don't—" She stopped herself. This was exactly what she wanted, wasn't it? An opportunity to do something for herself? To pursue her own interests? To use her mind to do something other than keep lists and manage domestic routine?

If there was one thing she knew how to do well it was keep a home. And decorate one.

"I don't know how long I'll be staying," she said, taking the card. It was thick cardstock, creamy white, and the raised font was in rose gold lettering. Effortlessly chic. She could almost picture her own name staring back at her as the idea the woman was offering began to take shape.

This island was full of potential. Beautiful, Victorian homes just aching to be restored to their former glory. It was a project that would inspire her. One that would make her feel alive. She felt more energized than she had in years just thinking about it.

"That's fine," Sheila said. "I could use the temporary help if that suits you. Though of course if this works out, I'd be sorry to see you go."

Hope would too, she realized. She'd be very sorry to go, but not because she didn't want to return to Chicago. Because she didn't think she was quite ready to leave the island. And more and more, she wasn't sure that she ever would be.

*

She left the shop a few minutes later, after exchanging phone numbers and agreeing to meet with Darcy

Ritter up on the bluff this Friday, something which seemed to bring as much relief to Sheila as it did excitement to Hope.

She fought the urge to hold in her news, realizing that she wasn't sure that there was anyone she could tell who would understand just how much this meant to her. Gemma seemed to think that her life was perfect; that she didn't need to seek change. And Ellie...well, Ellie was too wrapped up in Simon and the argument with Gemma to care very much about Hope having a meeting with Darcy, head of the local quilting club. Ellie had her paintings in stores, after all.

Her so-called friends in the neighborhood would be downright appalled. A job? That word ranked up there with snake pit when it came to fear factor.

And of course Evan. She hadn't even thought to tell Evan.

Sobering, she decided to treat herself to an iced coffee, and the girls to a baked good of their choice, considering they had behaved so well during that interaction. She pushed the stroller into the Cottage Coffeehouse off Water Street, her spirits lifting again when she saw John at the corner table, a laptop open and a bunch of paperwork spread out in front of him.

She stood in line, placed her order, wondering if she should bother him, questioning why she had a burning desire to share her news with him, when no one else felt like an option at the moment.

She glanced his way, waiting to see if he would look up, and then, when she collected her coffee, and she had to decide whether to take her own seat or leave without saying anything, he rubbed a hand across his face wearily and looked up. She smiled. He smiled. And then, with an unspoken invitation, she walked to his table.

"Hello." Was it just her, or did John seem happy to see her? His eyes were crinkled and his smile was broad and he pulled out a chair. It squeaked against the floorboards. "Sit if you have time."

She glanced at the girls, deciding the muffins would keep them occupied for a few minutes at least.

"Sure," she said with more excitement than she had planned, but she couldn't help it. Her good mood was bubbling up inside her; even her step had a skip in it.

John picked up on it right away and gave her an inquisitive grin. "You're awfully chipper today."

It was true. She was. And he was more used to seeing her frazzled and weary, wasn't he?

"I've had some good news," she said. She paused, fearful that once she made her announcement, her bubble would burst, that he'd let her down, the way so many had before. That he'd remind her that she was a mother, point out that the kids needed her, that she'd have time for all that other stuff in a few years. That he'd fail to recognize what this meant to her. That she'd feel foolish and regret all of it. "I've been offered a position, well, an opportunity, you might call it, to be a design consultant for the interior décor shop over on Main Street."

"That's wonderful!" he exclaimed, and Hope realized in that moment that she loved him for that, even though she shouldn't. After all, what did she know about this man other than that he was kind and helpful? And handsome, she thought. He was very handsome.

"Thanks," she said, licking her bottom lip. She took a sip of her coffee and leaned in. "You're the first person I've told. It just happened, so I'm a little frazzled."

"You? Frazzled?" He gave her a wink and she laughed out loud.

"Most people don't see that side of me," she admitted. Maybe that was the difference. With John, she was her true self, maybe even her weakest self. And she didn't mind. No pretense. No airs. And from him, no judgment.

If anything, she might even go so far as to say that he seemed to like her.

"So, tell me more about the job," he said, closing his laptop.

For a moment, she felt bad. She'd interrupted his work. But then she realized that he wanted to be interrupted. He'd chosen to give her his full attention. He actually wanted to hear her describe her passion, her interest, her knowledge.

She swallowed, her mind racing at how to describe her responsibilities. "Well, I'll be meeting with some of the local clients in their homes, to help them maximize their full potential. Some projects will be small, but it's the bigger ones, the ones that require more of a renovation that excite me the most."

"Keep talking like that and I might hire you to help with the inn that I'm planning to buy."

She blinked. Was he serious? That wasn't a job he was describing...that was a career! Her heart began to race when she considered what that implied, but then she realized she was getting ahead of herself. She hadn't even met with Darcy yet.

"Needless to say, it's a great opportunity and it was certainly unexpected." She smiled as she took another sip of her coffee.

"You look happy about that," he said, grinning. "It suits you well."

Her cheeks flared as their eyes caught and immediately John held up a hand. "I'm sorry if I overstepped."

"Not at all," Hope said. She wasn't used to compliments, she realized. She couldn't recall the last time she'd been given one by Evan. On their anniversary? She'd worn that black strapless dress that still fit, even though she'd bought it before the twins were born, for one of Evan's company dinners. When they'd first met, and even early into their marriage, he would compliment her when she made a special effort, but those days had faded. Life had become even more practical, and romance...well, romance wasn't practical at all, was it?

She glanced down at her rings. She saw John do the same.

No, she thought to herself, there was nothing *practical* about any of this.

"My husband isn't with me on this trip," she said.

He held up a hand. "You don't need to explain."

She considered that. Maybe she didn't need to explain. Maybe there was no need. They were just two people on a small island who kept bumping into each other. She was a lonely woman. And he was a kind man.

Except she didn't think it stopped there. And the look in his eyes told her that he didn't think so either. There was a sadness there, a resigned acceptance that she couldn't exactly place.

"I feel the need to, though," she said. "We're..." She didn't know how to finish that sentence. She didn't know what she and Evan were, only what they had once been. Once, they had been friends—the sort of friends who knew that they were a good match. On paper. But what about in real life? What about when it mattered?

They rarely laughed anymore. She couldn't blame Evan, not entirely. It felt like their entire life together was one long string of events, of things they were supposed to do, not things that they wanted to do. He worked hard, and she worked hard. Only more and more it seemed that while he could complain about a meeting with his boss or a difficult client, if she complained about Rose having a potty accident in the middle of a store or even being tired after a long day of taking the twins to all their kid-activities, that she was looked at as being a bad mother. Not a busy one. Not a person with feelings that mattered.

"We're taking a break," she finally said. It was an honest answer, and one that she hoped wasn't misleading. She liked John. She wanted to spend time with him. But she was still a married woman.

He nodded as if he understood, or perhaps had been through something like this himself. "So he's not coming here then?"

"No," she said. He was never there. And that was the problem.

And John...he was here. He was everywhere she turned. But more than that, he was present.

Chapter Sixteen

Gemma

When Leo said they should get out, he was true to his word. Out didn't mean sitting in one of the dimly lit pubs near the harbor, nor did it mean sipping coffee at the Cottage Coffeehouse.

She stood outside the Birchwood Stables, staring at the backside of a white horse named Sonny. "You can't be serious," she finally said.

He tossed her a grin. "You're going to tell me that you summered here every year and never learned to ride a horse?"

"Of course I learned to ride a horse," she said, throwing him a look of mock exasperation. She swallowed her nerves. They didn't go down easily. "It was just...a long time ago."

Back when she was scrawny, fearless, and...confident, she realized. The past year had taken a toll on her; made her question herself, not just her future.

"You should have no trouble then," Leo said, watching her expectantly. He gave his stallion a pat after adjusting the saddle.

Gemma saw no way out of this one. She looked worriedly up at Sonny. Would the poor animal even hold her weight? She felt guilty. She wasn't a skinny little kid anymore, and all that Thai takeout hadn't exactly helped her midriff area. Still, as she watched Leo hoist himself onto his horse and grab the reins, she knew she was just making excuses.

"Here goes nothing," she muttered as she slid her shoe into the stirrup and pulled up onto the horse. There. That wasn't so bad. It was just a lot higher than she remembered it being, or maybe she hadn't ridden such a big horse in the past.

She glanced to the barn door, where the ponies were eating hay. Ah, yes, those were the days. Small, less intimidating creatures. A few feet from the ground at best. Now, she was towered high up above the dirt path. It would be a long, hard fall down.

"Please don't trip," she whispered into Sonny's ear.

Leo was an expert, or a natural, she'd soon find out. He led them away from the stable, riding side by side with her on route to the wooded path where Gemma tried not to worry about fallen logs or other hazards.

Leo kept them going at a steady pace, but she could tell that he was itching to trot, and, as Gemma grew more relaxed, she almost felt the urge, too.

Almost. No sense in getting ahead of herself here. With any of it.

Still, her stomach stirred every time Leo caught her eye and gave her one of those warm grins, the kind that made his eyes go all crinkly at the corners.

"Where'd you learn to ride?" she asked. It clearly wasn't his first time on a horse, and she doubted it was a skill that he had just picked up since moving to the island, either.

He was quiet for a minute as he led his horse away from a pair of bicycles that were parked outside a picket-fence-lined home.

"I rode growing up. Grew up on a ranch." He glanced at her, as if not sure he wanted to tell more or needed to explain more. She focused on her horse, gripping the reins in her hands, trying to relax into the moment, and struggling.

Noticing, Leo grinned. "Anyone ever tell you that you have trust issues?"

Gemma laughed. "You're right. But I just met Sonny here. It's not exactly easy to put my life in her hands."

"Hate to break it to you, but Sonny is a boy."

"All the more reason then," Gemma snorted.

"You just met me too," he said, catching her eye, and something in the way he looked at her made her heart start to race. "And I'm a boy."

He was a man, through and through, and she couldn't help raking her gaze over the width of his shoulders, the muscles in his forearms as he led the horse.

"You saying I should be careful?" she asked, realizing, with mild horror, that she was flirting with him. A little.

"I've been known to let people down," Leo said, and by the way his brow drew together, she suspected that she had hit a nerve. They said nothing more as he steered his horse onto the wooded trail, and they rode single file for a while.

It was easier this way, Gemma thought. She didn't have to see his face, or his smile, or the warmth in his eyes. Didn't have to make eye contact. Maybe it was easier for him, too. He was a quiet man, and he didn't want to reveal much.

Not that she was up for sharing. After all, you just don't blurt out that your fiancé got cold feet without people wanting some explanation.

"So where's the ranch?" she asked, thinking this might be safer grounds, and he had volunteered it, after all.

"Wyoming," he said. "That's where my father was from, and how my mother ended up out there."

She knew that Edward had lived most of the year in Wisconsin until he became a full-time resident. "That's farther away than I expected," she said.

"Like I said, I needed a change."

She nodded, even though he couldn't see her. She watched him bounce a bit on his saddle, steer his horse to the right. She followed.

"You ever planning to go back?" she called out. He was gaining ground on her, and she wasn't yet ready to let Sonny loose.

The pause was so long that she assumed he hadn't heard her.

Finally, he said, "The ranch belongs to my brother now."

A brother. That was something. She realized that she wanted to know more. Older brother? Younger? Were there others?

"You two close?" she settled on, thinking of the bond she shared with her sisters, even though they had grown apart in recent years.

Even though Ellie was still upset with her.

"No," he grunted. He led the horse into a clearing and stopped. "You see that house over there?" He pointed through the dense trees. The trillium that was native to this region was still in bloom, a lush carpet leading up to a white carriage house. "That's my place."

She hadn't even considered where he might live other than with Edward, who kept a small cottage closer to town. She'd seen him so much at the Taylor house that she'd just connected him with the house, even though of course he didn't live there, he was just tending to it.

She took a good look at the carriage house that he had motioned to. It was freshly painted, with black shutters that flanked white paned windows. Underneath, where others might keep a carriage, were bales of hay.

"Whoa, boy," he said as he led his horse through the gate.

"Wait," Gemma said as it all started to come together. She forgot all about leading Sonny as she took in her surroundings. "That's *your* horse." No wonder the stallion had a shiny new saddle, she mused.

"I only have one so don't say I didn't share," he said, grinning. "Sonny here is the best of the herd from the Birchwood Stables."

"And he's a sweetheart," she said, giving her horse a pat.

"And here you weren't so sure about that," Leo said with a laugh. "Glad you decided to give him a chance?"

She caught his eye. Swallowed hard. "I think I am."

"Not all guys are bad," he said, giving her a cheeky grin.

She met his eye, felt a heat creep up her cheeks. "Never said they were," she managed, glancing away.

"You must spend a lot of time describing perfect men in your books," he remarked.

She shook her head. "That's fiction." And it was becoming increasingly difficult to write about a character that she had never met and may never hope to meet.

Still, Leo was right. Good guys were out there. And she was starting to think that he might be one of them. She watched as he dismounted with ease and closed the gate before helping her down, his hand warm and steady in hers. They lingered there like that, even once she was on steady ground, her legs a little shaky beneath her.

She licked her lower lip and pulled her hair away, wishing she could have held it for just a second longer.

It was cooler here, in the woods. She'd always loved this part of the island, away from the water, sure, but the way there were so many paths through the forest, so many houses tucked away, some were big and others small.

Leo's house was not at all what she expected. But then, she wasn't sure what she'd expected. She just knew that nothing about him, from his existence to this...*friendship* that they were forming was something she could have planned for.

"So...if you have a horse, I assume that you're not going anywhere anytime soon?"

"Don't plan on it," Leo said. He pulled a bushel of hay from the stack and tossed it to the horses. "Nothing to go back to."

Gemma peered at him. There had to be more to this story. What about his mother? His parents? And the ex.

No one just ran away to Evening Island without a purpose. It was too remote. Too cold in the winter. But it was beautiful. And not just beautiful. It was special.

"Shame you'll be selling the cottage," he said, as if reading her thoughts.

Her chest tightened as it did every time she thought about not returning to the island, because she wouldn't, she knew, once the house was gone.

"So caretaking..." she began, hoping to get off the subject of her own house's fate.

"That just pays the bills," he said, leaning against the fence. "My real plan is to turn this property into a proper stable. Get more horses. Give guided tours through the woods, all around the island. There's enough demand to support another business."

"You'd be good at that," she said, smiling at him.

"Like I said, I needed a change." He shrugged.

A change from what exactly? She nodded, imagining what it would be like to give up her routine and move to Evening Island where life was simpler, quieter, and slower paced. She'd thought that Ellie was selling herself short by residing here all these years, but putting it this way, a change sounded good.

Maybe, she thought, eyeing Leo, even tempting.

"Well," she said, clearing her throat as she took a step back, "I should probably get back to the house. Work and all. The books don't write themselves, and I've got a long way to go on this one."

"What has you so blocked?" he asked.

She pulled in a breath, not sure if she wanted to explain the reason behind her struggle, both personally and professionally. But keeping it inside, trying to deny the part of her that was at war with her own self, wasn't working out. She had spent too many hours staring at a cursor on a screen, trying to push aside her own feelings, and failing.

"I guess you could say that it's hard to write about love when you don't have it in your own life."

He was watching her steadily, his expression giving nothing away. "This has something to do with that ex you mentioned, I assume."

She nodded. "It's been difficult to be someone different on the page than I am in real life."

He shrugged. "So why not put more of yourself into the story?"

She stared at him. "Because I write romance." They do not expect the hero to call off the happy ending six months before the last page.

"And what you know best right now is heartache," Leo said matter-of-factly.

"Is it that obvious?" She winced.

"It's a universal theme, as common as love itself, even if it seems like the loneliest feeling in the world." He gave her a little grin, one that went straight to her heart and warmed it. "But I think if you put a little more of yourself into it, instead of trying to make it completely unrelated to what you're going through now, you might find that people connect."

She nodded slowly. He had a point. And a good one.

"Anyway, I'm not a writer, but I know a thing or two about moving on. I hope today helped," he said, giving her a lopsided grin. His gaze was steady on her, and for a moment, she fell under its spell, pulled into this world away from everything and everyone else.

"It did help," she said when she'd found her voice, and not just because she had finally really gotten out of the house or that Leo had given her the best advice she could have received about her book.

It helped make her think that maybe, just maybe, Hope was right, and that she could find love with someone else after all.

Chapter Seventeen

Hope

It had been nearly two weeks since Hope had decided to come to the island, and with each passing day, she felt more detached from her life back in Chicago. Truth be told, she wasn't exactly sure how she felt about that.

Today, though, she didn't need to think about it. It was Friday, and she had a meeting—an actual meeting!—at Darcy's house out in Forest Bluff. It was one of the prettiest parts of the island, on the West Shore, far from town, with a row of houses tucked behind a towering, thick hedge.

The house she was visiting had been in the Ritter family for generations. It had been built at the turn of the twentieth century, back when it became fashionable for people to build summer "cottages" on the island. Eventually, these turned into year-round residences when the owners retired, as Sunset Cottage had for her own grandparents. Now, the Ritter house was owned by Darcy, who was in her seventies by now and hadn't changed anything since she'd first taken over the estate.

Hope knew Darcy, of course, though she'd never been inside the house before. Darcy's children were older than her by at least ten years, and they hadn't played together on the Morgans' annual summer visits.

Still, Hope knew the neighborhood well. It was at the north end of the forest, off a path that she and her sisters used to like to ride their bikes. They loved spying through hedge openings onto well-manicured lawns, large homes, and a sweeping view of Lake Huron.

"I never thought I'd reach the point of selling this place," Darcy said sadly after she'd welcomed Hope inside.

Hope pushed back the thought that her own Gran would have said the same thing if she knew that Gemma was wanting to list it, too.

"It's a beautiful property," Hope said. And it was. It had potential. It just needed a little help. And she was here to offer that.

Hope still marveled at that. Her, hired to help another woman beautify her home!

"I thought my grandkids would want to visit," she explained when Hope stepped through the front door, still reveling in the odd sense of freedom she felt not to be maneuvering the awkward stroller or having to bribe the twins to behave while she had a few precious moments of adult conversation. The girls were with Ellie, who had kindly taken them to the studio for a few hours to give them a painting lesson. Hope didn't even want to think how that would go, and she hoped that Ellie had locked up all of her best work beforehand. "But they all want to go to Florida instead."

Darcy tossed up her hands with a sigh and shook her head as she led Hope through the house.

"I have quite a bit of experience with historic renovations," Hope explained as she inspected a bathroom, which was dark and dated. She was certain that the plumbing would all be needed to be brought up to code. "My own house is more than a hundred years old. We spent over a year renovating it." It was so exciting then, to plan the details, to prepare for their future, to feel like she and Evan were a real team. They were building their dream house, the foundation of their life together.

The life she had walked away from.

Heaviness settled over her chest. It was a feeling she couldn't quite identify, but one she'd experienced daily since coming here—one she was probably too busy to notice back at home. Yearning, she supposed, for that feeling of hope she'd once had, when everything still felt possible, not set in stone, or planned out for her.

Darcy led her up the stairs, which were covered in an unfortunate black runner that made the house feel so much darker than it needed to be. Yes, Hope preferred a light and airy style, but here on the island, that was almost a requirement.

"We could exchange this for something in the blue family?" she ventured, motioning to the carpet. "Navy if you want to keep things practical?"

"I don't have much reason for practicality around here these days," Darcy snorted. She stopped at the landing and opened the door to a sun-filled bedroom that faced the front lawn. The tree branches skimmed the window, and Hope looked out, imaging how beautiful the view must be in the fall. "This was my son Mitchell's room," Darcy explained.

It was done up in greens and browns, dated but tidy. Hope vaguely remembered Mitchell from her early summers here on the island. He must be in his mid-forties by now.

It didn't seem possible. Not any more possible than the fact that the last time she'd been to the island, she'd been twenty-two years old and now she was thirty-four. So much had changed. But looking around, she saw just how much remained the same.

Including her.

"You have two children, correct?" Darcy asked.

Hope smiled, as she always did when she pictured her girls. "Twins. They just turned four."

"Girls, right?" Darcy asked, and Hope nodded. "Good. They stick around a little longer, though not by much."

Hope frowned, considering her own family. When was the last time she had visited her childhood home? Christmas three years ago, she calculated, at the insistence of her parents, who had tried to reinforce their stifling traditions onto her family until she and Evan had argued about it. The following year, much to her mother's disappointment, she had put her foot down, said they'd be staying at home for the holidays. "But this is your home!" her father had barked down the phone line, and it had taken every muster of strength Hope possessed to say that she was referring to her house, the one she owned and lived in with Evan and her children.

The one that was not much different than her parents' house in the end, even if that was her own doing.

And maybe, her undoing, too.

"When they're gone, they're gone," Darcy said, pursing her lips.

Hope blinked, feeling affronted by that realization. Right now, every day felt long and tiring, but the years were passing quickly, and Evan had a point when he said that next year they'd already be preparing for kindergarten. This was the time she could never get back, that she would long for someday, only ten years from now, maybe less, when the girls preferred friends to her company, when they didn't want to hold hands or snuggle on the sofa with a book. When they would roll their eyes at what she said, not giggle when she quickly turned a bad situation upside down.

In that moment, standing in the room of this little boy who was now, no doubt, a grown man with children of his own, she felt a horrible, overwhelming sense of fear. Even though she had only seen her children an hour ago, and even though she had been downright giddy to speed-walk away from Ellie's art studio after Rose had upturned a cup of water and Victoria had started to paint on her own skin, she now longed to run straight back there, to gather the girls in her arms, to feel their soft skin and smell their strawberry-scented hair, and not even care if they got paint all over her white linen dress pants. She was never away from them, only when they were at school for a few hours each week, and soon, she would be away from them more and more, against her will, until they were gone. Gone forever. Like the boy in this room.

Her eyes prickled and she blinked quickly to make sure that no tears fell.

"Where are your children now?" she asked, hoping to buy time until she had composed herself, even though she wanted nothing more than to finish this meeting and leave. To go back to her life. To do what she was supposed to be doing. Taking care of her children. How could she have ever questioned it?

"Oh, all over. Mitchell is in California. My youngest is in Atlanta. My daughter is close. Chicago. You're there now, right?"

Hope nodded. "I live there."

And right now, she should go back there. Take the girls and leave.

But Darcy was still talking. "My children call this house the money pit."

"I would say that it could be worth a fortune," Hope said. "The land alone must be worth something?"

Darcy led her into another bedroom in shades of apricot and yellow. The daughter's room, no doubt, with a row of dolls on the double bed. Hope walked to the rear window, where the backyard led onto a large grass lot that extended all the way to the lake. A pool interrupted its path, and Hope could picture some colorful floats bobbing in the water. Some striped umbrellas over the iron tables that were perched at the end.

There wasn't beach access like they had at Sunset Cottage, but the view stretched as far as the eye could see. It would be stiff competition if this house went on the market, too.

As if reading her thoughts, Darcy said, "It will kill me to leave this island."

"Then why go?" Hope asked. "You've been a long-standing member of the community."

Darcy just clucked her tongue. "My husband has been gone for ten years now. My kids have their own lives. All that's left for me here are memories. I'll go to Chicago to be close to my daughter."

Darcy shook her head, her expression pensive as she looked around the room. "It all goes by so fast."

Hope's mouth was dry as she finished the tour and promised to call in a few days with some initial ideas. She waited until she was at the end of the long, neatly manicured boulevard before quickening her pace, moving as fast as her heels would allow on the dirt roads.

She couldn't get to Ellie's studio fast enough. She had to see her children. She had a horrible, sickening feeling that something had happened to them in her absence. That she had done them wrong by leaving them, even for only a couple of hours.

She felt wild as she hurried across the docks, her heel nearly catching in one of the wood holes and toppling her forward. She swung open the door, her heart feeling like it was beating out of her chest, as her eyes scanned the room for the girls. It was quiet. Too quiet.

"Hello?" she called.

From somewhere in the distance, she heard a muffled sound. Her sister's voice. "Out here! We're on the dock!"

She hadn't even realized there was another door to the studio until she saw it, half-hidden by a large, unfinished painting. She went outside, the relief that she was about to be reunited with her girls already making her shoulders relax, until she saw them.

They were standing on the dock. A bucket was at their feet. Rose was holding up a giant fish—in her bare hands—and Victoria was splashing about with two more in the bucket.

Ellie looked on gaily, while chatting with old Edward, who grinned broadly and said, "Teaching these girls how to fish! Good to see you, Hope! My, all grown!"

Hope took in the sight. She couldn't even prioritize her manners and make small talk with Edward, who had once been a handyman for the Taylors.

"I thought they were learning how to paint," she said faintly.

"Oh that." Ellie tossed a hand in the air. "Too much mess."

Hope's eyes popped. And this wasn't?

She stepped forward, reached for her girls and then thought the better of it. They smelled. They actually smelled like...fish. And Rose, she now saw, had things that she could only hope were not fish guts in her hair.

Hope felt the backs of her eyes prickle again, but this time it was not from feelings of regret or guilt. This time it was from exhaustion. Pure exhaustion at the thought of what it would now take to handle this situation.

She had the urge to turn around. To flee. To let Ellie help clean up the mess that she had made.

She wanted to go back to Darcy's peaceful home. She wanted to sit in silence and sip iced tea and talk about tile samples and paint swatches.

She did not want to touch her fish-slime-covered children.

Or deal with the fallout of taking them away from their fun.

"Looks like we'll be walking home." She hated the thought of ruining the stroller, even if it would take forever to walk home. Ellie had left it parked in front of the store, clearly having no need for it.

"What? A little fish smell never hurt anyone!" Edward began to laugh, a laugh that verged on a cackle, and Hope began to have the impression that she was the brunt of some joke.

Her jaw set as she stared at her sister, who was all too happily laughing along with Edward. Still, when Ellie caught her expression, something in her eyes flashed.

"They had fun, Hope," Ellie urged.

"Are you implying that they don't have fun with me?" Hope demanded.

Ellie opened her mouth to say something and then seemed to think better of it. Hope didn't wait around to continue the conversation. She had to pry a fish from her daughter's hands, then suffer through the inevitable tantrum that followed, then walk nearly a mile back to the cottage and then hook up the garden hose, if Ellie hadn't broken it.

That last thought was unfair, she knew. But it was also unfair of Ellie to create more work for her like this.

"I'm just saying," she said as she shook Rose's wrists until the fish fell into the bucket, "that I only asked for two hours of help. I cook. I clean. And I just asked for two hours of help."

"Hey, I never asked you to cook those breakfasts or dinners," Ellie said, her voice rising to a near shout as Rose's wails became shrill.

Hope didn't respond to that. There was no sense in pointing out that someone had to cook the meals in the house. Her girls had to eat. But did it have to be Hope, every damn day?

"I'm sorry," she said, stopping herself. She blinked, not liking where she had taken this conversation. She was talking to her sister as if she were Evan, letting out frustrations that were misplaced, and unfair. Like she'd done with Gemma last week. "I just...I need to get these girls clean."

She led her girls by the wrists into the studio, instructed them to wash their hands three times each—with soap!—and then did her best to dab at their arms and faces with soapy paper towels. Then she took the stroller and instructed them each to walk beside it.

Victoria had splashed her in the bathroom, and now her pants were wet, but she didn't care. What she cared about was getting home and getting these girls clean. Because someone had to care about that.

Unable to bear the thought of walking down Main Street to get to the west side, she turned east toward Lakeview Road, hoping to eventually cut up through the forest that divided the two halves of the island, even if it did add an extra ten minutes of walking onto her timetable. She glanced down at the girls, who inched along, still begging to go back to play with their fish, which apparently had names: Petunia and Anastasia.

Make that twenty extra minutes, she thought.

Still, the view was so lovely that she almost didn't mind. Lakeview Road was one of the quieter streets near town, full of residential homes, a few B&Bs, and anchored by one of the island's midsize hotels, and a personal favorite, the old Lakeside Inn.

Rose and Victoria screamed the entire time, "My fish! I want my fish!" and Hope didn't even try to bribe them into being quiet. She had no lollipops, and despite washing their hands, she didn't want their hands anywhere near their mouths at the moment.

"No, Mommy, no! Go back! Go back to the fish!"

"We're going to the house," she ground out.

Now it was Victoria's eyes that popped open in surprise. "We're going home?"

Hope wavered for a moment. She was so thrown that she didn't know what to say. The girls were used to Evan being away, used to it just being the three of them during most of their waking hours. But being away from their bedroom, their toys, from the only home they had ever known, that was different.

"Soon," she said as she started walking again, only she wasn't so sure about that. Now, with the opportunity she had here, she wasn't sure of anything at all.

"Hello!" a voice called out and Hope cursed under her breath, not wanting anything to postpone her getting back to that cottage and trying her hand at that outdoor shower, until she saw that it was John, up ahead.

Her heart lifted, and just like that, the noise didn't bother her, and she wasn't mad at Ellie anymore, and she almost forgot about the fact that her children—and possibly even she, at this point—smelled like a fish market.

He was wearing khaki pants, a white linen shirt rolled to the elbows, and a smile that was downright contagious. And he was standing at the gate of the Lakeside Inn.

She pushed the stroller to a stop and the girls reduced their crying to a sniffle.

"Don't ask," she warned at the questioning raise of his eyebrow. She jutted her chin toward the inn, curious now to find him here. "Is this the hotel you're thinking of buying?" she asked. She didn't know why, but she'd expected something large and more corporate. This was one of the more intimate hotels on the island. She didn't quite know what to make of that.

"I can't say anything yet," he said, but his eyes gave her the answer. He sniffed the air for a moment, looking perplexed, and then seemed to shrug it off. "These things don't always work out."

"Of course," she said. She'd been inside the Lakeside Inn a few times, to use the bathroom, to have lunch on the large front porch, to play hide and seek in the lobby when she was too young to know better. It had been family owned for as long as she knew, owned by the Altmans, who had a place at the northern tip of West End Road. "I hadn't realized that they were selling. You know that their family house is near my cottage."

"I might have put that together when you mentioned where you lived," he said, laughing.

"Are they selling that too?" she asked. She hadn't seen a sign, but if plans moved forward to sell Sunset Cottage, that couldn't be good for her or her sisters.

Although, selling the house meant leaving. No job. No getaway. No more summers with her sisters or even the hopes of one. No more memories that seemed to come alive at every turn.

No John.

For reasons she couldn't explain, even to herself, she suddenly said, "We're hosting a dinner at our house, actually. This Sunday. If you're around."

She didn't know where that had come from, but as she said it, the idea took hold, and it sounded wonderful. A dinner on the patio. She'd light tea candles and put out colorful centerpieces and a blue table runner to match the lake across the street. She'd make grilled fish and a strawberry pie for dessert. Her sisters would have to pull together for that. It would be fun—just the fun they needed to bring them closer again. And it might just make Gemma look at Sunset Cottage in a different light. Because while selling the house may be the practical thing to do, Hope was finding that following her heart was leading to a lot more happiness these days.

His gaze locked with hers. "Sunday night. I'll be there."

She pulled in a breath. He'd be there. Just like that. Just like she knew that he would.

"Sunset Cottage. There's a sign near the maple in the front. Seven o'clock."

"Looking forward to it," he said, giving her an unreadable look, but she could see the smile in his eyes as she pushed the girls on by.

A party. And this one didn't even feel like work!

She didn't even stop to think that her sisters would probably have something to say about a man who was not her husband coming to their house for dinner. She'd just have to conjure up a few more invites.

Chapter Eighteen

Gemma

Gemma finished replying to her editor's email and sat back with a smile. Leo had been right—getting out had helped her, and so had their conversation. She was finally making real progress in the book. Why not use some of her personal experience? It flowed from her fingertips and filled page after page. It was heartfelt, and real, and the more that she gave of herself, the less her chest ached. Life wasn't a fairytale, but if her heroine could come through a bad patch and find everlasting love, then maybe she could too. Someday.

She'd gotten out a few more days this week, too, taking her laptop to the Cottage Coffeehouse or working on the front porch when Hope took the girls out or settled them for their naps. And she'd taken walks, long ones, bringing a notebook to the beach and immersing herself in the setting of the story she was creating.

Why hadn't she done this in Chicago? She lived across from the park, not far from the lakefront either. Her neighborhood was full of cafés where other people seemed to have no problems being productive despite the chatter and the hiss of the espresso machine.

But she knew the answer. Because Sean was in Chicago.

And so was his new fiancée.

They'd gotten engaged three months after he'd ended things with her, meaning that they had now been engaged for two months. For two months he had called another woman his fiancée, when she'd never even made it to the altar.

That was the worst part of it, really. It wasn't that he'd gotten cold feet, wasn't ready to get married. It was that he didn't want to marry her.

She looked down at her ring finger. She'd been walking so much that she had lost some of the weight she'd put on, and the fresh air had given her skin a slight tan, even though there was still a slight chill in the air. The mark from Sean's ring was fading.

And slowly, the pain in her heart was too.

Gemma had just finished a chapter when there was a tentative knock at the door. She glanced at her outline, taking satisfaction in checking off another milestone. She was now more than two-thirds finished with the book. She could finish it—make that *would* finish it. It would happen. If she didn't get sidetracked, she thought, as her mind went to Leo.

She stood, stretched, and called out, "Come in!"

It was Hope, carrying a wooden tray by the handles complete with a glass of lemonade with extra ice, just the way she liked it, and a plate bearing a chicken salad sandwich with lettuce, and a side of sliced apples and plums.

"Brain food," Hope said, setting the tray down on the edge of Gemma's bed. "I take it you haven't had lunch yet?"

"I got busy," she explained. "I'm really making progress."

"Good!" Hope smiled. "So coming here was good for you then?"

"I never said it wasn't," Gemma replied, tilting her head. "You're not changing your mind about selling the cottage, are you?"

Hope glanced away. "I wasn't sure if you had."

The thought had crossed her mind, of course, especially when she was on the horse trails with Leo. And when she learned he was staying here.

She dodged the topic, refusing to even entertain the thoughts, and picked up the sandwich. "You didn't need to do this, but thanks. How was today?" Last night over a bowl of chowder and a glass of wine, Hope had told her about the offer from Sheila, keeping it vague and casual, and now Gemma was curious to know more. Both of her sisters were being evasive in their own ways—Ellie in the physical sense, and Hope, well, she supposed that Hope had never been one to share her emotions. She'd toed the line; she thought clearly, and behaved rationally. She would never have allowed herself to barely meet a deadline over a breakup as Gemma had. Hope didn't fall apart. Hope did what needed to be done.

Only now she wondered if that was true at all.

"Good," Hope said brightly. "I can see where I can really help Darcy."

"When you said you might want to go back to work, I assumed you meant back in Chicago."

"It's just a project," Hope said, her tone a little defensive. She walked to the window and glanced out it. "This window is filthy. It will be much clearer to see through it once it's been wiped down."

"It's fine," Gemma said. "You know who you sound like?"

Hope's eyes flashed. "Don't even say it."

Gemma had to grin. "You know it's true. You sound just like Mom."

"I'm nothing like Mom," Hope said in a huff. She crossed her arms tightly across her chest, practically glaring at Gemma.

Gemma took a bite of the sandwich. It was delicious, cold and crisp with just the correct ration of mayonnaise (which she knew that Hope made from scratch because she seemed to have an all-consuming fear of preservatives and processed food) and the crusty bread was distinctly from Island Bakery.

"This is delicious. Thank you." She took another bite, only then noticing that Hope was still looking at her, her expression turning to one of misery now.

"Take it back," she pleaded.

Gemma blinked. "Take what back?" Then, realizing that Hope meant the comment about their mother, she started to laugh. "Relax, Hope. You're not like Mom. You're...you're like a super-sized version of her. Is that better? I mean, this mayonnaise is fresh, and you know that Mom was never much of a cook..."

"I'm not a super-sized version of Mom. I can't be. I don't want that life!" And then, to Gemma's horror, Hope burst into tears.

"Whoa," she said, setting down her sandwich. "Where is all this coming from?"

Hope didn't cry, at least, not unless it mattered. Ellie was the one who cried, at a sad movie, when they found that birds' nest overturned in their backyard one day, the tiny blue eggs inside it cracked. And Gemma cried all the time recently. More than she smiled.

Until recently, she thought, once again thinking of Leo. She took a breath, and then, to distract herself, another bite of her sandwich.

Hope sat down on the bed and wiped her eyes. She sniffed hard. "I'm just...I'm tired."

Yes, Hope was tired. That made sense. After all, look at all she did! She cooked! She cleaned. She took care of those girls, all on her own. Evan traveled a lot, she knew, especially since he got that big promotion a few years ago. There was nothing wrong with their marriage. Hope was just tired.

"Of course you are. Look at all you do! You're the perfect wife and mother."

Hope slanted her a glance. "I'm far from perfect." Gemma opened her mouth to protest but Hope clarified, "I don't want to be perfect. I'm tired of being perfect. I'm so, so tired of being perfect."

"But—" But she had never complained before. Not even when they were kids and their mother would insist on matching outfits for the holiday card and Hope was way too old be dressed in the same tartan as Ellie, who was six years younger.

"I thought you liked being—" Seeing Hope's eyes flinch, Gemma searched for better wording. "You always did everything so well. Everything you tried, you succeeded in. Grades. Dating. School activities. Your house."

Hope was shaking her head. "It's not as easy as it all looks."

"I never said it was easy," Gemma said. "But you make it look that way."

Hope was quiet for a moment, her tears momentarily stopped. "You know how I told you that I wanted to do something else? Something for me?"

Gemma nodded.

"I might have found it. But it's here, on the island."

"I thought you said this project for Darcy was a one-time thing." Gemma frowned. "I don't understand."

"I'm thinking of leaving Evan," Hope said, and now Gemma set down her sandwich. Hope had her full attention and then some.

Her heart was pounding in her chest as she stared at Hope, searching for a hint of a smile, for an uncharacteristic flare for dramatics. But all she saw was sadness in her sister's eyes. "What? But you're the perfect couple."

"The perfect couple. Do you see a pattern? Nothing is perfect, Gemma. We may have been raised to think we had to be perfect, but there is no such thing. People get divorced. People breakup." She gave her a knowing look. "People don't wake up with perfect hair and walk around like smiling robots, hiding their emotions.

And...I've realized that some people even actually like me for just being myself, not the perfect version of it."

Gemma had never seen this coming. Evan and Hope had been together forever. They had a beautiful house, beautiful children, success and history and longevity and...She blinked. It didn't make any sense. "But a divorce?"

"I can't think of that word, not yet. But this relationship...I haven't been happy for some time, and I wasn't prepared to admit it to myself. Or Evan. Evan is never home, and when he is, he isn't really there, you know? He doesn't notice if the girls need a bath or if they're getting into trouble. I have to ask him to babysit so I can get my hair cut every six months! That's what he calls it! Babysitting! His own children! What does that make me?"

"Wow," Gemma said, trying to process what she was hearing. Hope never complained about Evan, other than a few little anecdotes when it came to housework or other things that women tended to joke about when they met for coffee. Now, she tried to remember if Hope had even mentioned her husband since arriving on the island. Or if they'd talked at all. She'd assumed that with Evan being overseas and with the reception here being hit or miss, that there was nothing more to it than that. But she'd assumed a lot of things, it seemed.

"I just assumed that you liked doing everything when it came to the house and the girls."

"Someone has to do it," Hope replied. "And Evan has his job, of course. And my job is to take care of the girls, but it's not the same. My day doesn't end, and I can't complain about it without looking like some monster. And he travels so much that when the twins were born, it just made sense that I would leave my job to take care of them. But more and more...I'm jealous of that career. I'm jealous that he has somewhere to go everyday, where people call him by his real name, not by his role."

Gemma nodded. "You just made it look so easy."

"And I love my girls," Hope said, brushing away a tear. "But...I need something else. I don't even know who I am anymore. I'm not sure I ever knew who I was. I just did what I thought I was supposed to do, without questioning anything. And I'm...I'm not happy."

"So this job?" Gemma eyed the sandwich as her stomach grumbled. It would be rude to eat in times of Hope's distress. But it would be just as rude to not take the food that Hope took such care to prepare.

She slid her hand onto the plate. Hope didn't seem to notice, or care. She was staring at her lap. Her cheeks were blotched. "I haven't decided anything yet. I haven't told Evan."

"I remember when you met him," Gemma said, giving her a grin. Didn't Hope remember that too? She used to talk about him all the time back then, always with a smile. She seemed to shine around him. To glow in a way that she never had before.

Hope managed a small smile. "He was so cute. And so attentive. He was everything I thought I wanted. Now I wonder if I was fulfilling the path that Mom and Dad laid out for me."

"You adored him," Gemma reminded her, realizing that she was speaking in the past tense and not sure how that made her feel. She'd been so caught up in her own breakup, she hadn't considered that Hope could be having struggles of her own. Had she not seen the warning signs? She frowned, trying to replay the past few months, but she was certain that she hadn't missed anything. That Hope hadn't let on. More than that, she hadn't shared.

Just like Mom, Gemma thought sadly. But the trait had carried down, to all of them in their own ways. They all hid their true fears, from the world, from each other, even maybe from themselves.

Hope was quiet for a long moment. "Yes. I suppose I did adore him."

She patted her thighs and stood up, as if that was that, the conversation was over. And just as quickly as she'd broken down, she had pulled herself together.

She was Hope again, with her honey-blond hair smoothed away from her face, standing tall and thin, looking elegant as always, even when she should have been a gawky and gangly teenager.

"I had a reason for coming up here, actually, and it wasn't just to bring you food. I'm having a little dinner party. Sunday at seven."

"A dinner party?" Gemma wasn't so sure what her sister expected from this. Usually her parties took weeks, if not months to plan. They were catered events with long invite lists.

"Something small and casual. I'll cook. But...I thought it might be a good way for all of us to spend time together. You, me, and Ellie."

Hope gave her a pointed look and Gemma knew better than to argue. It might be a good way to smooth things over with Ellie. A party, with other guests. A celebration of sorts. And now that she was further along in her book, she could almost look forward to a night off.

"Who would we invite?" Simon was the first name that popped to mind. Ellie would be happy about this.

Hope shrugged. "Invite the caretaker from next door if you want."

Gemma was flustered that her sister had even noticed her talking to Leo, but the idea was appealing. "I'll think about it," she said. "He might not be into that type of thing."

Hope gave her a sly smile as she set a hand on the doorknob. "I have a feeling it's exactly his type of thing."

Gemma didn't feed into that comment, even if she knew she'd still be thinking about it long after Hope had gone back downstairs. She felt a connection with Leo, and Hope had picked up on it too.

"Who are you inviting?" she asked. After all, it wouldn't be a party without guests.

Hope hesitated, then, in a carefully poised tone, said, "A friend."

"The lady from the shop?" Gemma asked. She took a big bite of her sandwich. God, it tasted good.

"No." Hope hesitated. "Someone I met on the ferry."

Gemma stopped chewing. "A *man*? Oh, Hope!"

"He's just a friend," Hope said, giving her a stern look.

Gemma felt uneasy about this, but she knew she was in no position to argue. She didn't know what went on in Hope's household anymore than Hope knew about what went on in the parts of her life she kept hidden from the world. It had all been as big of an illusion as her relationship with Sean.

"Just promise me you'll be careful," Gemma pleaded, and Hope let out a bemused snort.

"When have I ever been anything but careful? That's just the problem," Hope said. "I never took risks. I was never free to. Or, at least, I didn't think I was."

Gemma sensed that there was more to that last insinuation than Hope was saying directly. "I toed the line, too."

"Yes, but they didn't have the same expectations for you. Face it, Gemma. All the pressure was on me. And Ellie..."

They both knew that their father had expectations of Ellie, but that he'd given up.

"Dad always knew that you and Ellie were creative. But you were willing to make a plan for yourself. You stayed within the lines. Ellie did not." Hope raised an eyebrow, and Gemma knew it was true. She'd taken her creative energy and applied it to a corporate job, and then she'd stayed at that job, however miserable she was, until she had established herself. Proven herself. She could have taken something less conventional. Freelanced, or working for a small paper. But every step she'd taken had been deliberate, and designed to look...successful.

And recently, she understood firsthand how it felt to be anything but successful. It was uncertain. And scary.

And lonely.

"Maybe I'll go into town and try Ellie's art class tonight," Gemma said.

They exchanged a small smile, one that almost reassured Gemma that everything would be all right even though nothing felt right anymore.

"Let me know about the dinner and who you end up inviting," Hope said as she opened the door.

Gemma's heart sped up at the thought. She would ask Leo.

That's what friends did, after all...

*

Ellie was setting up for the class when Gemma arrived, carrying a box of cookies from the bakery, hoping that it was a worthy peace offering.

While she'd had every intention of visiting the studio sooner, she hadn't felt welcome to before now, and from the flash of Ellie's eyes when she entered, she wondered if she still wasn't.

"I come in peace," she said, handing over the bakery box. "And an invitation. To a party at the cottage. Sunday night. Seven o'clock. Hope's idea," she added, lest there be any confusion.

"Does that mean you've changed your mind about wanting to sell the house?" Ellie's eyes lit up with hope that Gemma struggled to look at.

She sighed. "Can we not talk about the house for right now? I'd like to enjoy each other's company a bit. I've missed you, Ellie. I want to have a nice time together here, the way we used to."

Ellie's smile was hesitant. "I'd like that too."

Relieved, Gemma looked around the studio. She'd always admired her sister's work, but the paintings she had hanging at the cottage were just a glimpse of what she had on display here.

"Oh, Ellie! This is amazing! I'm so impressed!"

Ellie's cheeks flushed. "You know my work."

"Yes, but this is all so..." She pulled in a breath, realizing now just why Ellie didn't want to sell the cottage. It wasn't about the house. It was about the life she had here. The one she'd created for herself.

"I wish Dad would see this," she said, giving her sister a long look.

Ellie's jaw firmed, and she began to unfold the stack of chairs she had leaning against the wall. "He wouldn't care. He's already made up his mind about me."

Maybe so, but Ellie should still be proud of herself. And their father should be proud of her too.

"So this party..." Ellie was clearly eager to change the subject, and Gemma didn't fight her. She took a chair from the stack and added it to the circle that Ellie was forming.

"It's small, but knowing Hope, she'll go overboard. She apparently needed at least forty-eight hours to prepare, hence the reason for Sunday instead of tomorrow." The sisters locked eyes and smiled. "She's inviting someone...a friend...that she met on the ferry."

Ellie looked curious, but didn't elaborate, and Gemma was grateful. The last thing she wanted was to explain what Hope was up to when she didn't even understand it herself. A divorce from Evan? Impossible. Knowing Hope, she would wake up tomorrow embarrassed at the omission, smooth it over with a laugh, and never speak of it again.

Like they'd been trained to do, she thought sadly.

"So we can each bring a guest?" Ellie asked.

Gemma nodded. Casually, she said, "I might invite Leo. He's done a great job with the yard and—"

"And he's super hot?" Ellie set down a chair and stared at her frankly.

"You noticed?" Gemma asked weakly.

Ellie laughed. "You'd have to be blind not to notice. Edward talks about him all the time, probably hoping that something will develop between us. He's not my type though. He's too much in his head for me. Besides, I saw the way you two were talking the other day. Before I interrupted," Ellie added.

An awkward silence filled the room. Finally, Gemma said, "So how many people come to the class?"

"As many as I have seats for," Ellie said briskly. After a pause, she said, "I happen to have one extra chair, if you're interested."

Gemma smiled. "I'd like that."

Together, they finished setting up the room, and they'd just put out the last easel when the door opened. Gemma didn't need to turn around to know who it was. The flush creeping up Ellie's cheeks said nearly as much as her smile.

Gemma suppressed a grin and turned to see Simon. Ellie was right; he had improved with age.

"Gemma!" Simon gave that dazzling grin of his that almost even made her swoon. "It's so good to see you again!"

"You too!" Gemma gave him a quick hug. After a brief exchange of how his parents and sister were, she said, "Are you...here for the class?"

She glanced back at Ellie, whose eyes were as wide as saucers now. Filled with light. And...hope. Almost enough to make her feel it too.

Simon sank his hands into his pockets and glanced bashfully from Gemma to Ellie. "If...that's okay?"

Ellie opened her mouth, but Gemma wasn't about to let her speak first. "Of course it's okay. Ellie was just saying she had one slot left. Popular class she's offering here."

She saw the look of gratitude that washed over her sister's face, and she gave her a quick wink.

"I was just helping to set up and drop off some cookies, but I've got to run now. More work to do tonight."

"My mom told me you're a writer now," Simon said.

Ah, the island. She didn't even mind the gossip tonight.

"That's right, and I'm afraid I'm on a deadline, so...I should probably run. And I told Hope I'd help her with the party."

Simon's interest seemed to pique. "Party?"

"This Sunday," Gemma said cheerfully. "Ellie will fill you in." She gave her sister a little wave. "Ellie, I'll see you back at home?"

Ellie nodded, giving her a wide grin that tugged at her heartstrings.

Home, she thought, as she pushed out the door, leaving Ellie and Simon alone in the studio. More and more, that was exactly what Sunset Cottage was feeling like, and she wasn't sure what to make of that.

Chapter Nineteen

Ellie

The weekend had passed quickly and in a few minutes the guests would arrive. Male guests, as luck would have it, because thanks to Gemma's nudge the other night, Ellie saw no way out of inviting Simon to the party, even if the rational side of her brain told her that she shouldn't.

But when had she ever listened to that inner voice? If anyone were to ask her father, the answer would be: never.

Besides, he *had* come to her art class. Ellie still couldn't stop smiling when she thought of the suggestive glances Darcy had given her all through the hour. At first she feared that Darcy would interrogate the poor guy, make things awkward for everyone, but she had behaved and silently observed instead.

The weather had held up, just as they all hoped it would, and if Ellie hadn't been home all day, helping her sisters prepare for the party, she would have taken her bike on a ride around the island with a canvas and her supplies in her basket, waiting for inspiration to strike.

Hope had organized everything, of course. She'd handed Ellie a list yesterday morning that Ellie took one look at and knew would require more than one trip to town. Her bicycle basket only held so much, and Hope was asking for several bottles of wine, various cheeses, grapes, figs, an assortment of crackers and bread—and that was just for the appetizer!

Still, they'd managed to get it all done, even when Hope decided a little late in the day this afternoon to send her back to town for more fruit, because she was going to make a cocktail from the wine, seeing as it was turning out to be such a warm night.

For now, the island felt quiet, even for a Sunday, like it was still theirs and theirs alone. And for the first time in months, Ellie almost dreaded the influx of people. Right now, the island was perfect, just as it was.

She came downstairs from getting dressed in one of her usual cotton sundresses and a bright pink cardigan and glanced out onto the porch, smiling in anticipation.

She could just picture them all sipping the sangria that Hope had made as the sun went down and the sky filled with rainbow colors that she would never grow tired of. Simon would remember what it was like to spend so many evenings on that very porch and question why he gave it all up and how he might get it all back. It was just the thing she needed to finally get him to admit that she was the one that he loved. That he'd always loved her and always would.

The wicker conversation set had been repositioned so that now there was a view of the lake from all angles. And the matching round dining table was now covered in a pale-blue tablecloth that Hope must have bought in town. White plates were already set up at their respective places, along with wine glasses, and in the center was a tasteful-sized arrangement of tulips, the colors of which matched some of the new pillows that Hope had set up on the armchairs and sofas.

"You've really made yourself at home here," Ellie said, and she wasn't quite sure how she felt about that, even if the cottage was just as much Hope's as it was hers. Maybe Hope wouldn't want to sell. Maybe they could keep the cottage and all would go on just as it was.

Only she didn't want things to go on as they were. She wanted change. She wanted more than what she'd had, even more than her art studio, she was beginning to realize.

She wanted love. Specifically, she wanted Simon. The island was better with him here. Her life was better with him here. For so many years, she'd abandoned the idea of finding someone to share her life with; she'd forgotten the excitement and fulfillment that came from connecting with someone.

"I'll light the candles closer to the time that everyone arrives," Hope was saying, more to herself than to Ellie. "And I should probably check on the appetizers."

"Let me," Ellie said. She was eager to help, but Hope gave her a knowing look. "Let me help, Hope. You take on too much sometimes."

Hope raised an eyebrow. "You know, you're right. I never thought of it like that, but yes. Thank you. Okay, the crab bites are in the kitchen, if you want to check on those and help with the salad? Maybe cut some tomatoes?"

She was happy to help, eager really. It would settle the nerves that had been bubbling inside her, leaving her restless all since Simon had said good-bye on Friday night, right after the class had ended, with the promise of seeing her tonight, at the house.

She walked into the kitchen, hoping she remembered where Gran had kept the cutting boards. Really, she'd had no personal need for such things recently.

But Hope had already found them and set them on the counter. The entire kitchen had also been transformed, and on the table was a cheese plate, complete with crackers, dried fruits, fresh grapes and figs, and sliced baguette and crackers.

Ellie's stomach grumbled as she reached for a slice of cheddar, but she heard a voice snap behind her, "Don't even think about it."

She turned to see Gemma standing in the doorway, grinning mischievously, and when Gemma looked at her like that, Ellie couldn't help but smile back. Maybe for one more night, she could put her hurt feelings aside. It was nice, spending time with her sisters like this, but she couldn't help worry what would happen when the party was over and the big, horrible thing they'd decided not to discuss right now reared again.

"You know that Hope will kill you if you mess up her cheese platter," Gemma whispered, darting her eyes toward the side door to the porch.

Ellie sighed and dropped her hand. It was true. And Hope tended to get wound up over formalities. Today, though, she'd been different. Ellie had even caught her humming while she lit the votive candles on the porch. "She seems to be in a good mood tonight."

"Hope loves to entertain. At least, I think she does."

"What are you talking about it?" Ellie looked at Gemma as if she'd gone crazy. "Hope adores entertaining. Why else would she have come up with the idea of having this party?"

Gemma said nothing as she reached for an already open bottle of white wine from the fridge and poured a glass. They both knew better than to taste the sangria before the guests had arrived. Hope would have their heads.

Ellie, feeling the nerves build up inside her, took a glass from the cabinet and helped herself too. "Simon's coming tonight," she said a little breathlessly.

"I figured as much, from the way he was looking at you on Friday," Gemma said, her eyes wide, waiting to hear more. Gemma was a good listener. Always had been. It's why Ellie had always been so drawn to her, why it was always so easy to look past the little hurdles that seemed to interrupt their relationship. Underneath it was a friend, a confidante, and someone who knew and accepted her, even if she didn't always agree with her. It was more than Ellie could say for the rest of them, even Hope.

Hope loved her, of course, but under it all, Ellie had always felt a prickle of insecurity around her eldest sister. After all, Hope was the perfect daughter. And she was...not.

"Thanks for the boost," Ellie said, grinning. "I might not have asked him if you hadn't mentioned things."

"Really? Why not?" Gemma looked so perplexed that Ellie almost told her that he was engaged. But telling her would mean having to think about it, and that would ruin the entire evening, and not just her good mood.

Besides, she was starting to wonder about this engagement, and not just because of what Darcy had said. Simon had come to her studio. Then her art class. And now he was coming here, tonight.

After all these years... Her stomach rolled over with excitement.

Before Ellie could respond to Gemma, Hope strolled into the kitchen, her cheeks flushed and the hair around her face coming free of her ponytail in wisps. But she didn't look tired or haggard, and she didn't look cool and calm either. She looked happy. Happier than Ellie had seen her look this entire visit.

"I think I might need one of those," Hope said, motioning to the open bottle of wine that was starting to sweat on the counter. Ellie hadn't gotten around to installing the window air-conditioning units, and the sun was blazing.

"So it's six of us then?" Gemma asked, a little pertly if anyone asked Ellie.

"Be nice," Hope warned as she splashed some wine into a glass and drank it back. She refilled it, and then popped the cork back on, raising an eyebrow at Gemma in the process.

Ellie frowned. "Did I miss something?"

Hope and Gemma exchanged a glance. Finally, it was Hope who spoke. "I'm bringing a friend as my guest tonight. A male friend. He's here on business. We met on the ferry. He helped me wipe vomit off my pants."

Seeing Ellie's reaction, Hope corrected: "He handed me napkins. A nice dinner is the least I can offer him in return."

Why was this the first time that Ellie was hearing of this mystery man? Gemma was clearly aware of something that Ellie was not. And she was worried.

Was there trouble in Hope's marriage? Was that why she was here? But that wasn't possible. Hope had the perfect marriage. She had the perfect life.

The diamonds on her ring finger sparkled as she picked up her glass again, and Ellie put her concerns at rest. Of course there were no problems in Hope's marriage. Hope had no problems, and for this, Ellie was relieved. Because if Hope's life fell apart...then what chance was there for her?

"To tonight," Hope said, lifting her glass to theirs.

"To sisters," Gemma said, giving each of them a grin.

"To Sunset Cottage," Ellie said, giving Gemma a poignant look.

"To memories," Hope said, and that was that. They clinked glasses and each took a long sip, and then, the doorbell rang.

They froze, and then, like teenagers waiting for their dates to arrive, started to laugh.

"I'll get it," Ellie said, feeling the need to establish that while Hope may be hosting the party, this was in fact Ellie's home, not just something she had a financial stake in.

She set down her glass and walked into the hallway, slowing only briefly to check her reflection in the hallway mirror. She looked flushed, happy, and there was a light in her eyes that seemed permanent now, and it wasn't because of the promise of good food and nice weather. It was because of the promise of good company. And maybe, something more.

She opened the door, already smiling, but her expression froze when she saw who was standing on the porch.

It was Simon. And, by the looks of it, his fiancée.

Chapter Twenty

Hope

Hope stood at the back of the hallway and watched as Ellie turned, flush-faced, her eyes glistening, and said, "I'll check on the girls for you, Hope."

Hope frowned, about to ask why, when she saw Simon. And another woman.

She glanced at Gemma, who gave her a wide-eyed stare and then disappeared into the kitchen, hopefully to fetch the sangria. Hope was happy right now that she'd had the sense to make a double batch. Already, things were off to a shaky start, and John hadn't even arrived yet.

"Hello, Simon." She smiled as she met him at the open door. She glanced at the woman, who was pretty, about Ellie's age, with a neat blond bob and a small smile. She didn't recall seeing her before. Or hearing about her, either. "I'm Hope Morgan."

"This is Erin," Simon said. He didn't meet her eye when he said, "My fiancée."

Hope could only pray that years of living under her father's roof and learning to be polite at the many stuffy events her parents hosted were adequate training for this moment. She kept her face frozen, resisting the urge to raise even a single brow, and smiled pleasantly. "Lovely to meet you," she said, shaking the woman's hand.

She stepped outside and led them deeper onto the porch, toward the conversation set. Gemma had come around the side and was already pouring glasses of sangria. Trained under the same household expectations, Gemma graciously chatted with Simon as she handed out the drinks.

Hope took a long sip before saying, "Gemma, this is Erin. Simon's fiancée."

Like her, Gemma was well adapted to hiding her true emotions, but Hope saw the flash of confusion pass through her eyes. So this was news to her, too.

But was it news to Ellie?

She pulled in a breath, no longer anxious about the thought of John coming to the house, but rather, eager. They needed a new dynamic. Something to break up this awkward moment.

To her relief, she saw Leo coming up the gravel path, looking much more polished than he did when he was working, wearing jeans and a crisp blue shirt rolled at the forearms, and carrying a bouquet of lilacs.

"The first blooms, I believe," he said, handing them to Gemma.

Gemma introduced him to Simon and Erin and said, "I'll put these in water," and then took him inside without another word.

Hope stifled a sigh and said, "I think I'll have one of those sangrias too."

Really, what was there even to say? It was only once she crossed the porch to the drinks cart that she saw her carefully set table. She'd need a seventh setting now. And a chair. The seating wasn't the issue. She'd only purchased six matching cloth napkins and brass rings. Well, she'd just have to do without. Couldn't have her unexpected guest feeling uncomfortable...even if her own sister did.

Worried, she decided to wait a few more minutes to check on Ellie. Hopefully she would come down before then. Hopefully, she wouldn't refuse to come down. Though that would solve the problem of the table setting...

Suddenly, she wished she'd never decided to have this party at all. She'd been impulsive. Carried away. She hadn't been thinking rationally. She'd been thinking with her heart. In the moment. Without a plan. And look what was unfolding.

She was still struggling with these emotions when she saw him. John, dressed in khaki pants and a white linen shirt rolled at the sleeves, carrying a bottle of wine, and wearing a grin that made her heart skip a beat.

"John!" Her voice was high pitched, she knew, and she blamed it on the nerves, but she no longer knew the source of them.

He handed her the wine and gave her a bashful grin. "Thank you for having me."

"Thank you for coming." She introduced him to Simon and Erin and said, "My sister Gemma is in the kitchen. And my other sister...I was just about to check on her."

He held up a hand. "I'll get myself a drink. And let me know what I can do to help."

She stared at him, and then, composing herself, said, "Of course. Drinks cart is right there. I hope you like sangria."

"Love sangria," he said, grinning, and something in her seemed to turn over. And for just one moment, she wasn't Hope with two girls sleeping upstairs and a house with pristine white slipcovers that she was forever throwing in the wash or scrubbing at. She was Hope, offering a drink to John, who was her friend, a person in her life. A life she hadn't even known existed two weeks ago. A life that she was starting to like an awful lot.

With a smile, she excused herself and passed the bottle off to Gemma. "I'll check on Ellie," she said.

"Good idea," Gemma said. She picked up the cheese plate and went back to the porch.

Of course, the girls had been asleep since six thirty. No nap and a long day playing in the sand had tuckered them out early, as Hope had planned.

She walked quietly up the creaking floorboards of the stairs, careful not to wake them. As expected, the second floor was quiet, and the bedroom door to the room that the girls shared was closed, along with her own.

Straining for any hint of sound, she tiptoed down the hall to Ellie's room and tapped quietly.

The door flung open immediately, and Ellie stood on the other side, looking a bit wild-eyed. Hope stared at her.

"Is everything okay?"

"Of course!" Ellie blinked rapidly. "Why wouldn't it be okay?"

"It's just that you've been gone for...a while." A solid fifteen minutes, really. Not that she was counting. "Are you coming down? John and Leo are here."

"Ah, so your dates have arrived." Ellie nodded.

"John is not my date," Hope clarified, even if she wasn't sure that was exactly the truth. "He's my guest." Yes, that was the best word for what he was.

Ellie was still nodding. "So now there are seven. Three couples. And me. And you don't need me making a scene."

Hope pulled in a breath and let it out. Now she saw where this was going. "This isn't about appearances. And we aren't three couples. John is just a guest," she clarified again. "And I'm pretty sure that there is nothing going on between Gemma and Leo either."

"Yet." Ellie raised an eyebrow and Hope had to grin. She'd seen the way that Gemma smiled when Leo came onto the porch. She was nervous; all signs were there.

"Did you know that Simon was engaged?" she asked. Of course this was news to her, but Ellie's reaction was one of such obvious disappointment, that she needed to be sure before she asked the guy to leave her house and never return again.

But Ellie nodded, slowly. "I knew."

Hope sighed and leaned against the doorjamb. "You knew? Oh, Ellie."

"I thought..." Ellie swallowed hard as tears filled her big, blue eyes. "I don't know what I thought. I just knew that I loved him."

"Oh, honey." Hope reached in and gave her sister a good, long hug, and she didn't release her until Ellie pulled back.

"I was so stupid," Ellie said quietly, brushing a hand from her cheek.

"People do stupid things when they're in love," Hope said, pushing away the frown she felt when she considered that she had invited John here tonight, not because she was in love with him—obviously! But because...she had been thinking with her heart, not her head. "Besides," she said, eager to focus on Ellie's dilemma instead of her own, "if anyone should feel stupid, it's Simon. He's here, with her, and he knows that wasn't how the invitation was made. You're in your house, and you should enjoy your party."

"I thought it was your party," Ellie grumbled.

"It's *our* party," Hope corrected. She tipped her head toward the landing. "Come on down," she urged, putting her arm around her sister's shoulder. "Hold your head up high. You've done nothing wrong here. Besides, I know you want that cheese plate."

She managed to get a grin out of her sister for that one. "Okay," Ellie said, a little reluctantly. "But only because you talked me into it. How do you do that?"

"I'm a mother," Hope said simply.

And as she walked back toward the stairs and passed the closed door to the room where her girls were tucked under the matching pink quilts, dreaming about unicorns and fairies and all the other wonderful things that little girls should dream of, for just one moment she wished she could go into their room, sit there for a while, or stay the entire night.

But a party was waiting for her. And so was her guest.

*

Any concerns that Hope had about John being the odd man out had been replaced with the obvious tension that was made by Simon's fiancée. Ever the hostess, she swiftly moved Ellie's place between her and Gemma when she added a new place setting for Erin beside Simon.

Simon had the decency to look as uncomfortable as he should, all things considered, because given how much time Ellie and Simon had been spending together lately, she couldn't completely fault Ellie for developing feelings for him again.

Gemma only focused on Leo, and Hope supposed that this was a good thing. She giggled a little too easily, and kept smoothing her hair, even though it was clear she'd taken greater care than usual in styling it. She liked him. And from the little smiles passed between them, Hope thought the feeling might be mutual.

From Ellie, however, there were no smiles.

Perhaps noticing the tension, John said, "This is a lovely house you all have here."

"Too bad that Gemma wants to sell it," Ellie said.

Gemma flashed her a look, but Ellie just miserably picked up her glass and took another long sip of sangria. Across the table, Simon adjusted the neck of his shirt.

"Is that true?" John asked. The space between his brows furrowed. "I guess that means you wouldn't be coming back to the island?"

But instead of addressing Gemma with this question, he was addressing her. Hope poked at her dinner—fresh Michigan whitefish in a light seasoning—and said, "Well, nothing has been decided yet."

If she didn't know better, she might just say that Ellie had slipped her a smile.

She pulled in a breath, deciding that really, it was almost time for dessert. Normally it would bother her to see a meal she had so carefully prepared be consumed so quickly, but tonight, she was rather pleased to see Simon all but inhaling his food.

"I'll get the tarts," she said, standing to clear.

"Let me," Ellie said, pushing back her chair with such force it almost tipped over. She gave Hope one of those silent, pointed looks that their mother used to give to them if they had their elbows on the tables, and Hope knew a hint when she saw one.

"Thanks!" she said brightly. She scanned the table. Even Gemma seemed tense now since Ellie had decided to resurrect their argument.

"So, Leo," Hope said, settling on the one person she knew least. "What brought you to Evening Island?"

Gemma turned to look at Leo with interest, as Ellie cleared each of their plates.

"That was delicious," Simon said to her, with a hopeful smile.

"Don't thank me," Ellie ground out. "Hope made it."

Oh dear, Hope thought, taking another sip of her drink.

Feeling the need to smooth things over quickly, she said to Simon, "I hear you have your own law practice now. What kind of law do you practice?"

"I'm a contract lawyer," Simon said. He gestured to Erin, who had been perfectly pleasant but very quiet all evening. "Erin is too."

An office romance then? Or perhaps they went as far back as law school?

Hope decided not to probe. "And Leo? Have you always been a..."

But Leo was shaking his head. "I'm also an attorney, actually."

"Really?" Gemma spoke with such shock that Hope wondered just exactly what they'd discussed in their little chats these past two weeks.

"What kind of law did you practice?" she asked.

His face turned a little ruddy as Ellie delivered him a slice of the strawberry tart that Hope had made this morning. "I don't practice law anymore."

"I don't think Evening Island has a lawyer," Hope said, wondering how much had changed in her absence.

"Don't look at me," Simon said good-naturedly. "I'll be going back to Philly at the end of the summer." He slanted a glance at Erin. "Well, more like the end of next month."

Ellie addressed him for the first time all night. A dessert plate was resting in the palm of each hand, and from the wrath in her eyes, Hope was a little worried that she might do something crazy, like put a pie in his face.

But she just said sweetly, "Is your mother feeling better then?" To the rest of the group, she said, "Simon came to the island to spend time with his mother. She was unwell over the winter."

"Nothing serious," Simon said as he accepted the plate from Erin—or rather, caught it before it hit the table. "But...it's time to get back to life."

Time to get back to life. Hope thought about that statement as she cut into her own slice of pie and let the conversation go on around her, sliding into safer topics like the most popular spots on the island.

She didn't relax again until Simon and Erin had left, and Ellie went up to her room, and Hope was standing on the porch alone with John. There was a sink full of dishes and a kitchen in need of cleaning, but for once, she couldn't let herself worry about any of it. That was part of her other life. A life that she didn't want to get back to any time soon.

"That was a wonderful party," John said, but his grin quirked and Hope squinted her eyes ruefully, giving him a playful swat on the arm.

"Please. It was a disaster. I'm a disaster every time I see you."

"Maybe I bring out the worst in you," he said, cocking an eyebrow.

"I actually think you bring out the best in me," she said, and just like that, all banter came to a halt.

"Well. I had a lot of fun," he said, his voice turning husky as the merriment was replaced with sincerity in his eyes. He reached down and took her hand, and for a moment she thought he was going to shake it, a proper greeting, and a proper farewell.

Only he didn't shake it. He just held it. And looked at her.

"Well, thank you again for coming," she said, clearing her throat. They dropped hands, and she almost wished that they hadn't. But staying that way...She pulled in a breath.

John seemed to hesitate, and for a moment, she was afraid he going to apologize, or take back the gesture. Instead, he said, "If you're free one day this week, I'd love to show you around the hotel. Get your thoughts."

She tried not to show how eager she was, or that this was all suddenly moving very quickly. She'd still promised some design ideas to Darcy early in the week, and she used that as an excuse to stall. "Wednesday or Thursday?"

He grinned, his shoulders seeming to deflate on her response. "Thursday would be perfect. Does two work?"

The girls would be napping at two. She'd go over then. "Perfect," she said.

Because it was.

Chapter Twenty-One

Gemma

The fireflies were out in full force, dotting the sky, and the only lights to be found aside from the moon in the distance were the dwindling candles that remained on the patio. The house was quiet, as quiet as all the other homes that lined West End Road, most of which were not yet inhabited for the season.

"I always forget how quiet it can be here," Gemma said, looking out onto what she could make of the water.

Leo was beside her, on the porch steps, his beer growing warm beside him. "It's a lot different than city life, I suppose," he said.

"In so many ways," she said, sighing. "I always wanted to live in a big city, you know." She gave a little laugh. It seemed strange in a way, like a different person, a person who saw the world differently, who didn't yet have enough experience to form a true opinion. "I wanted to be in the action. To be around people. Funny then, that lately, I've spent so much time alone."

"I don't mind it much," Leo said. "Being alone."

She frowned. There was still so much about himself that he wasn't willing to share, but she'd learned something new tonight.

"You never mentioned you were a lawyer," she said. It was a strange piece of information to withhold, and she couldn't help but wonder what else she didn't know about him.

He shrugged. "Didn't seem to matter much. That's all behind me."

"What kind of law did you practice?"

"State prosecutor," he said, and Gemma raised her eyebrows.

"I'm impressed!"

He gave a good-natured laugh. "You shouldn't be. It was just a job, but...I enjoyed it."

"So why'd you give it all up then?" she asked.

He was quiet for a long time. "I told you about my mom, and the garden."

She nodded. Smiled fondly. "It reminded me of my Gran. She taught us that sort of thing, too."

"And she learned from her father. From Edward." His own smile was sad. "My mother died a few years ago. My dad was gone long before her."

Gemma didn't quite know what to say. "I'm sorry," she said. It was obvious that they had been close.

He shook his head. "At the time I was working, and I was getting ready to propose to my girlfriend. And then..."

Then. That word said so much, didn't it? Everything could be going along fine, and *then...*

"My brother and I argued about the ranch and what to do with it," Leo said.

"Sounds like me and Ellie," Gemma said, feeling her stomach tighten.

"I got that distinct impression tonight," he said, raising an eyebrow. "Take it from me. These kinds of arguments can have lasting consequences."

She didn't like the ominous warning. It tapped into her greatest fears. What would happen to her relationship with Ellie if she pushed the issue? But to not push it made no sense either. Ellie needed a push; she always had. She needed guidance, and structure, and someone to ease her in the right direction.

She grew silent, thinking of the art studio, and Ellie's paintings, and everything she had created for herself all on her own.

Maybe she was wrong. Maybe Ellie was all right, all on her own.

Maybe, she was being selfish.

She swallowed hard, not liking that thought.

"I assume that your brother won the argument," she said, pushing away the thoughts of her own situation. "Seeing as you're here."

"He won. But only because he had support in the matter." He shot her a look. "My own girlfriend sided with him. The truth of the matter was that she didn't want to live on the ranch. She liked the other side of me, the buttoned-up side. When I found out...Well, I had to end it. Returned the ring to the store the very next day."

She set a hand on his arm, and he didn't move away. "That couldn't have been easy."

"It wasn't," he said. "I thought life was good. I had a family, a career, the family ranch...and then, well, it just seemed like there was nothing left for me there anymore. My brother wanted to take the ranch in a commercial direction. But to me...that was my home."

"So you came here," she surmised.

He nodded, keeping his eyes high, up at the sky. "Seemed like the only place that made sense. My grandfather is here, and he's getting on in years, and even though I never came here with my mother, I can sense her here. And the work is good for me."

He said it as an afterthought, and she eyed him for a minute, not entirely convinced.

"It's important to have roots," he said. "And the island has been good to me. No bad memories here."

None at all, Gemma thought, sighing as she looked up at the old Victorian house behind her.

"Do you miss it?" she asked. "The ranch?"

"No sense in looking back," he said gruffly.

"Easier said than done." She glanced at him, deciding she was willing to share more, too. "I was supposed to be getting married next month."

He looked at her with interest. "Now that couldn't have been easy."

"It wasn't," she said. "Especially when he got engaged to someone else shortly after calling things off. But coming here...I feel better. I feel almost...hopeful."

Their eyes met, and for a moment she almost had the sense that he was going to lean in, felt the brush of his arm against hers, saw the slight parting of his lips.

Just as quickly, it was over.

He cleared his throat. Looked up at the sky.

"You can see the entire Milky Way from here," he said.

"My Gran used to show us the constellations," she said, looking up. She could still remember gathering with her sisters, in their pajamas, on the front porch, Ellie always the most eager, and the most curious, so easily dazzled by nature when so many others took it for granted.

Maybe, like she'd taken this place for granted.

"I'm glad we met, Leo," she said, slanting him a glance.

He nodded. "Me too. And I'm sorry for what that guy did to you. You deserve better, you know." He gave her a long look. "You'll find it."

She frowned slightly at his wording. Here, she'd stared to think that she had maybe found it. With him.

"Do you think you'll ever want to share your life with someone?" she asked even though she wasn't so sure that she should be asking, or even if she should want to know. She felt a connection, one that she hadn't sought out or even hoped to find, but it was there, within her reach, and this time, she didn't want it to slip away.

"Nope," he said simply, and even though the word was small, the implication was huge.

She stared out into the distance, trying to process what he had just said, knowing that she had no reason to feel the disappointment in her chest that she did, but it was there all the same. The door had been shut. The intention was made clear.

"Look, it's nothing personal," he said, giving her a little shove with his elbow.

She didn't smile. "So you're giving me the whole it's not you, it's me speech?"

He winced. "Well, when you put it that way..."

She stood up and brushed the seat of her dress, even though she was fairly sure that Hope had swept the patio until every last cobweb or grain of sand was gone. "Forget it. You don't owe me an explanation."

"It sounds like I do," he said, looking up at her. He tapped the spot where she had just been, showing no signs of moving. "Sit, please."

It was tempting, but she knew that there was no choice. She had flashbacks of Sean doing the same thing, pulling her back, trying to let her down gently, trying to convince her that she was better off this way, that it hadn't been working, and that in time she'd see that too, when she was ready.

But what she and Leo had...that did work. It was uncomplicated. And easy. And natural. And fun. There was no pressure. No arguments. No expectation.

"Why shut down the possibility of something wonderful?" she asked.

"Why set yourself up for disappointment?" he countered. When she didn't respond right away, he stood. "You've been there, Gemma. You know how it feels to be let down, and betrayed. We're a lot alike in that department."

"No," she said, shaking her. "That's where we're different. When I first came here, I was coming to escape, and run away, it's true. But now, being here, being with you, it's made me realize that there are second chances. If we want them. We can punish ourselves, or shut ourselves off, turn our backs on what we love and who we are and what we want, or we can try again. And...I'd like to try again, because to not even try..." She shook her head. "I can't give up on myself like that. And I don't think you should either."

Leo looked at her sadly, and she knew that there was no sense in trying to change his mind.

Finally, with a heavy heart, she stepped back. "Good night, Leo."

Or maybe, it was good-bye.

She waited to see if he would say something, stop her, but he just stood there, at the base of the steps, looking like a man who had lost everything. And maybe he had.

The door closed behind her, and she walked into the house, expecting to find it dark, and just as quiet on the inside as it had been on the outside. She planned to go to her room, go to bed, maybe even pack her bags, board the ferry tomorrow. It didn't matter where she went. If she was in Chicago or if she was seven hours away on Evening Island.

She couldn't run from her troubles. She couldn't run from the pain in her heart.

Her hand was on the banister, her sandals slipped off into the pile of others that Ellie kept in a wicker basket and which Hope kept trying to line neatly, by pair, in vain, when she saw the glow of a light from the kitchen. She sighed, thinking that she should be an adult and turn it off for the night, even though what she really wanted to do was crawl under the covers and have a good cry.

She walked to the back of the house, seeing that it wasn't the kitchen light that was on at all, but rather, the old lamps that were set up in the backyard so that people wouldn't trip coming in from the outdoor shower. She opened the screen door, calling softly, "Hello?"

"Over here," a voice whispered back. Ellie. "On the hammock."

Despite the heaviness in her heart, Gemma smiled and stumbled through the cool grass barefoot until she found the hammock, tied between two old trees, whose branches extended high above the roof of this massive house.

She crawled on, settled in so she was facing Ellie, even if she could only make out shadows of her sister's face in the dim light.

"I'm sorry about Simon," she said, reaching out to squeeze her sister's hand.

Ellie was quiet for a long time. "Where's Leo?" she eventually asked, tossing her half of the old wool blanket that they used on evening bonfires at the beach.

"Gone," Gemma said flatly, as simply as Leo had answered the question she needed to ask.

Ellie nodded her head, no further explanation needed. They stared up, into the night sky, at the very stars they used to wish upon as young girls, back when they still felt full of hope and possibility, back when they were still bonded by childhood struggles and daily routine, not just the ownership of an old, run-down house.

Only they were bonded by more than that, Gemma thought. And it would seem that between the three of them, lasting love only did belong in fiction.

Chapter Twenty-Two

Ellie

It was early when Ellie arrived at the studio, but unlike the last couple of weeks, her heart didn't speed up as she passed through town, and she no longer viewed the hours that stretched ahead as being filled with possibility. It was another day on the island, same as always. She'd make some coffee. Some of the guys off the docks would come in to start their week off right. They'd chat about the weather, the choppiness of the water, and then they'd go on their way. She'd call around to the shops to see how her weekend sales had gone, and if any new inventory was needed. And then...

And then this was where things got lonely.

Before she could let her mood get the better of her, she started a fresh pot of coffee to brew and turned a sign on the door that led directly to the docks, letting all the regulars know that she was open. The coffee had only finished brewing when Edward came through the door, holding up his thermos.

"Happy to see you back in business," he said with a grin.

"I was never out of business," she said, filling his mug. He dropped a few bucks in her change jar, even though it wasn't necessary really.

"Well, you haven't been making your coffee these last couple days," Edward said, giving her a wink. "Made me drag myself all the way to Cottage Coffeehouse."

"Which is only around the corner." She laughed. "And they have the best coffee in town."

He gave her a wry look as he helped himself to the container of milk she kept in the mini-fridge. "Well, they don't have the best conversation."

She grinned. "Aw, Edward. You're too kind."

"Just being honest," he said gruffly, looking her square in the eye, and something in her melted a little. He was one of the fixtures of the island, the kind of local stock that made this place what it was, and she'd known him since she was a little girl.

The warmth in her heart lasted long after he'd taken his leave, after she'd promised to be here bright and early tomorrow, with muffins this time, and he promised to bring her some fresh catch to share with her sisters. This prompted them to share a good laugh about Hope that day last week, and Ellie was still chuckling about it when she was settled at her easel, only this time she didn't stay in her back room. She pulled her workspace into the brightly lit studio. The sun was reflecting off the water, and she wanted to capture the harbor before the light changed.

She was just sketching a few of the boats when the door opened. She expected to see Edward, back for a refill, but it wasn't one of the fishermen coming in off the docks.

It was Simon.

She frowned. She couldn't help herself, and he held up a hand before she could protest.

Still, she did. "Shouldn't you be with your fiancée?" she asked. She picked up her paintbrush, went back to the boats, but she was angry and her hand was shaking, damn it, and he'd messed up her morning. She wasn't going to let him mess up her painting too.

"You're mad," he said.

She flashed him with a look. "Gee, you think?"

"I'm sorry if you thought I was leading you on," he said. "That was never my intention."

"And just what was your intention?" she asked, but it was all so obvious now, so horribly, painfully obvious. She saw what she wanted to see even when real life was staring her in the face.

Simon had moved on. And she was still right here.

"I guess I wanted it to be like old times," he said. "Like how we left off."

She raised an eyebrow. "We left off with you saying that you'd be back next summer. And ten summers later, here you are. And here I am."

"And it was a surprise to see you, Ellie. A good surprise," he said.

She nodded sadly. She understood, even if she didn't really want to. "This island has a way of making you forget about the rest of the world."

"You knew I was engaged, Ellie. I never kept that from you."

True. He hadn't. She sighed, and this time she set her paintbrush down for good. "You didn't seem happily engaged," she said, looking him square in the eye. There. She'd said it.

He didn't argue with her. Instead he ran a hand over his face, looked at her with tired eyes. "I came to say that I was sorry for not giving you a heads-up that she would be at the party. She took the afternoon ferry in, she surprised me, and I told her I had this party, and well..."

And it had taken him until Wednesday to offer an apology. Not that she'd been waiting around for one. The apology she wanted was never coming. The apology for not returning all those years ago. And for breaking her heart.

"You're engaged, so it made sense that she came. That's what couples do. They spend time together. They go to parties together." Not that she would know. She hadn't had a boyfriend since Simon. Hadn't wanted to, really. Then she only wanted to focus on her painting, to throw herself into her art, and then, she was busy taking care of Gran.

But now, all of that felt different. She'd had a taste of love, even if it was unrequited. And now, now she couldn't bear the thought of never finding it again.

"I should have tried to reach you first," he finished.

She nodded. "Yes. You should have."

"She liked you," he said, raising his eyebrows, and to that Ellie gave a snort.

"And you? Do you still like me, Simon? All these weeks, all that time we spent together. That day..." She pulled in a breath when she thought of how close he'd come to kissing her, right here in this studio. Or maybe, she had almost kissed him. "I guess I misread things."

Simon thrust his hands in his pockets and nodded slowly. For a moment, she thought she'd overstepped, that he was agreeing with her. She'd been a fool. She'd tried to steal another woman's fiancé right out from under her. But then Simon looked at her, and she knew. She wasn't crazy.

"You were right when you said that I didn't seem happy. I....I wasn't. Erin and I got engaged and then everything seemed to change, overnight. She didn't want to spend the whole summer on the island, and I didn't want to keep rushing back and forth to Philly. We were arguing. A lot. And then there you were."

She gulped, and willed herself not to cry, because as much as she wanted to hear this, as much as she hoped that he cared, she also knew that it didn't matter. He'd made his choice. And she wasn't it.

"You know I always cared about you, El."

She turned from him, facing her painting, but all she saw was a blur of lines and colors. "Please."

He set a hand on her shoulder and then, perhaps thinking the better of it, pulled it back. "What we had was special. This island will always remind me of that time. But I don't live here anymore. And I can't take this place with me."

She nodded. Swallowed the lump that was rising in her throat.

"Please don't hate me for moving on. Or for caring about you. Because I'll always care about you, Ellie. And I'm sorry if I gave you the wrong impression."

She turned now, giving him a watery smile. "You didn't give me the wrong impression. I think I...saw what I wanted to see."

"Professional habit?" he grinned, but there was a sadness in his eyes that touched her.

"Could be worse things in life, right?"

They stood in silence, and then, without a word, Simon stepped forward and set his hand back on her shoulder again. "I'm proud of you, El. You did what you always wanted to do. You didn't care what anyone said. You didn't succumb to the pressure to do what others expected of you."

She frowned at him, wondering if there was more to what he was saying than just his own opinions of her life choices. He wasn't happy. She could see that. But she also knew that he had made his choice.

And she had made hers, hadn't she? She'd chosen to stay here, on Evening Island. To run this studio. To stay inside that huge, empty house all winter long. It was supposed to be everything she'd wanted.

She watched him go, until he was just a small dot out the window, until he was just a boy she used to know, back when they both had big dreams and big plans.

He'd followed his path. And she'd taken hers. And she didn't regret it.

But she needed something more to keep her here. And Simon wasn't it.

Chapter Twenty-Three

Hope

After last week's "fish situation," which Gemma did get a good laugh from, she offered to listen out for the girls during their nap, and in exchange Hope decided to pick up a fresh strawberry pie from Island Bakery on the way back to the house. It would be a reward for Gemma working so hard to finish her book, and an excuse for the sisters to sit outside and enjoy a fine, warm evening, hopefully with less drama than the weekend had brought them.

First, she had to get through her meeting (because that's what it was, surely) with John without letting the nerves get to her too much.

Only they weren't nerves, she realized, as she stopped outside the Lakeside Inn. What she was feeling was excitement. It was something she hadn't felt in a very long time, and damn did it feel good.

She walked up the brick paved path to the front porch, where John was waiting, tapping at something on his phone from one of the rocking chairs. He looked up when she said hello and immediately put his phone in his pocket.

"You can finish your email or text," she said as he stood.

"Later," he said, giving her a grin.

She sighed happily and turned to take in her surroundings. It had been a long time since she'd been to this inn and her memory didn't do it justice. Like many others, it was painted white, with crisp black shutters, and a wide porch lined with rocking chairs. The lawns were carefully maintained, the grass green and lush and the flowers so well taken care of that she didn't see a weed or wilting petal in sight. The inn faced the town, with its back against the lake, but standing here, from a distance, she could see the white dotted store fronts and flags and lampposts that made the island what it was. More than just a piece of land. It was a community, for those lucky enough to be a part of it.

"Should we go in?" John asked, and Hope nodded. She was eager to see what the Altmans had done to the place, and when she pushed through the door into the lobby, she realized that nothing had been done.

That the inn, much like Gran's house, and Darcy Ritter's house, was frozen in time. It was like walking into a memory. A place where everything had stayed the same in a moving world.

In some ways, that was what she loved about it.

She caught her reflection in a mirror near the umbrella stand, John at her side.

So much was the same, only so much had changed. Before, when she visited the island, she was a girl. Her life, while planned out for her in so many ways, was still wide open. She didn't have to follow the carefully laid course—it was just easier to do so. She could have veered to the left, at any moment, and chosen her own path.

Like she was doing now.

"Thoughts?" John slid her a wide-eyed look, and she did her best to suppress a laugh.

"Carpet needs to go," she whispered in his ear.

He laughed. He had a great laugh: rich and loud and warm. The kind of laugh you yearned to hear again. The kind of laugh that said so much about his character. He was honest, sincere, and kind.

And in another lifetime, he could have been someone she loved.

"Wait until you see the dining room," he said, motioning for her to follow him to the back of the lobby, where the floor-to-ceiling windows boasted a view of the lake even if they were flanked in heavy gold drapery.

Merriment made his eyes twinkle as he turned to look her way, and she could only shake her head. Really, what was there to say?

They continued their tour to a few of the unoccupied bedrooms upstairs, each done up in heavy wallpaper with matching fabric on the upholstery and bedding, and only once they were outside, on the back deck that dropped down to the pool area and beachfront, did they allow themselves to speak freely.

"It needs a lot of freshening up," she confirmed. "But so much potential! Do you think the new management has any ideas?"

He gave her a funny smile. "Oh, I think they could be convinced."

She spread her arms wide, taking in the view of the South Bay lighthouse in the distance, and the harbor on the other side. "I mean, look at this! Think of what this place could be!"

"Oh, I know what it could be. And I was thinking that you could be the design expert. If you're interested."

She blinked and turned to stare at him. Giving her ideas for the place was one thing. Working on a project of this scale was another. "Me?"

"Why not?" He shrugged. "You know the island. You know the people and what they like. You'd be true to the history, authentic to the charm of the place."

She would. She could. She could be everything that he was describing. But taking on a job like this was a commitment—it meant more than asking Ellie or Gemma to watch the girls for a few hours. More than helping people like Darcy freshen up their homes. It meant...It meant a whole new life. A whole new set of possibilities.

"I need some time to think about it, if that's okay."

He held up a hand. "Of course."

"And thank you. For thinking of me. I just don't want to give my word unless I can truly commit."

"Do you mind me asking what's holding you back?" He stopped himself, shook his head. "Sorry. That was unprofessional and I overstepped. But, this meeting wasn't purely professional, if I'm being honest."

"Neither was my dinner the other night," she said gently.

They locked eyes, and what she saw in his, she realized, was hope.

She cleared her throat and began walking down the steps, eager to keep moving, even if a part of her was anxious about what would happen next.

"So, how is it that a guy like you isn't already married?" she asked, giving him a rueful look.

"I was married," he said simply, and she tried to hide her shock. Why hadn't she considered this before? A man like John, patient, kind, supportive...he wouldn't have just sat on the market, and he didn't seem like the type who was set firmly on being an eternal bachelor either. "It was short lived. No children, much as I would have wished," he added, casting her a glance.

Something in her tugged. He would have made a great father. He still would. After all, he was only a couple years older than she was, from what she knew. He'd be the kind of father who got down on the ground and played with the kids, who helped not just wrap the birthday presents but pick them out too. The kind of husband who'd hold doors and get the strollers through them.

"Katherine and I married young, right out of college," he elaborated.

Hope nodded. "Evan and I met in college too." He'd been cute, interested, and he'd seemed like the perfect choice. Her parents' approval had only confirmed that. Made her think she was on the right path.

But had her heart ever raced, or her stomach ever fluttered, the way it did now, talking to John?

She wanted to say that it must have. But she couldn't be so sure.

"It's all so much simpler when you're young, isn't it? She was my first serious girlfriend. I didn't know any other way. I didn't even know who I was or what I really wanted from my life."

Hope nodded. Yes. Yes. Yes. He understood. So, so well. What she thought she wanted was just the comfort of what she'd always known. And now...now she wanted something different.

"So we got married, and let's just say that it was a lot tougher than we thought it would be. I was trying to move my way up at the company and I was working a lot, and Katherine struggled to find work, and that made me work even more, and then she complained that I wasn't around, and, well, the long and the short of it is that she left me."

Hope stopped walking. She stared at John. Possibly, she gaped. "She left you?"

The astonishment must have been clear on her face because John gave a low laugh. "Don't look so surprised. To hear Katherine spin it, I was an absentee workaholic husband who didn't treat her like she deserved." He shrugged. "Maybe I didn't."

"I find that very hard to believe," Hope said, shaking her head.

They had reached the beachfront now, and a breeze was blowing in off the lake. Hope slipped off her heels and let them dangle in her hand.

"Going through a divorce that young changed me," John said. "At first, I threw myself even more into work. Told myself that I wouldn't be punished for working too hard. Told myself that I was good at something, even if I'd failed in my marriage."

"And now? Did you ever date?" she asked, even though she almost didn't want to know. The thought of John with another woman bothered her, even though she knew it shouldn't.

"Some. But none of it really stuck. And as the years went by, more and more women were already paired off." He gaze pulled her in. "But I'd like to have a second chance. I've changed my ways. And I know what's important now. I just sometimes wish I'd learned that lesson a little sooner."

He stopped to face her and grinned, and Hope felt a strange sense of propriety toward him, a tenderness that extended beyond her own desires, a need for him to find what he was looking for.

A second chance. After all, wasn't that what she was hoping to find for herself?

"Well," she said when the shoreline turned rocky and it made sense to turn around. "I suppose I should head back and check on the girls before they do something like turn my sister's novel into confetti."

John laughed, and she did too.

"They wouldn't really," he said, but there was enough hesitation in his tone to prove he'd met her kids.

She raised an eyebrow. "Oh, they would."

"They're sweet kids. You're lucky, Hope. I just...well, hope that everything works out for you."

"I feel like it might," she said, slipping him a shy smile. The inn was behind them, tall and white against the clear, blue sky, and she blew out a breath, imagining all the possibilities that lay inside. And right here, on the island.

"Well," she said again, meeting his eye as she pulled herself back to the present. "I'll see you soon?"

"I'll be here," he said, backing away.

Yes, Hope thought to herself. She had a feeling that he would. And that he always would.

*

Hope's mind was spinning with possibilities by the time she reached the cottage. She could picture the inn, transformed, light and airy with shades of blue and green and gray and the big dining room windows open to show off the sweeping view of the lake.

And she could picture John, with his kind eyes and genuine smile. She could picture herself, talking to him, getting to know him even more than she had in this brief amount of time.

She was smiling as she walked up the porch steps. Gemma had offered to watch the girls for her past their nap time, claiming she needed a day off from writing that Hope prayed had nothing to do with Leo not stopping by in a few days, or Gemma's reluctant to offer more than a grunt when Hope mentioned him by name. Gemma had let herself be derailed by matters of the heart once before and Hope could only cross her fingers that Gemma wouldn't let that be her guide again...

Except—wasn't that exactly what Hope was doing now?

She pushed that thought away as she opened the door and stepped inside, taking in the sounds for a moment. No screams coming from inside. That was a good thing. Still, the afternoon was getting on; surely the girls were up by now.

She'd take them down to the market; get some fresh produce for a salad for dinner. Maybe some good bread, too, if there was any left. All the food from the party had been eaten, and the house was clean, as if the night had never happened, and was instead some strange sort of dream—an alternate existence. Hope of Evening Island. Not Hope of Willow Lane. She felt restless, and excited, and she knew that she wouldn't be able to sit still, not when she couldn't stop thinking of all the ways she could revive that historic inn.

When she couldn't stop thinking of John, and the way she felt when she was with him.

She climbed the stairs to the landing. "Gemma? Girls?"

"They're visiting some horses," a deep voice said behind her.

Alarmed, Hope turned around, and came face to face with her husband standing in the front hall, looking up at her.

"Evan," she said breathlessly. He felt out of place here in this house where he had never been, that represented a life before him, a life without him. A life where she was free to be herself, just Hope, not the roles that had come to identify her since they'd been married.

"What are you doing here?" she asked, and then, seeing the hurt in his eyes, she corrected that statement. "I mean...how did you get here? I thought you were in Singapore until at least tomorrow." Often, the trips ran longer than originally planned.

"I came back early," he said.

She dropped her chin and stared at him, gripping the banister. Evan didn't come home early for anything. Not when she had influenza and a fever and was too sick to make the girls dinner, let alone get out of bed. She'd had to call Gemma to come up and help her, because Evan had a big client meeting and couldn't cancel it. Not when she had a migraine and asked him to get home early to pick the girls up from preschool. Then he'd had another client meeting. He couldn't leave his client in a lurch. She'd had to put on her darkest sunglasses and deal with it, even when he hadn't come home until well after the girls were in bed (client dinner).

"You came back early?" She narrowed her eyes at him. "Why? Deal fell apart?"

Evan had the decency to look ashamed. "That's a fair statement, but no. I came back because I missed the girls. And I missed you, Hope."

She stared at him for a long time. He was still handsome, tall and fit, with the same dark hair and eyes that had caught her eye all those years ago. He was familiar. But right now, standing here in this house, on this island, in the life she had created for herself here, he looked strange and out of place. She knew the correct response would be to tell him that she was thrilled, that she missed him too, and not long ago she might have done just that.

But she wasn't that person anymore. And the truth was that she didn't know who she was anymore. Or where that left them.

Chapter Twenty-Four

Gemma

Gemma was working at the table on the porch the next afternoon, a glass of lemonade at her side, the sunshine on her face, and the wilting bouquet of lilacs from the weekend's party front and center, pulling her thoughts away from the chapter she needed to finish by end of the day and back to other, personal matters. Conversations she'd rather forget. Feelings that never should have crept up in the first place.

What had she done, allowing herself to develop feelings for Leo, of all people, just because he was friendly, and cute, and...something else. Something she couldn't quite put her finger on, something that defied all logic and tapped right into the part of herself that she no longer trusted, and shouldn't have trusted. Her heart.

Exasperated, she finally lifted her fingers from the keyboard, pushed back her chair, and grabbed the vase. She marched it through the side door to the kitchen of the house and crossed through to set it in the center of the underused formal dining room, and then walked purposefully back to her computer.

There. Out of sight, out of mind.

If only it were that easy.

She posed her fingers over the keyboard and skimmed her last paragraph, trying to get back into the feel of the story. After taking a day off yesterday to help with the girls, she was now nearly three hundred pages into the story. She knew the characters. She knew what would happen next. She had one week to finish the draft, and then...then she could fall apart.

She wrote two more lines—slowly—and then looked up when she heard something crunching over the gravel driveway. It was Ellie, home early, it would seem. She dragged her foot across the kickstand and left the bicycle at a precarious angle on the front path, waving when she saw Gemma sitting on the porch.

"Writing?" she asked.

Gemma smiled. "I was. I could use a break if you want to join me for some lemonade." She motioned to the pitcher on the table.

Ellie grinned and pushed her long braid over her shoulder. "I'll grab a glass."

She went inside and returned a moment later. She filled her glass and took the seat next to Gemma, staring longingly at the water in the distance.

"I feel bad about how I behaved the other night at the party," she said, darting a glance in Gemma's direction.

Gemma hadn't been pleased that Ellie had tried to argue with her in front of their guests, but she had bigger problems to deal with. Besides, she understood. She saw the hurt in Ellie's eyes every time that Simon spoke, and when he and his fiancée left at the end of the night, hand in hand.

"We don't need to talk about it," Gemma said. She gave her sister a reassuring smile. "And I'm happy you joined me. There's no sense enjoying such a beautiful view alone."

"No," Ellie said a little sadly. "It's probably my favorite thing about this house."

"Same here," Gemma said.

"Is Hope here?" Ellie asked.

Gemma shook her head. "She's out with Evan and the girls. They left this morning, so I'm surprised they aren't back yet."

"I don't think Hope was expecting him," Ellie said. "She seemed more flustered than usual at dinner last night, and then they disappeared. Do you think...do you think it had anything to do with that man she brought to the party?"

Gemma sighed. She didn't think it was her place to share what Hope had revealed, especially not with Evan being here.

"Hope's a big girl. If anyone can figure out her life, it's Hope." After all, what chance was there for her if Hope's life fell apart?

"Unlike me," Ellie said, frowning at the table.

Gemma looked at her. "What's that supposed to mean?"

"I mean, that my life is a mess. It always was. It still is. Dad was right about me."

"Don't say that," Gemma said firmly. She leaned forward in her chair, stared at Ellie until she was forced to look up at her. "Look at all you've accomplished. You have your own art studio. You sell your paintings all over town."

"I barely make any money. It's just pocket change. I'm living off that trust. Without this house..."

Gemma grew quiet. "Is that why you're so against selling it? You know you'd get a third of the sale price. You could go anywhere, and put down a deposit."

Ellie shook her head. "It's not about the money. It's that...Well, you have your apartment in the city. Hope has her mansion in the suburbs. And I have...this. I don't have anything else of my own other than the studio, and I'm barely keeping the lights on over there. You're right that I let this house go. It's old. Repairs are expensive, especially when materials have to come in from the mainland. But I've tried my best," Ellie said, and suddenly her eyes teared up.

Gemma reached out and took her hand. "Of course you did. And this house is a third my responsibility too. Hope and I should have sent money for repairs. We just didn't know..."

Ellie angrily brushed at a tear. "I didn't want to tell you guys what was going on here. I just figured you'd think what Dad always does. That I'm irresponsible, that I make poor choices."

"Don't listen to what Dad says," Gemma said, but she knew that this was easier said than done. "And if anyone makes poor choices, it's me."

"You? But you have a career, one that you are earning a living wage from. And you can always go back to advertising."

"But I don't want to," Gemma said. "And I'm scared that will happen if I can't make a success of my writing."

Ellie cracked a smile. "We were warned..."

"You followed your heart, Ellie, and that is a very brave thing to do."

"Oh, I followed my heart all right," Ellie grumbled. "And now...Now I guess you could say that it's broken."

Gemma nodded. The expression on Ellie's face at the party had been obvious to everyone there, even, she feared, Simon's fiancée.

"You may not want to hear this, but I don't think Simon was the right guy for you. He balanced you out, maybe, and you have good memories with him, but he didn't want what you wanted, and you need to find someone who does."

"Dad approved of Simon," Ellie said a little begrudgingly.

"Maybe that's why you liked him," Gemma said, giving her a knowing grin. "Or maybe you liked that Simon was a little bit like Dad, in the conventional sense, only unlike Dad, he supported you."

"Forget my comment about advertising. You could find a job as a therapist," Ellie said ruefully, but she was smiling. "Maybe that's true. I don't know what made Simon so appealing. Maybe I'll never know. I just know how I felt when I was with him."

Gemma considered this. "I can't make sense of my love life either. Or lack thereof."

The sisters were quiet for a moment until Ellie said, "Dad probably wouldn't approve of Leo."

Despite herself, Gemma laughed. "Probably not. But, it doesn't matter anyway. Leo isn't looking for a relationship."

Ellie raised an eyebrow. "Are you?"

Gemma nodded slowly as she gathered her thoughts. "I didn't think I was. I wasn't sure I ever would be, after Sean. But meeting Leo made me realize that I can have feelings for someone again. And that's...scary."

"But what's the alternative?" Ellie asked. "To never try at all? Although, that's sort of what I've been doing all these years. Until Simon came back."

"At least you can say that you tried. You followed your heart, Ellie. You did everything you set out to do."

"You both did," said a voice behind them.

Gemma turned to see Hope standing in the doorway, looking weary. "I didn't realize you all were back." Normally, the girls made their presence known.

"Just me," Hope said, coming to join them. "I walked home, slipped in the back door. Evan's still in town with the girls."

"Everything okay?" Gemma asked.

Hope shrugged. "Yes. No. It's like you said. You did everything you set out to do. Both of you. You always wanted to be a painter, and you are, Ellie. And you, Gemma, you were miserable at that advertising agency and you always wanted to be a writer, and look at you.

Published. Under contract. You were able to quit that job you never liked."

"Only because of Gran," Gemma said, giving Ellie an apologetic smile. "She helped all of us out, Ellie. We're all better off because of how much she supported us, then...and now."

"She was a wonderful woman," Ellie said as her eyes filled with tears.

Not wanting to go down a dark path, Gemma veered things back to steadier ground.

"Besides, I may have to find another job I don't like if I don't pull off this book in time," she said.

"But you will, Gemma," Hope said, with a smile. "I always knew you would. And I think deep down you knew it too."

Gemma thought about that for a moment. It was true, she supposed, that even in her panic, and even in her sleepless nights, she knew that she would get the job done. She'd finish the book. She'd find a way. It was the one thing in her control when the rest of the world was not.

"But you got everything that you wanted," Ellie said to Hope. "You always got good grades. You went to the best college. You married Evan, for Pete's sake."

A strange look came over Hope's face. "I'm not saying I'm not grateful for everything I have, I...I never had dreams like the two of you did. I never wanted something, specifically. I guess that all I ever wanted was Dad's approval." She laughed softly, shaking her head. "Sounds pretty lame, doesn't it?"

"That's all I ever wanted," Ellie said. "It still is."

"What?" Hope looked at her with astonishment. "But you...Sorry, El, but you sort of rebelled."

"I did what I wanted to do, yes, but I thought..." Ellie glanced at Gemma. "I thought that if Dad could accept Gemma's career that I could find a way to make him accept mine too. Someday."

Gemma shook her head sadly. "I think he would have, if things had been different. But our roles are already defined, aren't they? I'm the smart one. Ellie is the—"

"Black sheep," Ellie said, frowning. When Gemma and Hope didn't react, she said, "Face it. I am!"

Gemma couldn't argue. She glanced at Hope. "And Hope is..."

"Perfect," Hope said. "Even though I'm not. I was a perfect daughter. Perfect student. And I married the perfect guy. Now I'm just a mother. Not a perfect one."

"Just a mother?" Gemma repeated. "Hope, you are a world-class mother. Look at you! You had a unicorn at their birthday party."

Ellie's eyes lit up with interest. "You did? I can't believe I missed that."

"Much like something Mom would have done," Hope said. She shook her head. "You were right, Gemma. I am just like Mom."

"No," Gemma said, realizing her error. "Mom would have had a unicorn for show. You had it to make your girls happy. That's the difference."

"I do want my girls to be happy," Hope said pleadingly, and Gemma reached out to squeeze her hand.

"Of course you do. And they are!"

"Do you think...?" Ellie chewed her lower lip. "Do you think that Dad ever cared if we were happy? Or was it all just about making him happy?"

Gemma looked at her sisters. She wanted to say that of course their happiness mattered, that they had been loved and cared for, and given opportunities for successful lives.

"I think," she said carefully, "he thought he knew what was best for us. But I do think he knew what he wanted was different. He didn't like coming here, but he knew we did. So he let us come."

"Why do you think Dad never liked coming here?" Hope asked. It was something they'd never questioned, but now Gemma saw the situation differently. This house, it was so full of memories, it could soften even the hardest heart.

It had softened hers.

"I think it made him sad," Gemma said. "Gran moved in full time when her husband died, and I think that was when Dad convinced himself that he hated it here. I think it just hurt too much."

Hope locked Gemma's gaze. "This place does have a way of stirring things up."

"It stirred us up," Ellie said, flicking them each a glance.

Gemma nodded sadly. "Where do we go from here?"

"I don't know," Hope said, "but I hope that whatever we all end up doing, we'll be doing it for the right reasons."

"From the heart," Gemma said. "Even if it is sometimes the hardest path."

"But it's the only one worth taking," Ellie said, sighing deeply. "I have to get back for my class tonight, but I need to get this out first. I think you're right," she said, a little breathlessly. There was fear in her eyes, but a determination that Gemma had always loved. "We should sell the house."

Gemma set down her glass of lemonade and looked at Ellie for a moment. "And here I was thinking that we should keep it."

Chapter Twenty-Five

Ellie

Ellie loved each part of the island for its own unique reason. There were the lighthouses at the north and south shores, standing tall and proud, a beacon over the lake waters. And the dock, with its boats and activity, and the promise of adventure. She loved Main Street, with its lamps and benches and the buckets of flowers that flanked each shop door. She loved the smell of fudge and waffle cones and the crowd that gathered outside Main Street Sweets to watch the taffy being pulled.

But most of all, she loved Sunset Cottage. Not because it was where she'd lived the past few years. Not because of the summers she had spent with Simon, or even her sisters.

She loved it because it was the one place in the world where she was free to be herself.

And that was why her decision to leave it didn't come easily.

But once her decision had been made, she stuck to it. That was one thing she was sure of, one thing that she had lived by. She was true to herself. Even when it hurt.

Ellie closed the door to her studio with a sigh. She was lucky that the landlord had been willing to let her break the lease without a penalty since the month was drawing to a close, but then, this was Evening Island, and everyone here looked out for each other.

It was comforting, in many ways. Secure. But as much as she'd dared to follow her own path, she'd always stuck to the safe side of it. Until now.

There was an entire world out there. A world of oceans and mountains and tiny villages that were all waiting to be seen, and captured. And buoyed by her sisters, she was going to do just that.

"Heard you're leaving!" a voice called out, and Ellie felt her shoulders droop. She'd only talked to the landlord this morning. She'd been hoping to see Edward today and tell him herself before the word travelled, but that didn't mean it would be an easy conversation.

"Only temporarily," she said, as he came to meet her.

"But you're closing the studio?" Edward asked.

"I thought I needed a studio of my own to be a real artist," she said, setting a hand on the door. "But the truth is that I only need one place on this island. Sunset Cottage." She grinned, and he gave her a nod of approval.

"That's a mighty fine house," he said.

"It's a wonderful place," she agreed.

"So where are you headed?" he asked.

"Europe," she said. Gemma had been the one to offer up that idea. Said that Ellie could use her honeymoon trip, put it to a better use. "I've always wanted to go."

"Don't stay away too long," Edward said. "You know we'll all miss you around here."

The truth was that she didn't know how long she would stay. The voucher was open-ended, and without the rent on this place, she had a little money in her pocket. But she did know that she would be back. Even if it was just for next summer.

Ellie leaned in and gave the older man a hug and only wrinkled her nose a little at the smell of fish coming off his clothes. She didn't mind. Not really. It was the smell of the island. And she loved every inch of it. Even the not so pretty parts.

She gave one last look around her lovely, light-filled studio, with the view of the harbor and the sound of the waves lapping at the rocks along the shore. "I hope whoever ends up taking this space puts it to good use."

"I'll see to it that they do." Edward was a man of his word.

"See you when I get back?" she asked.

"I'll be here," he said, and she grinned at that, because she knew that he would. And it was nice to have something to count on. Like Sunset Cottage.

Next she walked into town, past the shops that sold her paintings, stopping to admire the setup in Hill Street Gallery. The owner had placed a little sign next to her bright and cheerful watercolor: "Local artist Ellie Morgan."

Artist. She'd never called herself that, not really. Never allowed herself an official title. She'd always given a description of her job instead. "I paint," she'd say, or "I do watercolors." But seeing this sign, here on display, with her name, made her realize that she was an artist. That she was exactly what she'd set out to be.

She carried on her way, finally stopping at Lakeview Gifts. She pushed through the door, glanced at Jewel who gave her a beady stare, and then walked over to the counter, where Naomi was wrapping up a figurine of a lighthouse for a young couple.

"Tell me the rumors aren't true," Naomi pleaded as soon as the door closed behind the tourists.

Ellie had to laugh. "News sure does travel fast around here. How'd you hear?"

"Your landlord told Darcy that your studio was up for rent! Did you really close it down?"

"I did," Ellie said, and then, seeing the dismay in her friend's face, said, "I don't need a studio to make me an artist. I can paint from Sunset Cottage. I can paint anywhere. And I can still offer my classes. That house is so big, it needs a bigger purpose."

Naomi's grin was rueful. "I like the sound of that."

"But I am going away for a while. There's more out there that I want to capture. And I could use a break from the island for a bit," she said, thinking of Simon, and his fiancée, and the wedding that was lurking around the corner. She'd run into him again someday, she was sure, but by then, with any luck, she would have moved on, rather than stayed behind, waiting. "I'm not leaving until the end of the week," she said.

"And I'm heading to Blue Harbor tomorrow to help my sister with her new baby," Naomi said with a frown. "I figured this was the last week I could get away before the summer season is in full swing. But you will be back?"

"Soon," Ellie said.

"Promise?" Naomi asked, and Ellie had to grin at that.

"I always keep my promises."

With a heavy heart, she leaned in and gave her friend a long hug, telling herself that this wasn't a good-bye. It was just a so-long for now.

She swallowed the lump in her throat and turned as the door opened and another customer walked in, bright-eyed and eager, probably their first time on the island.

"Welcome to Lakeview Gifts!" Naomi called out with a smile. She held up her hand, giving Ellie a heart-felt wave.

"Hello!" the customer called out before Naomi could stop her, and at once, Jewel cocked his head with interest.

Ellie locked eyes with Naomi, and even though this might usually elicit an exasperated sigh, or sometimes, actual tears, Naomi burst out laughing, and Ellie did too. And she smiled the whole walk home, the sound of Jewel's squawking still fresh in her ears.

*

Ellie made one more stop at the studio before re-turning home. As much as she called Sunset Cottage her home, she'd really kept it as Gran's home, leaving so much of it as it had been, almost afraid to change it. Slowly, over time, she'd replaced some of Gran's heavy-framed oil paintings with her colors, but only with her absolute favorites. All except for one.

Now, she picked up the painting that she'd brought from the studio, her favorite, the one that showed Main Street in the snow, all soft and grey with hints of green and blue.

Few people had the pleasure of seeing this island as it was in this painting. And she had. And she would, again. Because she'd be back.

She hung it on the wall opposite her bed, took one last, long look at it, and walked out into the hall. The house was lighter now, and not just because of the watercolor paintings of the island, but because of the improvements that Hope had made, replacing the heavy throw pillows with pops of blue and green, opening the blinds to let all the light in, adding bouquets of fresh flowers in every room, even the ones she picked from the bushes that were starting to bloom, and the kitchen, where, other than the porch, all of them seemed to gather at least a few times a day.

But it wasn't just this house that was lighter now. It was her step. Her heart. She had a chance now, not to prove herself to anybody, but to do what she'd always wanted to do. To paint. To follow her heart. To live her dreams. To be happy.

She walked into the kitchen, wanting to be around her family, thinking how different it all was just a short time ago when she could hear every creak, every shift in the house, because that was the only thing keeping her company. When each room was dark before she entered it to turn on a light. This house needed life.

And she...she needed to live.

Hope was at the counter, slicing apples and setting them on a plate for the girls, along with cubed cheese and carrot sticks. Through the window, Ellie saw Evan mowing the yard. Bless him!

"Is everything okay?" Hope asked.

"I was just thinking how much I'm going to miss you all," Ellie said. They had an entire day of fun planned, a picnic on the beach, a Sunday night bonfire with marshmallows and everything, just like the old days, but she couldn't stop thinking that this time next week, she'd be somewhere else.

"You'll be back," Hope said with a reassuring grin.

Ellie breathed in that thought and nodded her head. Her sister was right. But then, Hope was always right. And try as they might to change themselves, for better or worse, they were exactly who they were, and who they always were, and she wouldn't have it any other way.

From the kitchen table, Rose spilled milk and Victoria started to cry and then, seeing Victoria cry, Rose started to cry, and then Hope was dashing for a dish rag and wiping it up and Gemma was trying to grab her pages from the table before they got wet and muttering something about just needing a few minutes to finish one chapter, and Ellie could only stand back and take it all in.

Really, this house may be large, but they weren't the same young sisters they had been all those years ago and there was only room for one of them here now.

And that was just as it should be.

Chapter Twenty-Six

Hope

Monday, it rained. They stayed inside, reading old magazine and pouring over Gran's albums, and later moved outside to the porch to play cards. Ellie won every hand. She'd clearly been busy up here on the isl-and, even if they hadn't realized it at first.

But Tuesday was a bright, sunny day, and Hope and Evan decided to take the girls up to the North Shore Beach, away from town, and away from the cottage. Away from the inn or any chance of running into John.

She hadn't seen him since their meeting at the inn, when she'd told him she'd give him an answer soon on his offer. But his offer wasn't just a professional one, even if that wasn't directly spoken. If she stayed on the island, and took the job, then this—this family life she had with Evan and the girls—would be over as she had come to know it. She'd be starting a new chapter, the life she thought she wanted, maybe even the life she had always wanted, if she'd ever dared to ask herself what that was, exactly.

She owed John an answer. And she owed Evan one, too.

He hadn't said when he was leaving the island and she hadn't said when she was either. It just hung there, unspoken. Like a lot of things.

"You're awfully quiet," Evan said, coming to sit beside her. The girls were happily playing in the sand a few feet away. Every once in a while they stood to gather rocks to decorate the castle they were making, that looked more like a few lumps and hills than a royal residence.

"Just thinking." She dragged a finger in the sand, finding it hard to look him in the eye.

"This is a beautiful place," he said, almost pensively. "Why didn't we ever come here before?"

She gave him a long look. "Our lives are busy. There was never any time."

He nodded. "I know what you think. I heard what you said that day, after the girls' party. I know you think I'm not present when I'm home, but I guess it's because I always thought you liked being in charge of everything with the girls and the house. So I let you do it."

"Oh please!" Hope said, but as she looked at him, she realized that it was true. It wasn't a lame excuse to get out of being less than helpful. And she did like things a certain way.

"And the truth is that you're better with them than I am," Evan said, frowning a little. "You know the times that I tried to put them to bed, they kept saying they wanted you. That I read the stories wrong. That you did it right."

Hope felt something in her heart thaw a little. This was the first time she was hearing this.

"And that time you went to that party and I had to get the girls dinner? They refused to eat what I made. They said it was gross, that you're a better cook. I got so fed up that I took them out for fast food."

She had to hide her smile. She didn't have the heart to tell him that the girls had told her all about their trip to get french fries and burgers the next morning.

"Well, I'm sure they loved that," she said, sliding him a smile.

"They love you, Hope." Evan pulled in a breath. "And I do, too."

She blinked, not knowing what to say, not even sure what she felt. She was so caught up in the strange imbalance of their relationship—of their lives—that she hadn't stopped to ask herself if she really still loved her husband, because wasn't that what it all came down to?

"I could have helped more," he said. "I should have helped more. I should have been there when you asked me to come home when you were sick. You're just...so capable that I figured you'd be able to handle it. But I should have come home. I should have made you the priority, not my client. Because you are the priority, Hope. You always were. You always will be. You're...you're my wife, Hope. But you're more than that. You're my life."

Hope swallowed the knot that had wedged in her throat. He was saying everything she wanted to hear, and she wanted to believe him, so badly, but she just didn't know if she could.

"It's easy here, on the island, to focus on the things that matter. To unwind, to not pick up a call from a client, or disappear into the living room to watch the game. The girls aren't being run around all day, there aren't playdates and class parties, and bake sales, and dishes to wash." Well, there were dishes to wash because that dishwasher was still broken, she thought. But that was beside the point. "It's easy to say all this now, Evan."

"But I mean it," he said, holding her eyes. "I want us to do things like this. Take trips. Do you think I like travelling across the world with coworkers? I'm doing it because of you guys. Because I want to provide for you. Because I thought you wanted to be a stay-at-home mom."

"And I do," Hope said, blinking. "I want to be with them. I just..."

"You just needed a break." He grinned. "I get it."

"Do you?" She wanted to know. She needed to know.

"You're so good with them, and they adore you, Hope. And I thought you wanted to take it all on. But now I see. I'll be there more. And if you want to work, then work. I support your decision, Hope. I've never wavered from what we decided, all those years ago."

They locked eyes for a moment and a hundred thoughts flooded her at once. It was the same face she had looked at day after day for years and years. The same man who infuriated her. The same man who had been there for moments that mattered more to her than anything else ever could.

The same man who hadn't been there when she needed him the most. But who might. Or so he said.

"I guess we've both struggled with finding balance in our roles," she said. "I wanted to do it all. I wanted to take on the role of parenting like I did everything else. But, I could have included you more. And I could have taken more off my plate." She eyed him sidelong. "I mean...the girls didn't need a unicorn."

"Nah," Evan said grinning. "They needed one. And you knew how to make it happen."

A smile of understanding passing between them.

"Daddy!"

Hope jarred to the right, seeing Victoria standing with a bucket, holding it up in the air expectantly. "We need your help!"

Help. Yes, that was what Hope had needed, wasn't it, even if she hadn't directly asked for it, even if she'd maybe been a little too passive aggressive, taking it all on herself, and feeling resentful later.

Evan grinned and said, "Sure thing!" and got to his feet.

He took the bucket in one hand and Victoria's hand in the other and joined Rose near the lakefront, where the water was lapping their toes. It was early in the season, and still cold, and it made Victoria squeal.

She could have stood up and joined them, but right now, she preferred to sit back and watch.

Her heart pulled tight as she watched the girls instructing Evan on how to create a proper moat, explaining in great detail that the princesses would need to get in and out of their castle for shopping trips, and that no, they could not take a boat, their dresses might get dirty!

Evan played along, joked with them, teased them until they squealed in frustration and then began explaining again, more insistent this time, until Evan helped build the moat and a drawbridge.

He glanced over at her, caught her eye and winked, and her breath caught in her chest. She wanted to capture this moment, hold onto it, remember it on the long, hard days when she felt weary and exhausted and started questioning her choice.

She wanted to remember that this was how she felt when she was on the island. How she'd always felt, ever since she was a little girl. At peace. Happy. Fulfilled. Free of worry and pressure and expectation and the daily responsibilities that had defined her life for as long as she could look back, from the time that she was eight years old and had received a B in math and had to explain to her father when he got home why that grade had not been an A, and promised, solemnly, to do better next time.

She would do better next time, she thought now.

John was right about something he'd said to her. Everyone deserved a second chance. Even her.

Chapter Twenty-Seven

Gemma

Leo hadn't been at the Taylors' house since the night of the party, not that Gemma had been checking. Much. Still, every day, when the sun began to set over the water and she knew that he had not come by West End Road, her heart seemed to sink along with the sun, only to rise again the next day when she woke up in her third-floor bedroom, renewed with hope that today might be the day that he came back, and everything could go back to how it was.

Only life didn't work like that, and she'd been through enough to know it.

You couldn't go back. Even here, at Sunset Cottage, everything had changed from the last summer she'd been here with her sisters, when they were all young and innocent, when they hadn't yet had their hearts broken or their dreams shattered. When time was on their side, spread out before them as vast as the great lake. When anything seemed possible.

She wanted to get back to that place. She wanted to believe that despite everything, her future was wide open, full of great things waiting to happen. That there was another path for her, after the one she'd been taking had come to a dead end.

She stayed in her room and worked through the morning. With her book due in only three days now, she was scrambling, but it felt good to pour her energy into something other than her heart. And it felt good to be here on the island, with the sunsets and the water right there, just a few yards away.

Everyone was out, making the most of their last few days on the island, and Gemma had the entire house to herself. She could sit out on the front porch until they all came back. Or she could go down to the coffeehouse. Or out back to the hammock to read over some of her pages.

She decided on the porch. It was the defining feature of this home, the gathering place, where so many happy memories had been made.

With a glass of lemonade in one hand and her notebook in the other, she pushed out the side door of the kitchen onto the porch, looking out over the water as she rounded to the front.

And there he was. Standing outside the front door, wearing khakis and a button-down shirt, not the usual jeans and T-shirt she had grown used to. His expression was wary. His eyes unsure.

"Leo."

She swallowed hard, catching herself. She had wished for this moment, just as she had wished at first that Sean would change his mind and come back. But unlike with Sean, a part of her, however small and however hard she tried to deny it, had thought that it might just happen.

That she hadn't been wrong about Leo. That maybe, just maybe, she'd been right.

"Sorry to startle you. I was just about to knock."

She nodded, wanting him to say more. "If you were here to mow the lawn, I'd tell you that you were too late."

"I'm not here to mow the lawn," he said.

She swallowed hard. Gathered her wits. Told herself it didn't mean a damn thing. That she shouldn't open herself up to disappointment. But then, that's what she didn't want to do. She had closed herself off for too long. "I can see that. You're all dressed up."

He gave a bashful grin as he looked down at his shirt. "Yeah, I was thinking about something that was said at the party. About how there isn't a lawyer here on the island. And I was thinking about something else that was said that night, too. Something you said, about not turning my back on things that made me happy."

She blinked, trying to understand where he was going with this. "Are you going back to your old career?"

"In a sense," he said. "I still want to open the stables, but I rented out a storefront in town. A law office, I suppose you could say. Actually, I rented out your sister's studio. It was my grandfather's idea. He seems to think that place has a special purpose. Helps lost souls find their way."

Gemma grinned. "You could say that about this entire island."

He sank his hands into his pockets. "So Ellie's really moving out then?"

"Of the studio?" Gemma nodded. "She's going to travel. I think it will be good for her, to see the world, to experience new things, and meet new people."

"So you guys are on good terms with everything then?" he asked.

Gemma grinned. "We are. This house was a lot for Ellie. I think she was afraid to let go of it, but now she's ready to embrace the next phase of her life."

Leo nodded slowly as he thrust his hands into his pockets. He looked over at the lake and then back at her. "So I'm too late then."

She blinked. "Too late for what?"

Leo took a step toward her. "What you said the other night really sank in, Gemma. I had a rough go, and I felt let down by a lot of people. And for a while it was easier on my own. I like it here. Really like it. And I like the work I've been doing. But..."

Gemma felt her breath catch.

"But I was denying an entire part of myself. And I wasn't being fair to myself. Or you."

She stared at him, not sure of what to say, or if she could even speak.

"I spent so long trying not to think about my ex, trying to push aside any feelings that I had for her, that I didn't even realize that my feelings had changed, and that the person I was pushing away wasn't her." He looked at her steadily. "It was you. And...the way you made me feel. It was a feeling that I didn't think I'd find again and honestly, didn't really want to."

She nodded. She understood that much.

"Being here...it's made me see that my old life was never going to work for me. Even if I'd kept the ranch instead of my brother, things still would have fallen apart with my girlfriend. I can't blame him. Or her. She just wasn't the one for me."

Gemma's heart was pounding as she looked up into his eyes, daring to believe that he felt the same way that she did.

"The truth is that I like it here. I'm able to be myself. Now I can even think about practicing law and running my own stable, something I couldn't balance before. And I've found someone who likes me just as I am."

She nodded, because it was true, every word he'd said. "Just as you are."

"Look, I'm not good at speeches. And I'm not good about talking about my feelings either. And I'm sure you could have said all this a lot better than I have."

She shook her head. "You're not a character in one of my books."

But he had been the inspiration.

"Besides, what I write is fiction. This is real life. And it's messy. And it's complicated. And it's far from roses and sunshine. But right now, it's pretty damn close." She met his smile, feeling her heart fill with joy.

"What do I have to do to convince you not to sell the house?" he asked.

She looked at him in surprise. "We've decided to keep it."

There was a pause as he digested this. "You did?"

She nodded. "Some things are worth holding on to, even when times get tough."

"They are." He looked around the porch, from the chipped paint on the posts to the worn whitewashed floorboards. He seemed to want to say something, but took a step backward instead. "Well. Tell Ellie to give me a call when she gets back to town then. I'll see what I can do about some of these repairs on my free time."

Now Gemma grinned. "Oh, it's not Ellie who will be staying on the island."

He looked at her, his brown eyes deep and steady, as if he knew what she was about to say. Maybe even hoped for it.

"I'm staying," she said. She'd reached the decision easily, so easily that perhaps the idea had been in her head all along. "There's nothing for me in Chicago anymore."

He nodded, his grin starting to quirk. "And here?" he asked.

"Here I at least have hope," she said, stepping toward him. "And that's a pretty good feeling. And...I have you."

He smiled broadly, all the way up to his eyes. "You sure about this?"

Maybe she was foolish, or maybe, this time, she was right to listen to her heart, because it had never felt more full, or more sure, and if she couldn't trust herself, how could she ever trust anyone else?

"So I was thinking that maybe we could strike an arrangement," she said, struggling to hide her grin.

"Are you speaking to my professional side or my personal side?" His eyes twinkled with amusement.

"I was thinking that maybe you could help fix up the house, and in exchange, I could help you get your stable up and running."

He looked at her in disbelief, and then burst out laughing. "You? I saw you on that horse, if you've forgotten."

"I'm not saying I'd be a riding instructor." She pursed her lips. "But I used to work in advertising. I know how to market a place like this. I know how to get the word out, and I definitely know the people of this island, because I'm one of them."

His eyes were steady, as unwavering as his words. "Why are you doing all this for me?"

She shrugged. "Because we're friends, and that's what friends do."

"That's where you're wrong," he said, taking her hand and stepping toward her. "We're not friends, Gemma."

He was close, so close now that she could see the freckles on his nose and cheeks from too many days in the sun. See the golden highlights that streaked his brown hair. The little scar under his right eye that told a story that she didn't yet know, but wanted to. Badly.

"We're not?" she whispered, swallowing hard.

He shook his head and reached up to push a loose strand of hair from her cheek. "We're a hell of a lot more than friends."

She grinned as he wrapped his hands around her waist and pulled her close and kissed her in a way that she had never been kissed and had been waiting to be kissed...even if she hadn't known it until now.

Chapter Twenty-Eight

Hope

Hope stood at the gate of the Lakeside Inn, knowing the chances were high that John was inside at this very moment, if not in his room, then maybe in the lobby, or in the dining room enjoying breakfast—it was early. This conversation couldn't wait any longer. She'd waited a week to tell him what she'd known in her heart she would tell him all along.

She let out a shaky breath, asked herself for the hundredth time if she was really going to do this, and then, mostly because a few of the guests had started to stare at her as they waited for her to move to the side so they could pass through the gate, she began to walk toward the inn.

The cobblestone path to the front porch was flanked with flower beds, and near the door was a bike stand, full of mint and teal and hot pink cruisers. She'd recommend keeping all of that. She'd recommend keeping a lot of things the same, actually. That was what made people come back to this hotel year after year. It wasn't the fresh décor they sought, or modern amenities, it was the nostalgia. The reassurance that came with knowing that while everything else in life moved quickly and moved forward, that some things would remain the same, and that there was one place they could always come back to and know that it was just as they remembered it would be.

Inside the lobby, people were already filling the couches and the chairs, and there was a lively buzz to the room. It smelled of coffee and the warm cinnamon rolls that the inn was famous for, not just on the island but all over the Midwest—people brought boxes home and froze them. She knew, because her mother did this every year. And Hope would probably have done the same, if things hadn't gone the way they had these past few weeks.

Her heart was heavy as she walked through the lobby and into the dining room, but there was no sign of John. No warm smile and sincere eyes. She decided to have one last sweep of the back porch before she pulled his card from her pocket and tried his phone.

But then she saw him, on one of the deck chairs looking out over the grounds. His laptop was open on a table in front of him, but when she called out his name, he closed it.

He grinned, and just like that, every part of her turned from heaviness to joy. But it was fleeting, so fleeting, and she hoped, that like this hotel, it was something that she could hold onto, in her heart. Because the rest of him, she had to let go.

She blew out a breath and walked toward him. She closed her eyes when he stood to greet her with a peck on the cheek, and then she took the chair beside him when he motioned for her to sit down.

"Coffee?" he asked, motioning to his own cup.

She shook her head. She needed to get her words out. She needed to say it, because it had to be said, even if it hurt, and even if, one day, she knew, she might look back and wonder if she'd made the right decision.

"I can't stay long," she said.

His expression changed from one of expectation to one of resigned acceptance. "I see."

"I'm going back to Chicago, John," she said. And even though she knew he was from Chicago, too, she knew that she had been direct. She was going back to her life. To her husband. To her family. She'd already told Sheila, who took the news in stride. She'd speak to

Darcy personally before she left, with some tips, of course, and an invitation to visit her when Darcy was in town near her daughter.

But this was the hard part.

He nodded. “Is it okay to say that I’m disappointed?”

“I didn’t want to lead you on—”

He held up a hand. “You didn’t.”

She hadn’t. She knew that. But she also knew that the bond they’d formed had happened all on its own. They were two people that clicked. Maybe it was the circumstances. Or maybe in another lifetime things might have been different.

“Evan came to the island the day that I was here. That’s why I haven’t given you an answer yet about the project.” She looked around, the vast white porch, to the lush green grass and the flowering trees, to the lake, vast and blue and calm. “You offered me a whole new life. A life that I really thought I wanted.” And maybe, in her heart, still did. But her choice was made. It had been made a long time ago.

“I love my family,” she said. “It’s not always easy, and it’s not always perfect, but I’m not willing to let it all go.”

“Some things are worth holding on,” John said, nodding slowly.

"Maybe I'll..." She trailed off. What was she saying? Maybe she'd see him in Chicago? That one day she'd be walking down the street and their eyes would meet and...no.

He seemed to know what she was about to say because he said, "Actually, I'm staying on the island. This inn isn't just something I'm investing for my company. This is a personal investment. I'm going to take over the inn and stay here."

She blinked and took a step back, looking around her in wonder. "I hadn't realized that."

He gave a little laugh. "I hadn't either. But I'm happy here. And I think this is where I belong."

She bit her lip, holding back tears. "I was happy here too."

"You're an amazing woman, Hope," John said, and the kindness in his eyes had returned with the sincerity in his smile.

"Thank you," she said, but not for the compliment. For all of it. For lifting her spirits when she needed it the most. For being a source of support when she felt so alone in this world. And for making her believe that her marriage could work, if she really wanted it to.

And she did.

"I hope you find everything that you're looking for, John," she said, swallowing back the lump in her throat. "Because you deserve it."

He nodded. "You too, Hope. But I think you're going to be okay. You've got a lot of good things going on in your life."

She gave a sad smile, thinking of Rose and Victoria, and Evan, who was back at the cottage right now. Waiting for her. And her sisters, who hadn't all been together on this island in over twelve years, but who now had promised to meet back at Sunset Cottage every summer.

"I do," she said. She pulled in a breath as he reached out and patted her hand and she looked down at her fingers, at the diamond ring sparkling in the morning sunlight, and she knew that she had said all there was to say, and that their time together had come to an end.

"Life has a weird way of bringing people into our lives when we need them the most," she said, pushing back her chair.

He rose to stand beside her. His gaze was intense, but for the first time since she'd met him, it hurt to look into his eyes, to see the warmth there, the comfort.

"Some people are meant to be together for a lifetime. Some people are only together for a short time, but that doesn't mean they'll be forgotten." He grinned. "I'll miss you, Hope."

"And I'll miss you," she whispered.

She turned, before the tears could fall, but they were hot and thick, filling her eyes as she walked down the stairs to the lawn because she couldn't bear to go back into the lobby around all those people. They slipped down her face, one after the other, and she didn't brush them away, because she couldn't.

She cried for the man who had first approached her on the boat, when she was so flustered and scared and confused. And she cried for the man who was gentle and kind and had listened to her talk through her problems. And she cried for the man who had offered her the world and asked for nothing in return.

Maybe because he knew, in his heart of hearts, that there was nothing she could offer him.

*

The house was quiet when she stepped inside and she called out the names of the children, Evan, her sisters, but no one was there. Had they gone for a walk?

She went back out to the porch and looked across the road at the beachfront, but it was empty, aside from the seagulls creeping near the water's edge.

She walked back into the house, and that was when she saw them, gathered on the hammock in the yard. Her sisters, laughing and smiling, as if they hadn't spent a fair bit of time arguing these past weeks, or even this past year.

And her husband, tending to Gran's vegetable garden with Leo at his side.

And her children, making mud pies.

And all she could do was smile.

Epilogue

Hope

The line for the ferry was short. Almost too short. And as Hope watched the boat dock and the tourists and summer people here for a new season depart, she felt a sharp sting in her chest.

"Is it terrible to say that I'm a little envious of all these people just arriving?" she asked Ellie, but it was Evan who replied.

"Why don't we come back? In August? When the weather is warmer?"

She blinked up at him. She hadn't been expecting that. Not when he'd just come, given up his time from work, when a seven-hour drive home was still ahead of them. She'd assumed at best that she'd come alone next summer, for a week with the girls, or that they would talk about returning and get too sidetracked with all the things that filled that calendar on her pantry door.

She thought about that for a moment. She was just as guilty of being too busy as she accused Evan of being half the time.

"You really mean it?" she asked, smiling up at him.

"I meant everything I said, Hope," he said, leaning in to kiss her.

Ellie rolled her eyes and said, "Please! Do I really need to be subjected to your eternal bliss? It's bad enough that the four of you look like you're ready for a catalogue shoot, but do you have to remind me that I am the only one here with no prospect of romance in my future?"

"Says the girl who is leaving for Europe on Sunday," Gemma pointed out as she maneuvered her luggage farther down the pier.

Ellie gave a small smile. "True. And there are men in Europe."

"Hot ones," Gemma said.

"Thanks again for giving up your ticket to me, Gemma," Ellie said, setting a hand on her sister's arm.

"You'll put it to far better use than I would have. Taking a honeymoon alone is hardly every little girl's dream," Gemma replied with a snort. But she was smiling, just as she'd been smiling a little more every day since she'd arrived on the island.

"How long do you think it will take you to pack up the apartment?" Hope asked her. She grabbed two handles of the suitcases while Evan pushed the double stroller.

Gemma shrugged. "Not long. I'll try to get a sublet-ter through the end of my lease. It's such a beautiful view and location that I shouldn't have a problem."

She looked so wistful that for a moment, Hope wondered if she was going to change her mind, but then Gemma hoisted her bags onto the luggage cart and said, "That apartment has nothing but bad memories. But this place, the island, it's full of happy ones. And that makes all the difference, doesn't it?"

Hope felt a pull in her chest as she stepped onto the ferry, feeling the unsteady floor beneath her, knowing that she was taking the last official step away from eve-rything that had happened here this past month, but not completely.

This place was full of happy memories; Gemma was right about that. And she knew that she was making the choice she could live with, not the one she would come to question or regret.

This time around, she was following her heart. Not doing what she should, but what she really, truly wanted to do. She took a seat next to Evan and the girls. Where she was meant to be.

The boat hitched and ever so slowly pulled away from the dock. The island grew distant, and smaller, until they could see the entire mass of it, sitting long and proud in the water, and everything on that island, everything that had happened, and everyone who was still there, left behind, felt like a strange sort of memory that grew smaller and smaller, until she couldn't see the rooflines of the houses anymore, or even the outline of the Lakeside Inn.

"I know I couldn't wait to leave," Ellie suddenly said, "but now I can't wait to come back."

"You can come back whenever you want," Gemma said. "After all, I may be the one living there, but the house belongs to all of us. It's our home."

Hope slipped her hand into Evan's and their eyes met, full of new understanding, and new appreciation.

Her home was on Willow Lane, with Evan and the girls. But a part of her heart would always be at Sunset Cottage.

ABOUT THE AUTHOR

Olivia Miles is a *USA Today* bestselling author of feel-good women's fiction with a romantic twist. She has frequently been ranked as an Amazon Top 100 author, and her books have appeared on several bestseller lists, including Amazon charts, BookScan, and USA Today. Treasured by readers across the globe, Olivia's heartwarming stories have been translated into German, French, and Hungarian, with editions in Australia in the United Kingdom.

Olivia lives just outside Chicago with her husband, daughter, and two ridiculously pampered pups.

Visit www.OliviaMilesBooks.com for more.

Made in the USA
Middletown, DE
11 April 2020

89025975R00215